# Twice a Prince

# Look for these titles by *Sherwood Smith*

*Now Available:*

The Trouble with Kings

*Sasharia en Garde! Series*
Once a Princess (Book 1)
Twice a Prince (Book 2)

# Twice a Prince

*Sherwood Smith*

A Samhain Publishing, Ltd. publication.

Samhain Publishing, Ltd.
577 Mulberry Street, Suite 1520
Macon, GA 31201
www.samhainpublishing.com

Twice a Prince
Copyright © 2009 by Sherwood Smith
Print ISBN: 978-1-60504-296-1
Digital ISBN: 978-1-60504-073-8

Editing by Anne Scott
Cover by Anne Cain

First Samhain Publishing, Ltd. electronic publication: July 2008
First Samhain Publishing, Ltd. print publication: May 2009

# Dedication

For M. She knows why.

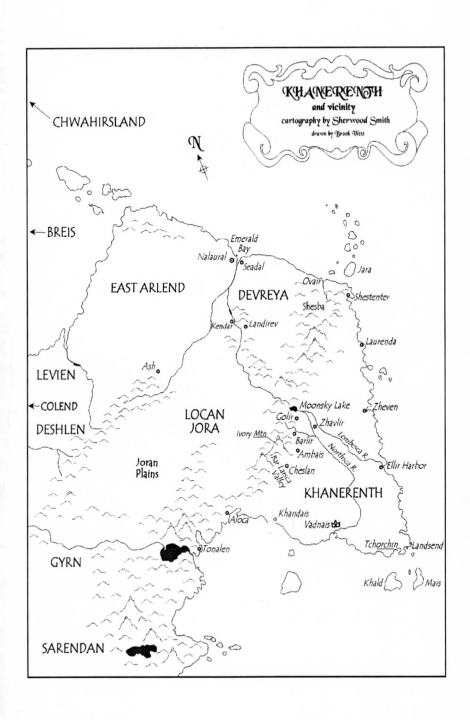

KHANERENTH
and vicinity
cartography by Sherwood Smith
drawn by Brook West

CHWAHIRSLAND

N

BREIS

Emerald
Bay

Nalaural    Seadal

EAST ARLEND    DEVREYA    Ovair    Shestenter

Shesha

Kendar    Landirev    Laurenda

LEVIEN    Ash    Zheven

COLEND    LOCAN    Moonsky Lake    Zhavlir
    JORA    Golir
DESHLEN    Ivory Mtn    Barlir    Lembeca R.    Ellir Harbor
    Ambais    Northca R.
    Joran    Far Larca Valley    Cheslan
    Plains    KHANERENTH

    Aloca    Khandais    Vadnais
    Tchorchin    Landsend
GYRN    Tonalen

    Khald    Mais
SARENDAN

# Chapter One

"Prince Jehan did *what*?" King Canardan exclaimed.

Magister Zhavic, one of the king's mages, stroked his gray beard, making sure his tone was detached. Disinterested. Academic. "After the academy cadets finished the midsummer games, His Highness Prince Jehan had himself rowed out to his yacht. In the middle of the harbor. He'd had it moved out there earlier. No one knew why."

"Probably in hopes of a breeze. If it's been half as beastly hot in Ellir as it's been here. Even my son," he added wryly, "is not too dreamy to overlook this weather."

The stars shone in the rain-washed midnight sky over the royal palace in Vadnais, but the palace room was still too warm. Magister Zhavic resisted the temptation to wipe his sleeve over his damp forehead, and got to the important part of his report. "When he heard that the prince had gone out into the harbor for the night, War Commander Randart rowed out with a force into the harbor after him."

Canardan sighed, his gaze straying to the pile of papers waiting on his desk. "Randart's orders are to set sail at dawn, in pursuit of that curst pirate Zathdar. What's he doing chasing after my son? Did he decide to commandeer Jehan's yacht? Or maybe he's taking Jehan out to help catch the pirate?"

"The war commander did not see fit to inform us. He just left, and was seen rowing back again, without the prince, just before I transferred myself here to report. They might be docking right now. If the threatened storm did not slow them up. He did not have the prince with him. I made certain of that before I left." Master Zhavic lifted his left hand, on which lay the magical transfer token, bespelled for a trip to the royal palace and back again to Ellir Harbor.

The king's attention flicked from the brassy token to the tall, lean, gray-haired man sitting before him. "You have no idea what Randart was after, then?"

"There is speculation, of course. But the war commander did not inform us directly. All I can tell you is that he ordered his nephew to accompany him."

The king regarded the mage with brooding question. Magister Zhavic sat squarely on his chair, his face stiff, gaze diffuse. But Canardan, used to listening for clues, heard the subtle satisfaction emphasizing certain words. Zhavic was *gloating*. "All right, let's hear the speculation."

"According to Patrol Leader Hathmad, the war commander and his force rowed out to the prince's yacht to make a search."

"A search? For what?" The king leaned forward. "My son's art collection?" Despite the joke, the king did not smile.

"They weren't told, just ordered to search for anomalies. The war commander's own captain seemed to have private orders, but the others weren't given those orders."

"What did they find on this search?"

"Nothing. The prince had gone to his yacht to get one of his, ah, female artists to paint a fan for her majesty. The entire force overheard that."

Huh! If Randart was still rowing back yet Zhavic had this fresh report, that meant one of those men—probably this patrol leader—was a paid informer to the mages. Canardan was not surprised at that so much as at the fact that Zhavic was in such a hurry to tattle on Randart that he revealed the existence of the spy.

"Female artist?" Canardan repeated. Could that possibly be the reason behind the search? There was only one missing female of import—Sasharia Zhavalieshin, daughter of Princess Atanial, whom Canardan had closely guarded up in the tower, as a cherished guest.

But if her daughter, who had been captured by the pirate Zathdar at last report, was at large, and War Commander Randart was searching for her, surely, *surely*, the war commander would report that to his king. Wouldn't he?

"What did this female artist look like?" Canardan asked. "Tall? Frizzy hair? Hawk-nosed?"

"Small, short red hair, very attractive. Perhaps Colendi. The only other female on board was the cook. She was quite tall. Hathmad didn't remember her hair, so it must have been unremarkable. She was also drunk, covered with flour and wine, so they couldn't really see her features."

Hathmad was the spy, then. Canardan repeated the name to himself to commit it to memory. He frowned. "I could have sworn last year Jehan treated me to a meal prepared by a Colendi master cook named Kial...Kaer...ah, I don't remember his name, but in any case this was a man. I can understand that a Colendi master cook might get tired of sitting around on a yacht that sees its owner once or twice a year. Did Hathmad observe the cook working?"

"Said she prepared an exquisite meal and served it like an experienced steward."

"Which the cook has to be, on a yacht that small. Very well, we'll set aside the fan artist and the cook. Randart certainly seems to have. Go on with the report. Does anyone have any worthwhile speculation on why the war commander had them searching for anomalies on my son's yacht in the middle of the night?" Canardan rubbed his jaw, wondering if Randart was ruminating on heirs again. Maybe it was time to send Damedran on a long, long journey, to learn diplomacy or observe armies or whatever.

"Something having to do with the prince having arrested or almost arrested or attempting to arrest, a cutpurse, as near as I can tell. There was very little information to be found out about that. Everyone wanted to talk about the games and those mysterious youths who carried every single prize away from our cadets."

"Yes, just what we needed. Another mystery," Canardan said with heavy irony.

He turned his gaze back to the papers, but he didn't see them. Magisters Zhavic and Perran, the king's mages, both hated the war commander and his brother—a feeling that was mutual. None had any use for the others, which had suited Canardan fine. You don't want your military leaders and your strongest mages allied.

The cost was that they spent a lot of time that ought to have been dedicated to his own concerns trying to prove the others false. Canardan knew that Randart was behind recent whispers that the king "should" disinherit Jehan and put his nephew in his place. He blamed himself for speaking aloud in extreme exasperation once, when Jehan had done something particularly fog-headed.

However, the idea had obviously stuck, and Canardan didn't like that. Damedran was a military man's ideal candidate for royal heir: handsome, strong, tough, courageous. But his knowledge of trade, of diplomacy, of all the other aspects of kingship that his father and uncle scorned was even sketchier than Jehan's.

What bothered the king were these sporadic secret missions, as though Randart had gotten wind of actual treason. Not that chasing a cutpurse was treason. Neither was chasing a cutpurse any reason to take a handpicked war band out for a tedious harbor trip after a long day spent outside in the broiling sun. Nor was it a reason to institute a covert search, his target not a suspected pirate or shady trader, but no one less than the crown prince.

Canardan rubbed his eyes. His own ambivalence gave him pause. A part of him *wanted* Jehan to be conniving behind his back. That would mean the boy had his brains after all, and his ambition. Jehan when small had shown a distressing tendency to mimic his mother's impossible ideals, which was one of the reasons Canardan had sent him west to get some sense knocked into him as well as some training. The other reason had been to protect Jehan somewhat when Canardan had parted with his mother.

Jehan had had plenty of time to get used to that. He'd returned beautifully trained, obedient, cooperative...but without ambition.

If Jehan was really conniving, hey, that showed the rudiments of ambition! But why not on his father's side?

Canardan scowled at the papers, still not seeing them. Unlike his own monster of a father (until the old man was killed by Canardan's siblings, who were both far worse) he gave Jehan a free hand. Unlimited money. Rank. Even some responsibility—as long as he followed orders. And Jehan did follow orders...when he remembered them.

No, Randart had to be inventing shadows to jump at. He'd always had a suspicious nature, which had saved Canardan many times in the past.

Still. Taking Damedran out to the yacht? That was very odd.

Canardan returned his attention to Zhavic. "I want someone trusted on the flagship. Reporting every day."

Zhavic bowed in his chair. "It shall be done."

"Meanwhile, you return to searching for Atanial's daughter. I can't do anything until I have her. The old castle with the World Gate is warded, isn't it?"

"Perran is there himself, right now. No one can possibly transfer between worlds without our knowing immediately." Zhavic hesitated, then made a tentative gesture upward, toward the tower above them. "You are content with matters here?"

"You mean Princess Atanial?" Canardan grinned wryly, thinking, *You mean her magical tokens.* "Oh, I think so. Carry on." He twiddled his fingers in dismissal.

The mage rose, bowed, murmured and transferred by magic, leaving a puff of displaced air to rattle the papers still gripped in Canardan's hand.

So exactly where was the missing tall, wild-haired, hawk-nosed daughter of Princess Atanial?

I left off standing there in Jehan's arms while we lit up the sky with a supernova kiss.

At least, that's what it felt like.

The thing about sensory firestorms is, there's that rock of common sense sitting somewhere in the center of all the heat. Or so it is with me. Because when I came up for air, the rock was right there inside me with all its insistent weight, and I gasped, nearly choking on rain, and pushed Jehan away.

"Sasharia?" he asked.

Lightning crackled, striking the sea not far away. He held his hands out to me, but when I braced myself to resist, he dropped them to his sides.

In the glow from the cabin door, his eyes looked black, his expression changing from passion to puzzlement. "What's wrong?"

I looked at the fine strands of white hair lying across his brow. Tenderness made the insides of my arms ache to hold him, and my fingers twitched, wanting to smooth back his hair, which (I had discovered) was as soft as a bunny's fur, only long. I clenched my hands behind my back, wishing the lightning would do me a big favor and strike me now. "I hate *Fatal Attraction* movies," I snarled.

Of course that made no sense to him whatsoever.

I shook my own wet mop impatiently out of my face, but did not move, despite the lightning and thunder, and the stinging needles of rain. The thunder smash had died away to a distant growl. "I was going to make a joke about sleeping with the enemy and being stupid, but it's not funny, is it?"

"Enemy?" He stepped back, his chin jerking up as if I'd slapped him.

"Oh, Jehan, I didn't mean that. I mean I did, but not—oh, I don't know what I mean." I gave a strangled excuse for a laugh and tried desperately to smooth a horrible moment over with a joke. "So what's your place in"—*my life?*—"Great Events? Did some mysterious mage cast a Shadow of Destiny on you when you were little? Or some weird prophesy turn up with your name in it in reference to a Path of Fate?"

"Fate? Destiny?" he repeated.

The words had come out in English, and I remembered Mom telling me years ago they didn't have any such concepts. Nor did they talk about luck, either bad or good. Chance, yes.

My "joke" was about as funny as mud, but I kept trying to turn the most serious conversation of my life into light banter because if you laugh you can't get hurt, right? "I mean do you have a life membership in the Villains' Guild? Now would be the time to zip it from your wallet and get started with the har har har."

"Villains?" He looked skyward. "How can you think that, Sasharia? What have I done? What have I not done?"

Lightning. Thunder. Neither of us moved. We stared at one another, as if anger and passion and desperate questions could reach past locked gazes into skulls and decode the thoughts there. But though people walked in the world who could do that, neither of us had been born with that particular gift. Or curse.

"Call me Sasha." I knew it was inane, that I was being the kind of weak female I despise. But I so wanted to hear him say my name. Just once more. Because I was going to stick to my guns, and leave as soon as I could.

"Sasha." He said my name on an outgoing breath, which sent shivers all through my nerves. "Why won't you let me explain the pirate disguise?"

The rainsquall ended abruptly, a wave of slanting gray diminishing over the sea, leaving us standing under the dripping sails on the wet deck. I fought to keep my voice steady. "You. Are. Your father's. Son."

His eyes closed. Then opened. "Didn't you listen to anything I've told you?"

"Oh, I listened. Heard everything you said. Which was, mostly, everything I want to hear. Just as your father talked to my mother twenty years ago your time, using every smile, every charm at his command."

He gripped the rail with both hands, and looked at me over his shoulder. "You're never going to trust me, are you? No matter what I do. What I say. Because of who my father is."

"Let's skip right past the fact that you lied to me about who you really are, when we first met. Privateer or pirate, you are attacking your own side. Your lying to Randart I have no problem with. But you're also lying to your dad. I know you don't want anybody killed, but for whose good? Here's the real question: what would you do with your dad if you won some kind of battle against him? Put him on trial for his life, or stab him in the back?"

"Neither." Jehan faced the sea and let his breath out slowly. "But you won't believe me even on that. Will you." It was a statement, not a question.

"So how do you propose to take away the kingdom? Last I heard he was decades away from a convenient death of frail old age."

"That's not for me to decide, it's for Math," Jehan said. "Don't you see? I am on your father's side. I want Prince Mathias back on his throne. I want the kingdom reunited. Everything I do is to keep Randart on the hop, keep my father busy, which will make it all easier when Math does return. If Math returns, then maybe my father will listen to sense. There doesn't have to be any killing."

"Yes there does, because your father has Randart as his right arm. He likes killing," I retorted. "And your father lets him do it."

"That's why the guises, don't you see? If I can just hold off Randart while finding Math, maybe, maybe, there is a solution without another Khanerenth bloodbath. But as Jehan, I have no freedom."

"A *prince* with no freedom? Then it must be really tough to be a peon!" I could see how much my words hurt him. Or did he want me to see that? "I'm sorry for my sarcasm. I'm not trying to be a crank. It's just that everything you say, I hear my mom warning me...and more questions sprout like tentacles in my mind. Like, why didn't my father tell you where he was going, if he really trusted you?"

He did not answer, just stared at me, grim in expression, his mouth a white line.

My righteous anger vanished like the heat in the sudden thunder, leaving me just as unhappy. "Don't you see, Jehan? I *wish* I could believe you. I wish I could *trust* you, because there's no denying we've got some major chemistry going between us." *Chemistry* didn't have a translation any more than *peon* had. He didn't seem to need it. "But all I can think of is my mother's stories about Canary trying to seduce her over to his side. And, well, there we were a few minutes ago—"

"I follow." He flung up a hand. Looked out to sea. "You've said enough."

He lifted the other hand, turned away, and I heard his quick steps crossing the deck and the door to the cabin shut.

Leaving me standing there in the dark, with about as toxic a Pyrrhic victory as anyone ever...lost. Because I sure did not feel like a winner.

After a couple thousand years I crossed the deck, which was silent except for the creaking of the wood, the wash and hiss of the restless sea, the distant mutter of thunder. I shut myself into my cabin.

And sat there, waiting—arguing both sides for when Jehan came back.

But he didn't come back.

The next noise I became aware of was the thump and swish of the boat being lowered. I moved, aching and cold, to the leaded glass window, in time to see him drop down into the boat and raise the single sail, which filled and carried him toward the shore on the making tide.

Behind me, in the east, dawn smeared, a bleak smudge, against the horizon.

# Chapter Two

King Canardan was still thinking about Atanial the next morning, when he was supposed to be looking over Randart's requisitions for the army war game. When an aide announced that Magister Zhavic had just appeared by magic transfer, Canardan decided to use his appearance as an excuse to find her. He was certain he knew where she was.

The aide held open the door and the gray-haired mage dropped unceremoniously into a chair to recover from the sickening wrench of being yanked out of one space and thrust into another. As soon as he drew a deep breath and looked up, Canardan forestalled the usual amenities and said, "Let's take a walk. You get over it faster. Report as we go."

Zhavic was not about to say anything to a king about his theories on recovery from magic transfer. "Very well, your majesty." He struggled to his feet again, breathing deeply against a surge of reaction nausea. "You wished me to report when War Commander Randart departed. He has just done so."

Canardan nodded and walked out of his private chamber.

With a rustling of papers and a thumping of feet, all the aides and runners in the outer office leaped up and bowed. Canardan waved a hand in a big circle, acknowledging and sending them back to their tasks. A very long time ago he'd loved these signs of respect. Showed in outward form everyone knew who was king. Now he wanted them back at work. Work that was *always* behind.

Through the barracks command office he paced, and again

the leaps—this time military salutes—the wave of the hand. Into the hall looking onto the back court, and there she was, with the kitchen helpers.

Atanial was laughing, wisps of her hair coming down around her face and shoulders as she churned butter. He grinned, remembering when she first came, and she'd shown a tendency to go around to the servants and lecture them on workers' rights and women's liberation, asking excruciatingly personal questions with the earnest air of a crusader. Math's pride and embarrassment. And her delight and then chagrin when she discovered that whatever "rights" she'd been extolling had long been a part of life here. Delight, chagrin, but no pride, no affront. Skewed as some of her notions were, she really had been an idealist.

"She obviously has no communications device," he said to Magister Zhavic.

"No, we're fairly certain now that the magical object she keeps hidden has to be her World Gate transfer, given her by Magister Glathan."

"As long as she cannot get to the old castle tower she cannot use it, so we can safely let it be, I think." Canardan knew he was disappointing his head mage, who badly wanted that little bit of powerful magic to use for his own purposes. Canardan regarded it as safer where he knew the mages couldn't get their hands on it, but he could if he really had to.

He watched Atanial working away, laughing, chattering, as everyone went about their business. At the sight of her shapely arms, her long body, the familiar tightening of desire wakened, to be quashed. *Don't look at her, look at what she's doing.* The problem was, she wasn't really doing anything but talking and being her usual friendly self.

Impulse again. "I think I'm going to give her a party. No, let's make it a grand ball, a masquerade. She used to love those. My chief allies will like it, she can think it's a courting gesture if she likes, but I want them all to see her being obedient and content under my hand." Another thought occurred. "Yes. And let's have Jehan here. That will be the

19

excuse, the two of them meeting. He's supposed to be good with women, maybe he can win her over for us. Find out where the daughter might be, or at least find out more about her. Let's do it. End of the week."

Zhavic said, "Is that enough time?"

Canardan gave him a wry look. "Whenever I want is enough time. Go back to the harbor. You know your orders. Tell my son I want him here as soon as possible. I'll go get the heralds sending runners out to my other guests. It's a good way to shift the gossip away from whatever happened at those damned games as well."

Zhavic, seeing that the king had quite decided, bowed and left, sourly thinking of all the extra work that would fall on the mages, warding the castle, the guests to get ready so hastily, and all of it because the king had rediscovered his twenty-year-old hankering for that troublesome woman.

Canardan had already forgotten the mage. He watched Atanial straighten up, arching her back. Was the daughter as smart, as incomprehensible? She couldn't be as beautiful, not if she'd inherited Math's and Ananda's wild wooly hair, the Zhavalieshin bird beak of a nose.

Atanial wouldn't talk about the daughter at all. Any questions he asked, she deflected.

Well, maybe it was time to ask again, but not by himself. Jehan, worthless in matters military and diplomatic, ought to be able to manage sweet-talking a woman about her marriageable daughter.

As for him, he might begin their first dance by asking why she liked churning butter.

He walked on, the morning sunlight in the windows outlining his form, shadowing it to silhouette, and outlining it again. Everybody down below in the courtyard had seen him appear in the hall above. They all knew he was there and had redoubled their efforts.

Atanial finished stretching her back and watched him until he vanished into the heralds' wing. If he'd noticed her down here, what did he think? Oh, he noticed. Just as his servants and guards were aware of his presence, very little escaped his eye, she'd learned that much. So if he did ask, she'd tell him it was fun.

It wasn't fun, but the talk was. The butter churning, she'd discovered, was a splendid upper-body workout without being obvious. She didn't dare demand a sword-fighting session. Canary seemed to be on the watch for her to try something stupid like trying to kiss up to the guards; anyone she spoke to at length was rotated elsewhere.

*I wish I had a plan of action,* she thought as the second pastry cook tested the butter for color, consistency and taste.

Guilt tightened her throat, made her stomach roil.

*Everyone seems to assume I'm happy to be here. I've given in, given up. But what else can I do? Yelling about treachery and treason and betrayal would win me a free ticket to a cell all to myself.*

No, now she was on sure ground, even if only a few inches of it. Make trouble, and Canary removes the troublemaker. And she wouldn't get anywhere near her friends in the detention wing. Friendliness hadn't accomplished it, but threats and heroic speeches definitely wouldn't.

The kitchen workers headed back inside. Instinct so far had prompted her to make friends with everyone, but then that was an easy plan because she would have done it anyway.

Instinct, not duty. She winced, a sudden memory throwing her back to her very first days in this palace, when the old king was alive, and Math running around doing his jobs. *You don't need to wear those tight dresses with all the frills,* she'd said to one of the young aristocrats at her first ball. *Women are as good as men, and no one will be convinced of it while we're serving as male sex objects in clothes like this.*

*But I want to be what you call a "sex object" if by that you mean I dress to attract,* was the reply. *I want the attention of the man of my choice. And I want him to dress to attract me. What would be the fun of flirting at a ball if we all dressed in sacks?*

Atanial laughed at herself as she made her way upstairs. How long ago that was! Surely Canary didn't give her this much freedom because he thought she'd go right back to lecturing everyone on self-actualizing and consciousness-raising...or did he?

*At least if he thinks I'm a fool he won't see me as a threat.*

Fool. Threat.

She frowned, thinking over the queen's words.

As she lowered herself into her bath, she thought wistfully, *a threat would have a plan of action. All I've got is a silly reputation.*

Her mood was somber when she emerged from the bath. Feeling she'd betrayed Mathias, Sasha, almost everyone with her total lack of success at coming up with a working plan, she reached for the first gown in the chest, then paused when she saw the heavy cream-colored linen paper resting on her little table by the door.

After pulling her robe back on, she retrieved the note. It was sealed with a silvery wax imprinted with the royal cup. She slid her finger carefully under it, her nails still soft from her bath.

She frowned at the script she hadn't read for years.

*His Majesty...invites you to honor him with your presence...masquerade ball...week's end...in order to meet his son and heir, Prince Jehan.*

Canardan had written this invitation by his own hand.

Zhavic winced away from the brilliant sunlight of a rain-washed morning. Transfers always gave him a headache. At least there didn't seem to be any trouble. He squinted against the dancing points of light reflecting off the deep blue waters of Ellir Harbor, where the fleet was pulling their anchors up and lowering sail. The tide was on the ebb.

His mage-apprentice on duty, a trustworthy, sober girl, had informed him as soon as he entered the mage room in the command tower that Prince Jehan had been seen disembarking from his boat after dawn at the height of tidal flood.

"Send someone—no, better go yourself. Find him, request

him to meet me, everything polite. King's orders," Zhavic said, and the girl was gone with two quick steps and a swing of rust-colored braids.

Zhavic sent the senior cadet on duty at the door to fetch him some breakfast. He knew by the time anyone found wherever Jehan was moping about and he actually made his way up, the mage could eat a good meal and maybe get rid of the transfer malaise.

While he waited for his food, Zhavic stood at the window and watched Randart's fleet begin its slow departure. He had a mage safely aboard—and at Randart's request, which was far better than having to try to arrange a covert role. Zhavic had chosen a quiet, steady, untoward mage, her area of expertise being woodwork. The commander would not suspect her of other orders.

Everything was as it should be.

Sunlight reflecting off the glass in a merchant's window below in the street lanced at his eyes and he turned away, thinking of Randart's brother in the command suite directly overhead, probably dealing with the results of the disastrous games. The king had been disappointed, but Zhavic, in the safety of an empty room, could permit himself to smile. What could be better for keeping those Randarts busy? One off chasing pirates, the other facing an academy of angry youths who'd been trounced by those mysterious boys from the hills.

Magister Zhavic's breakfast arrived moments later, brought by a breathless weed of a cadet. The boy set the tray down, bowed and backed outside the door to his post, and that, too, made Zhavic smile. The cadets as well as their masters were all afraid of mages. Good. Healthy attitude.

He'd not taken two bites before he heard the familiar lounging footfalls of the prince, who sauntered in, dressed in his usual brown velvet, his eyes tired, his face tense. Zhavic, looking for mere sulkiness and perhaps the nausea of a hangover, thought he saw the signs. Drunk again. Typical.

But then, if Math turned out to be dead, a future drunken king would be so easy to guide.

Zhavic smiled a welcome. "I am sorry to disturb you, your highness. It was at your father's request. First, would you care for refreshment?"

"No thank you." Jehan seemed to gather himself inwardly, then he looked up. In his hands he carried something with ribbons dangling. Seeing the mage's gaze go to it, Jehan snapped open a fan with expertise. "I brought this for the queen. Do you think she'll like it?"

"Queen Ananda...seems to have departed. No one knows where. Your father has given us to understand that she retired into the countryside."

The prince's eyes narrowed. For a moment he almost looked intelligent. But then a hangover would probably look the same. "I see. But he doesn't actually know that?"

"No. No one knows where she went. However, your father requests me to convey his wishes. He is giving a masquerade ball at week's end for Princess Atanial. It is his desire to introduce the two of you to one another at this event, which is intended to honor you both. He desires your presence directly back in the capital."

The prince turned his head toward the window, as though the emptiness out at sea would fill the emptiness of his head, the mage thought wearily.

Then Prince Jehan gave Magister Zhavic an airy salute. "It shall be as he wishes. I will depart at once."

# Chapter Three

Jehan's boat vanished in the fleeing darkness of the west along the coast.

I stepped out onto the deck of the yacht. No one in sight except for two figures at the wheel, who looked up.

I said to Owl, "Can we talk?"

He led the way to the cabin, where my coverlet was still spread on the obviously unused bed. I gathered it into my arms, hugging it close. Then I faced Owl. "You've got a couple of choices here. Either you're going to have to put me in irons, and I'm gonna fight you every inch of the way, or else let me dive over and drown. Because I'll keep trying to get to shore. Or you can give me the rowboat and let me go."

"I'll tell Zel to fetch your gear," he said.

Oh. Okay. That was...easy.

I retreated, feeling inexplicably awful. I was still wearing clothes belonging to Kaelande, the Colendi cook. I skinned out of those, put on my shirt and trousers, and shoved Kaelande's things through the cleaning frame. It was disguise time for me— a thought that gave me pause, seeing as how I'd just been dinging Jehan for his false faces. But I shook it away. *He* was a prince, after all. *I* was a fugitive.

Owl rejoined me and gave me my little box of mementos and coins. I checked. Everything was as it should be. "Ready."

Owl indicated the yacht's tiny hold. "He wanted me to offer you your choice of weapons. Anything you think you might need."

"That's all right. Please let me take the boat."

"I'll row you ashore."

"That's all right—"

Owl raised a hand. "The launch is already there. I would really rather not be stranded here without a boat, leaving him with two to bring back."

"Oh. Right."

"I have some shopping to do before the tide turns anyway. You can go your way, I'll go mine."

I felt highly uncomfortable, but was too tired to do much beyond climb down and take my place in the boat. We scarcely spoke on the long row in. When we came to the dock, Owl said, "Farewell, Princess."

"You too," I managed, and I climbed up the barnacle-dotted ladder between the tide-marked pilings, and hastened down the dock without looking back.

Once I reached the street, though, I *did* look back. Not once but several times. I bobbed and weaved, trying to stay as unobtrusive as I could. My rain-washed hair was drying in a massive cloak of frizzy curls, but I left it that way. If they were still going by the description of me at the old castle, they were seeking a woman with braids. Just once I'd wear it down, but next time I was in public it would vanish under a sober cap, foiling any possible new descriptions going out.

I made my way up the street, so tired by now that the sunlight sparkling off glass and metal along the market street seemed to jab my eyes. But I made it to what I was seeking, an unobtrusive-looking inn, where I paused in the doorway, doing one last sweep for long white hair and brown velvet.

Though I didn't know it, Jehan was at that moment galloping to the southwest toward the capital at the head of an honor guard containing his father's servant and Randart's handpicked spy.

Satisfied that Jehan was not lurking somewhere about, I entered the inn. They had rooms to spare (in fact they were all empty, what with the fleet having sailed) and so I bought myself a night, stopped only long enough to help myself from the magic-cleaned water bucket they put out for guests, and then I retreated to the bed and was soon asleep.

I woke at dawn the next day, feeling more human, if not in a better mood. But the inn provided a breakfast of fresh buttered biscuits with honey, crisped potatoes with cheese and eggs, and plenty of hot liquids to drink. My mood altered gradually from *Just kill me now* to *Well I might as well live* as my body responded to the food like a dry garden under a fresh rain, and by the time I was done eating I had a plan of action.

The idea was not to draw attention to myself. So I was quite methodical. I straightened out my clothes (which looked better after a trip through the cleaning frame), braided my hair tightly in a single tail down my back like I saw both women and men wearing, and made my way back down to the moneychangers. This time I cashed in three of the smaller stones, each at a different booth, so no one would remember a handful of jewels or vast amounts of money and equate it with a tall woman yadda yadda.

After each stone, I moseyed up the street, past handwoven fabrics of every imaginable type and color, baskets, shoes, gear. I stopped to make carefully planned, sober, unostentatious purchases.

After that I retreated to the inn and changed. When I emerged again, my braid was wrapped round my head under a plain scarf of blue, I wore a long robe of pale blue heavy cotton over riding trousers of forest green.

By the end of the day, as vendors were finishing, I made my last purchases, a sword and a horse, having spotted what I wanted earlier. But now, in the flurry of closing, the tired vendors seemed to be distracted. After a very short dicker and a good price, I found myself the owner of an older cross-country mare who seemed to be mild and well cared for.

I bought her a good saddle pad. Onto it I hooked my new tote bag carrying all my goodies wrapped round my rolled coverlet, which in turn held the box of mementos. On the other side of the saddle pad, I'd hung the saddle sheath containing my new sword, a good dueling rapier.

As the sun began to set, I rode quietly out of the harbor city with the departing marketers. My mare ambled not ten paces from the top of Market Street, where I'd confronted Zathdar—Prince Jehan—what seemed a hundred years ago. Was it really only two days ago?

No answer.

I rode until well past dark, stopping in a small market town that had its own inlet to the sea. The inn was full of merrymakers celebrating a wedding, but they had a few hammocks slung for desperate travelers and I slapped my cash down before anyone else could claim one. For an extra charge, a stablehand tended to the mare's food, another got out curry brushes and a third checked her feet.

Satisfied that the mare, at least, would sleep in a good mood, I retreated up to my hammock, and despite the singing, rhythmic stomping, roars of laughter from below, and the sounds of people breathing, sighing, rustling around in the attic around me, I dropped into sleep.

The next day, I began my long journey toward Ivory Mountain, where I hoped to find my father.

# Chapter Four

The lookouts on the towers at the royal castle in Vadnais sent runners below to announce that the prince was arriving.

More correctly, the dust from the road was spotted by the guards on the walls just about the same time two outriders appeared on foam-flecked horses.

By the time Jehan and his honor guard trotted tiredly through the outer gates and up the streets to the castle, the brown and silver banner indicating the Crown Prince in Residence hung below the king's banner, limp in the humid air.

A small army of stablehands waited to take the drooping animals in hand as the guards dismounted, everyone weary from the grueling pace the prince had kept. (Why did they volunteer for honor-guard duty? Hadn't everyone said he always stopped at every inn to get drunk and flirt with the prettiest girls around?) But no one was more weary than Jehan, who hadn't let himself sleep more than a couple of hours at a stretch for several days.

His mood was vile. Not because he was hot and tired, but because he had tried to outrun his thoughts. He knew better. But the chattering voice in his head had kept pace right with him, whispering all the things he should have said to Sasha to convince her, leaving him with the even more depressing retort: *Doesn't matter. She wouldn't have believed anything I said.*

That was the worst of it. She didn't trust him, didn't believe him. He'd never cared what anyone thought before. There were six people who knew his secret identity—well, nine, with Sasha and the Ebans—but somehow, in a matter of days, Sasha's opinion had come to matter the most.

Canardan, glancing out of one of the windows above the military courtyard, was shocked at the grim tension in Jehan's face. He sent a runner to bring his son upstairs at once, and so Jehan appeared in his private room not long after, bowing his head in salute, his tangled white hair imprinted with the dust of the road.

"Jehan?" Canardan said, puzzled. He'd never seen his son this—this angry, no, this *present*. His mood altered to uneasy question.

"You summoned me, Father."

"You seem to have ridden as if all Norsunder was on your heels. What did Zhavic say to you?"

Jehan blinked, seemed to gather himself, then his face smoothed into a semblance of his customary lack of discernable expression, despite the dust smudges. "A party. I must get to my tailor. I would not dishonor your guest by appearing in last winter's masquerade costume."

Canary was relieved, and irritated. "So you nearly ran the horses to death to get to your tailor?"

"We changed mounts at dawn. Had a race the last way, but it began to get hot," Jehan said, with his usual maddening habit of answering someone else's question, and not the one his father had asked. "The horses were all right, hot but not blown," Jehan added, and Canary nodded. That was true enough.

So Jehan wasn't angry, only overheated from the summer sun. Probably had an aching head. Canardan had had enough of those of late, and not just from the weather. "Well, get yourself some fresh clothes. Eat. I want your report on what happened at the games."

Jehan bowed and left, determined to get a grip on his mood before he faced his father again. He could see questions there.

As soon as he was gone, Canardan turned to his chief valet, a slight man of indeterminate age who went unnoticed by all who did not know him. The other servants, who did, were afraid of him. "Chas. Make certain he and the princess do not meet. Unless I am there to witness it."

Chas did not speak, only bowed, and effaced himself, smiling as soon as he was alone. He seldom spoke, but when he did, the other servants listened, for they never knew when it was his will or the king's being expressed. Either way, whatever they said or did was sure to reach royal ears.

While Jehan was taking a cool bath, Atanial moved from the upper reaches of the castle to her own rooms. She'd heard the horns, and watched from the window at the staircase as the boys assigned to banner duty put up the prince's flag in the place she used to see Math's hanging.

She went out onto the nearest balcony that overlooked the courtyard, but all she'd seen was dust and milling horses and military people, with stablehands dashing about in between. Once she thought she caught sight of white hair gleaming in the sunlight, but almost immediately the figure vanished below.

She crossed back to her room and summoned her maid. "If the prince has a free moment, I would very much like to offer him some refreshments."

"If it pleases you, your highness," the girl said nervously. "I can ask permission."

Atanial smiled. "Whenever the king wishes."

Interesting. So Canary didn't want them meeting on their own, then. But what did *that* mean?

Now, for the first time, Atanial looked forward to the ball whose preparations had thrown the entire castle into a state of madness.

She went to the window, looking down into the garden court.

All the servants had brought in relatives to help clean and decorate the ballroom with the summer blooms raided from gardens outside the city. The air smelled day and night of baking, and everywhere one encountered the sounds of brooms wisping, the squeak of vigorous polishing, the slosh of windows being washed. The one time she ventured into the anteroom to the great chambers, a horde of little girls leaped to their feet, flowers drifting into piles on the floor, half-fashioned garlands dropping, as they stared at her in dismay. She retreated rapidly.

She moved to the balcony again. *In all this craziness I bet I could slip away.*

*Okay. Then what?*

Trouble for all the servants, that's what. And maybe threats against those in the dungeon or wherever Kreki and the others were stashed. Meanwhile, exactly what would she be doing, other than lurking around the countryside?

No, much as she longed for it, escape right now would be a bad move. She longed to get away and find Sasha, but she would not risk others.

Besides. She remembered the glimpse of white hair in the courtyard below and remembered what Ananda had said about Jehan.


Jehan longed to be standing on the captain's deck of the *Zathdar*. He longed to be asleep on the *Dolphin*.

He longed to be anywhere but here.

But there was no leaving, and certainly no sleep. He bathed, dressed, drank the hot steeped listerblossom brought to him by servants familiar with his tastes. That at least reduced the headache.

He checked, making certain his magic-transfer notecase went directly from the pile of dirty clothes into his new, because the moment he left, someone—probably Chas—would be searching his things.

Standard, all of it. Meanwhile his father awaited him for lunch. After that everyone would be expecting him to fuss over his clothes, so he had to find the energy to give them what they expected.

The lunch was being served on the shaded private balcony overlooking the back garden, where stooped backs worked among the roses and other flowers, busy trimming, weeding, sprucing up. Some of the flowers looked withered. There'd been no rain here for almost three days now, and dust rose everywhere, shimmering light brown in the dazzling sunlight, settling to the distantly heard dismay of sweepers, dusters, cleaners.

"Welcome back, my boy," Canardan greeted him.

"Thank you, Father." Jehan bowed.

They sat down to eat, and Jehan faced his father's searching gaze. "Tell me about the games," the king said.

"Shambles." Jehan broke a biscuit fresh from the oven. "We had four outsiders join at the last moment, who took all the prizes they competed for. Then they vanished before the awards."

Canardan rubbed his jaw as Jehan dug into his meal. "What happened to Damedran?"

"Thumped repeatedly. But that did not prevent him from riding in the relay even so."

"And still he lost?"

"Yes."

"Who were they, any idea?"

Jehan had thought this aspect out very carefully. "I know one of them from my training days in the west. He recognized me. Came up beside me when I was going down to visit my yacht, said something about assessment. Said word is out west, Norsunder will be moving against the world soon. Said we should be better trained in defense tactics."

There it was, the truth.

Canardan waved a hand impatiently. "Every court is yipping about Norsunder. I did it myself when I pressed the guilds to up their tax share to me."

"You hold that view despite these warnings?"

"What warnings? It's all rumor, innuendo, nonsense. Excuses for other plans. If Norsunder's mages do start sniffing around, we have Zhavic and Perran to ward 'em. Last I heard, no one has actually seen the Norsundrian army except down there at the southern base, which concerns itself with Sartor and its environs. I want Locan Jora back. We need it. They interfere with Colendi trade, causing me to spend time and energy with these constant negotiations. That's enough to worry about." His voice sharpened, warning that he would no longer listen, only demand.

Jehan deferred yet again, hating himself, the situation, and the entire world. But as usual, hid it. "I had commissioned a gift for the queen. Magister Zhavic told me she vanished. What does that mean, vanished?"

"I don't know myself. One morning she wasn't in her rooms, and no one had seen her depart."

"Magic?"

"Could be, though Zhavic went over her chambers himself, and insisted he found no traces of transfer. But then the magic would..." He waved his hand. "Dissipate? Sounds like fog, not spells. Anyway, the residue of major transfers only lingers for a time, they all say. And we don't know when she left. She stayed in her rooms, never came out except to walk in the gardens."

Jehan nodded, satisfied that the queen had gone of her own free will, however mysteriously, and had not been conveniently dispatched. Now that there was a potential queen around.

Speaking of whom, it was time to mention her. "When do I meet Princess Atanial?"

"Officially, at the ball. But if you like I can invite her to supper. She has nothing else to do. I caught her, I might add, having made straight for those fools around that troublemaker Kreki Eban. Who is sitting down in the lockup right now, with the rest of them, awaiting my pleasure."

"What is your pleasure?" Jehan asked.

"That they all drop dead. But they won't. I don't know what to do about them. I can't figure out if I should hope someone runs a rescue raid so I have an excuse to kill them all, or if I should make them disappear. But whether there was dirty work or not, you can be certain rumor would smear me. As usual. So they sit there. And Atanial up here. None of them making trouble." Canardan grinned.

"I am to understand you summoned me here to meet her?"

"To talk to her." The king threw up his hands. "You like women. You chase women. They must like you, or you wouldn't catch them. Atanial is likable, but too old for you to chase. Talk to her instead. Ask about her daughter. What she looks like, what she's been taught. Where she might be. I want that daughter here, and I want you to court her."

"Court her?" Jehan repeated, aghast.

"Court and marry. Zhavalieshin name and ours twined, very romantic and might just settle down this curse-blasted kingdom."

Jehan felt the headache looming. "What if she won't have me?"

"Of course she will," his father countered. "You have success with all these artists, surely you can romance her. You're handsome, you're rich, you've got a title. If she's romantic, you give up your artists for a little while. If she's sensible, you don't even have to do that."

From a certain point of view, it sounded reasonable. Kings and queens negotiated just such marriages all the time. But Jehan never felt farther from his father's view of the world than at this moment.

"Do you know where she is?" he asked, thumbs at his temples.

"No, but if the pirate's got her, Randart will soon take care of that. If not, the mages will track her down on land."

"What if she won't cooperate?" Jehan asked.

Was that irony in his voice? Canardan eyed his son, then shrugged. Imagination. Maybe the boy hesitated for his usual stupid reasons. She might not be pretty, or more important, might not like art. "She'll cooperate."

They both knew he'd use persuasion, and then threat.

The rest of the lunch was about details—the ball, taxes, decisions. Canardan did not expect any intelligent response. He probably did not want it. He only wanted acquiescence, and that Jehan gave him with his usual air of absence.

Sherwood Smith

Seeing it, his father relaxed. When Canardan was finished, he rose. It was time to get on with his busy day, and for his son to carry out his assigned tasks.

Jehan crossed the long halls to his seldom-used rooms, now filled with people patiently awaiting him: the two tailors, a model his height and build, a dozen apprentices standing ready with swatches of cloth, and servants hovering at the back.

Jehan submitted silently to their ministrations, his thoughts extremely bitter. They stayed that way until evening, by which time his head ached like a hammer on metal.

So he was in no real mood of appreciation when he sat down to dinner with his father and his prisoner, Princess Atanial, who was tall, built on slighter lines than her daughter, though not by much. They had the same light hair and the same light eyes, though there the resemblance ended. Sasha, Jehan thought, was a real blend of her parents' features, Math's distinctive bones made beautiful by Atanial's spun-sugar prettiness.

He hated her laugh.

"So *nice* it is to meet you *at last*." She giggled. It really was a giggle. "You *do* have white hair. Not light blond, or what we call *platinum*, it's so white it's blue." And the trilling giggle again.

"All the morvende are like that." Canardan didn't seem to mind the laugh. "You should see a room full of 'em. Like snow statues."

The princess leaned forward and pressed Jehan's fingers. "Oh, but don't think I don't count you as handsome. Woo-hoo-hoo! Why, the girls must simply *swoon* over you."

He tried not to show his wince.

"But I'm told all the Merindars are as handsome as your father."

He braced himself—and there came the laugh.

How could his father possibly admire this woman? But he was staring at her with a peculiar bemusement Jehan had never seen in his face before.

36

The signal for the servants at least quieted the laugh as food was handed round and everyone ate. Atanial plopped her elbows on the table the same way her daughter did. This breach of manners lessened Jenah's irritation enough to make her voice bearable.

Just as well, for she chattered through the entire dinner, running on about masquerades, the castle, music, Math, and ending with, "So what will your costume be, dear?"

Dear? "Not much I can be." He felt measurably better now that he'd eaten.

She chuckled, a soft, even attractive sound that suddenly shifted to the piercing giggle. Jehan's nerves fired. Was it possible she was faking that horrible laugh?

He fought back the tiredness settling like cloud-blankets over his thoughts now that the headache had receded, and forced himself to pay attention. "Not many famous morvende in sunsider history."

"Sunsider? Oh! You mean we who live in the sun and not in your caves. Woo hoo! But you could wear a wig. Some sort of disguise along with your mask—"

And put that idea in everyone's mind? He marshaled the last of his energy and waved a languid hand. "Loathe disguises in any form. Any mask I wear must be a work of art."

"Oh, I *see.*" She trilled coyly. "*Art,* yes. I think your father told me you are sensitive to all forms of art. That must be your morvende heritage." And the laugh again.

What a stupid remark! Yet Math had admired his wife's brains, and Sasha thought highly of her mother.

If so, why?

His interest sharpened. Seeing his father gazing at her with a slight furrow between his brows, Jehan said, "Does your daughter like masquerades?"

"My daughter?" Princess Atanial looked around as if a daughter were hiding behind the chandelier or under the table. "Oh yes. That is, she does love a good romp. When in the mood. Though she is not much one for costume. They do so rip and tear so easily. Hee-hee-hee!"

"In the mood?" Jehan persisted, after his father made a motion with his hand, waggling the fingers. *More, more.*

"Well. You know," Atanial said airily, looking at the light through her glass. "Not angry. Or sullen. She does have her very good days, and on those, she can be as sweet as roses, and for longer than many give her credit for. Why, are you interested in my darling Sasha? Oh, you young men, always with the young, but I'm only an ugly old woman, and I don't count. I know, it's the way of life." A bosom-heaving sigh.

Canardan sat back, gazing at her in perplexity. Jehan winced when she trilled again. "Oh no." He forced a smile. "Quite the opposite, I assure you. It's only your beauty that has me hoping your daughter might be a candle to your sun."

He felt a pang of self-loathing, knowing how false he sounded.

She twiddled her fingers at him demurely. "Go along, then. Beautiful indeed! They do say that poor Sasha inherited her father's looks, but we who love her think her beautiful, and as for that terrible Kickpail epithet, well, it's simply not true. Quite unkind, put about by jealous minds."

"Kickpail?" both men repeated at the same time.

Atanial looked skyward. "Oh dear. *Don't* tell me you hadn't heard about everyone calling her Clumsy Kickpail. Naughty me! But how was I supposed to know? I assure you the stories about how ungainly she is are quite exaggerated. Quite. She only broke that table once, and it was already old and ready to fly to pieces at a touch. As for those windows, why, that can happen to anyone. And it's not true she flung the serving maid through one. Stupid girl tripped all on her own, not moving out of the way fast enough." Atanial thumped her elbows back onto the table, chin resting on her laced fingers. "When my daughter has a sword in her hand, it's art to watch her. Though it's better not to watch when her temper is, ah, somewhat peppery. But that's true of anyone. An-ee-one!" She blinked rapidly.

Jehan was stunned. A more false word picture of the Sasha he knew could scarcely be found—except for the sword. *The single true observation reported to my father.* Surely Atanial had to be playing some sort of game, right under Canardan's nose.

"Oh, I do so hope I can introduce the two of you." Atanial gave a coy little bat to Jehan's sleeve. "I can give you some little teentsy hints on how best not to set off, that is, how to please her the most. She is the best company if you don't anger—ah, when in her wonderful social mood."

Jehan was sure of it now, Atanial was lying. To what effect? His father made a surreptitious encouraging motion.

Jehan turned back to Atanial. "Teentsy hints like?"

"Never talk about flowers with her. She hates the sight of them for some reason. Oh, and rain. It puts her in such a dour mood. That's natural, isn't it? Everybody hates rain. She also hates snow, hot weather and wind. Horses. She despises their smell, and their noises. Talking about any other woman will miff her, oooh, the tiniest bit. She's been so sheltered, she never really learned social graces. We were on the run for so many years, and then she had to adjust to another world at the most awkward age, and the awkwardness, I fear... Her family loves her dearly, and we don't count any of these faults against her thousands of good qualities." Atanial sighed, looking up again. "But oh, I must admit to the teeniest bit of jealousy myself! That's the way of it. When a young woman enters the conversation, if not the room, the old woman is quite forgotten. I must get used to it, I suppose."

There was more obvious digging for compliments, which Canardan, bestirring himself at last, gave with grace, evoking that head-shattering laugh. And then—none too soon—they all parted, to the sound of hammering and muffled swearing from below as servants muscled garlands out to decorate the walkways leading to the grand chambers.

Canardan put a hand out to keep Jehan from leaving. When they were alone, he said, "She's never spoken so much about the girl in all the days she's been here."

"Is she always like that?" Jehan asked, too tired to think.

Canardan rubbed his jaw. "No. But I think, I think she was flirting with you."

Jehan stared, appalled. "That was flirting?"

"What else could it have been? You're young, almost as handsome as I am, and who knows what sort of customs they get up to in that other world?" Canardan took in his son's honest disgust and amazement. "The important thing is, she hasn't said as much in all the weeks she's been here. I want you to take her out for a ride. Let her flirt as much as she likes. Get more out of her, especially about Math."

Jehan forced himself to bring up the subject of Sasha, dangerous as it was. Much as he hated himself for his astounding failure in every particular of their relationship— except for one incredible kiss. Maybe that had been a mistake as well, but one he'd never regret... *Focus, idiot.* "Do you really want me to marry someone called Clumsy Kickpail?" And then he had it, Atanial's reasons for the lies. "She sounds terrible. We should be glad she's gone."

But Canardan just grinned. "What could be better? The worse this girl is, the more popular you become. She can always sustain an accident when convenient. From the sound of it, no one would even mind. Better and better."

Jehan almost felt dizzy, his emotions veering between revulsion and laughter at how wrong that vivid word picture was of Sasha. How to let Atanial know her ruse was not working? He couldn't. He hated the pretense, the lying, but as he crossed to his rooms, the soft summer air bringing the sounds of workers singing tunelessly a ballad from Sartor, he knew he would lie—cheat—steal, if he had to, if it meant he could protect Sasha from discovery by Randart. Even though she didn't want to be protected.

He also would lie—cheat—steal in order to protect the kingdom.

It needed protecting badly.

Once he reached his room, he dismissed everyone but gangling, tuft-haired Kazdi, his cadet runner. It took only an exchange of looks and Kazdi prowled around watching for spies, especially Chas.

Jehan shut himself in the bath chamber and pulled out his

magic-transfer case, which he had not been able to check for days.

Several tiny folded pieces of paper awaited him. The first, from Elkin, his mage-student friend doing his journeywork as a mage-scribe at the academy.

In ancient Sartoran, he'd written: *Damedran put in for changes. Dannath rescinded them. Tension between masters and seniors.*

There was one from Robin, leading the fleet.

*The* Skate *is leading the Aloca fleet after us. We think they're going to try a pincer. We'll hang them up around the islands.*

One from Aslo, the ally he'd planted in Randart's fleet carrying the invasion weapons, now the liaison with Tharlif, the tough old woman who'd been privateering for most of her life. One of Zathdar's staunchest allies. *Our contact agrees, purpose of shipment is to stockpile weapons. Much speculative war talk.*

So far, as expected.

The last one, the smallest, he unfolded, his heart hammering.

There were no words, only a tiny drawing of an owl in flight.

He smiled for the first time in days, left the bath for his waiting bed, and was soon deep in long-postponed sleep.

# Chapter Five

The weather did not relent.

In the gardens the blossoms drooped, looking papery and withered, the edges of leaves yellowed, and a silted pall of dust shimmered in the air above the roads. But the night of the masquerade, a couple thousand candles softened the dust and dryness of the city with a forgiving, golden shimmer. Lights were everywhere, candles in cut-glass holders, their flames glittering in infinite reflection against paired mirrors down hallways. Outside, candles glowed in lamps of colored glass that were hung in trees and set along stone walls.

The king watched his guests arrive from his private balcony overlooking the broad entryway to the grand chambers. His son was with him, observing the press of open, light carriages rolling up to release fantastically groomed and glittering guests. Atanial listened through the open doors of her room to the echoes of musicians tuning instruments, servants calling last-minute orders and bustling about on last errands.

All three knew the setting was right. Why shouldn't it be, after uncounted hands had labored all week to get it that way? All three of them reflected (Canardan briefly, Jehan brooding, Atanial with resignation) how the decorations, the clothes, the starry night with its colored lights, hid the parching drought— as the prospect of a party hid the tensions between people.

The king had to wait until everyone was there, for his appearance signaled the beginning, and afterward arrivals were officially late. Being late to a party given by a king would get you talked about, and not in a good way, for months afterward.

So Canardan stood out on the balcony, which was at least somewhat cooler than indoors. He wished he'd not chosen a heavy robe, splendid as it had looked in the heralds' drawings. Yet his costume was a message, a subtle reminder of his own heritage, for he was going as Matthias Lirendi, the last and most famous (some said infamous) emperor of Colend. Who was a Merindar ancestor. Of course he was an ancestor of most of the royal houses in the eastern part of the continent, but that also underscored Canardan's royal antecedents.

Jehan had chosen the guise of an old Sartoran poet-prince, known for his complete disregard for the invisible boundaries of politics as well as for his visionary works of art. The long paneled robe worn over loose trousers was cool and easy to move in; the colors, sky blue and black, complemented his white hair.

He knew the costume would annoy his father, good as it looked. But its purpose was to deflect interest in him as a political figure. Though in truth, he thought sourly as he reluctantly started downstairs, every single thing he did or said had political repercussions.

The costume and his rank would at least hold importunate guests to discussing any subject he chose, and he chose to stick with poetry.

As his shoes whispered over the marble steps, he considered Atanial. The question was, what would he say to her?

He thought back over their ride earlier that day. They had talked little, both agreeing that the heat was too breathless. In reality, Jehan's planned words had zapped away when he discovered that Chas was to accompany them, ostensibly to see to their needs.

The few words they'd exchanged had been masterpieces of dullness, punctuated by Atanial's horrible giggle. As Atanial commented with excruciating detail on everything she saw, right to the types of grass growing on the roadside, Jehan enjoyed the jaw-locked tedium in Chas's face.

Obedient to his father's wishes, he'd asked about Sasharia, to be regaled with giggle-punctuated stories not really about Sasha at all, but about Atanial. She'd described little anecdotes even more pointless and tedious than her chatter about grass, often correcting herself several times in the maddening way of the crashing bore. "Was it five? No, no, I state it wrong, it was four. No, it was five, for I remember the moon that night, and I was wearing my new gown...four...my friend—you should meet her some day—anyway she said, 'Four more times,' I remember it like it was yesterday. Or was it five after all?"

Jehan had kept Chas in view just so he could count the man's attempts to swallow yawns. Jehan was now convinced Atanial's chatter was a performance, and it was brilliant.

He was convinced when he realized that Atanial was willing to lie about Sasha when alone with the king and himself, but in front of all those other ears, she never quite brought herself to say anything at all. And so, mindful of Chas behind him, he'd contributed his mite by boring on until his throat was parched about styles of Sartoran versus Colendi art.

They'd all been glad when that ride ended.

Snapped back to the present by the sweet, brassy peal of the King's Fanfare, Jehan took his place in the grand ballroom. Around him hissed the breathing of far too many people, all shifting and rustling as they tried not to sweat into their good clothes.

The promenade introductory music prompted the company to assemble, and because this was a masquerade where the customary order of rank was somewhat relaxed, those more bold, more confident or more desperate all tried to get to the front without unseemly haste.

Atanial, at the king's side, observed the prince's distracted blue gaze as he fell in behind. She raised her hand to meet Canardan's palm at shoulder height, distracted momentarily by the fall of the splendid sleeves of his robe, all blue and gold, embroidered with highly stylized, gracefully attenuated lilies.

He did the king thing well, she thought with private irony. He looked good from his fineweave boots to the waving auburn hair brushed back nobly from his brow—not a hint of balding, either. The angle of his chin, his slight smile convinced her he knew it. He was *preening.* That sense of irony became an inward laugh.

As for arrogance, she knew she looked good all in midnight blue velvet, edged with crimson, and the high medieval headdress like nothing in the room, her mask being (for she knew she was the center of attention, and she'd play along) the sheerest of veils.

It was enough to hide her inch-long grayish silver roots. She remembered that people did color their hair on this world, but it was done by magic, not chemicals. She did not want to risk inviting any of Canardan's mages to perform magic over her. Who knew what kind of spell they might slip in besides the hair color?

Therefore the veil. Even if she was the only one amused, going as Maleficent from Disney's *Sleeping Beauty* definitely gave her secret enjoyment.

The promenade began with a flourish of brassy horns and a clash of cymbals, all the guests pacing in time, chins high, backs straight, toes pointed.

"You look lovely, Atanial." Canardan smiled. "Is that a guise from your world or ours?"

"Oh, mine," she said cheerily, noting the "your world or ours". "Maleficent is a very, very wicked woman."

"Ah, and by that you are suggesting?"

"Nothing. Do you think me wicked? You know better than that, Canardan. I like her style."

"I sometimes wonder if I know you at all, Sun. But a wicked queen who reigns in a ballroom, it's a fine touch. Danger with dance, without destruction. Would that the world were conducted the same." He smiled, saluting her hand with grace.

And—they were quite aware—every pair of eyes in the ballroom took in that hand kiss.

Snap. The trap she'd helped him to build closed round her, just as she became aware of it. *I ought to have been Clarabelle the stupid cow.* She realized at last what a masquerade *meant.* She was on display, everyone knew who she was, but the very fact that this was a masquerade meant she could not actually speak to anyone about anything real.

She was stuck in a Disney guise, but this was no Disney film, with a handy fairy godmother or blue angel standing by to waft the hapless heroine to a happy ending.

Furious with him, with herself, she stared straight ahead and worked on her breathing, as Canardan looked round to the formed circle of his guests. He caught at least four meaningful glances, people who were going to single him out for A Little Talk.

He faced forward, setting a slower pace. When you're a king you can slow up an entire circle of people and no one will make a peep. The gap between them and the last couple widened. Speaking low so that Jehan and the duchess behind them could not hear—not that they were listening, for he could hear the duchess talking about her daughter's stunning talent in the arts—he said, "I take it you feel more comfortable among those of rank than you once did?"

"Oh, I got over the rank thing really fast in the old days," she responded with forced cheer. "As Math often said, princes have to put on their pants one leg at a time, same as do poets. Or poulterers."

"I remember you brought that up during one of our first conversations. Such sayings sound earnest and egalitarian, but are they really believed? There is a such thing as protesting too much."

"Then I'll drop the sayings. I see your aristocrats as human beings raised to certain customs, ways of speaking and thinking, that become habit. It's partly training that sets anyone apart from anyone else. And training means you're taught to do something, whether it's making lace or running a kingdom, but whether or not you do it well is up to the individual," she said.

Before Canardan could answer, the musicians shifted up half a key, and he realized they'd been patiently playing the same phrase far too many times. He was not being a good host. He lengthened his step, Atanial matched his pace, and they obligingly closed the distance with the rest of the circle.

Atanial turned gracefully to the right as the king turned to his left, and her palm met the prince's. They completed their half turn and began pacing in the opposite direction.

Everyone's attention was distracted by their new partners. She snapped her gaze back to Jehan and was surprised by a narrow, assessing gaze that was, for a moment, startlingly like his father's.

She murmured without moving her lips, "Ananda said to trust you."

And heard him draw in a breath.

No more. Already the couple ahead had glanced back, and she felt the weight of the king's gaze behind her. She turned her attention away from Jehan, smiling vapidly into the room as they trod the measures until the next chord change, half a key up the scale.

Again they changed partners and direction, leaving her facing a man her own age. She recognized a duke from what used to be the west, before Locan Jora forced a treaty onto Khanerenth, dividing the kingdom into two. Thus truncating most of the duke's land. His spare form was barely in costume, more of an old-fashioned court outfit. The "mask" was the visor of his helm, which he'd lifted.

Obviously he was only paying lip service to the masquerade rules. Being a duke, he could. Atanial remembered the unspoken but iron-strong custom: if someone of higher rank broke a social rule, you could too. But you didn't do it first.

It was up to the duke to choose whether he would speak to Atanial or to Maleficent. She wasn't really a princess, not with the Zhavalieshins deposed. It was a mere courtesy title, her privilege (or lack of same) dependent entirely on the king's whim.

"Is Prince Math alive?" he asked, his brows bristling.

"I don't know."

"You trying to find out?"

Step, step, dip—step, step, dip. The music changed, but the duke gripped her hand. "Are you?" He let her go and growled, "Never mind. I think I have my answer." He turned away.

Atanial also turned, not really seeing her next partner. She felt sick, certain the duke had implied she had forgotten her husband and was angling for a king. No time to consider anything except that, so far, the masquerade was a disaster. *I'm a failure without having spoken ten words.*

Her next partner asked who she was.

"Maleficent."

She did not know the man, but he was polite, asking one or two suave questions about Maleficent that were easy to answer, and the dance whirled him on.

The next two partners accepted Maleficent at face value, and embarked on light flirtation with this fantasy wicked queen. She answered in kind, which was easy, but as the long dance wore on she was more and more aware of just how badly she had fumbled.

A new partner leaned close as they placed their palms together. "Do you remember me, your highness?"

She faced him, to encounter her new partner's mask. Through the eye holes she made out familiar gray eyes. He had a heavy jaw, and iron gray hair.

Resisting the impulse to rip aside her veil and his mask so they could be two real people, she sifted memories. Those eyes. Younger, browner hair—someone around Canary—yes, one of the captains in his own private guard during the old king's days, now obviously titled with land of his own. For Canardan did not invite mere guard captains to masquerade balls in the royal palace.

Above her rank? Below it? What *was* her rank in their eyes, anyway?

Whatever. She was not about to frost him by pretending he'd broken the blasted "rules". "How nice to see you." She smiled. "You've flourished, I see."

"Old count of Shesba died. No heirs. So I am still in the saddle, but now riding my own lands, so to speak." The familiar voice brought back Math saying *...and he's one of the quiet, honest sorts, warrior captains who would carry out their duties no matter who was in charge. If left alone, good, reliable people.*

Atanial now remembered Shesba as a difficult area way to the north, squished between mountains and the vile coastline. She congratulated him, the music changed again, and she found herself with another partner, this one tall, old, unfamiliar, their voices blending with the hum of conversation and the music. Then the entire company sighed as, at last, the unseen mages got their magic spells working and a breath of cooler air teased her already moist flesh, followed by a gentle, steady breeze.

Almost everyone visibly relaxed, some faces turning to the open doorways, through which the mages had drawn their invisible tunnel of colder air from high in the sky.

The short, stout Chief of the Guild Council was her next partner, followed by another landowner of some degree. Other men danced with her after that. Everyone knew who she was, but stayed on their side of the Maleficent pretense. They were all polite, two or three friendly. But, clearly, the king's men. Not allies. And in their eyes, Prince Math's wife was flourishing here in her gilded cage.

Step, step, turn, step, step turn, the promenade sped up now, always climbing half a chord. They were nearly at the end of the circle, the talk the most superficial exchanges of politenesses. Her exchange with that duke lingered, making her wary. How many of these smiling men thought she'd abandoned Math to his fate in order to catch a king?

Canardan watched her from across the room. She danced with those entrancing moves she'd always had. Sometimes she spoke, but judging from the lack of reaction in her partners, everything was as it should be. Let her trip prettily around his ballroom and show everyone how well he treated her. He hoped she'd enjoy it. Thinking about her was more pleasant than listening to the obviously rehearsed compliments and broad hints for returned compliments of his current partner. *Fishing for royal catch*, Canardan thought sourly. Here he'd invited this baroness—old family, good lands, good support, rich—because her daughter might be a fallback for Jehan. He'd forgotten she was a widow.

"May I honor your majesty with a reminder of how famous were your splendid regattas through the city of Alsais? We still read the poems all these centuries later," she whispered, fluttering her fan.

What regatta was she dropping her not-so-subtle hint about? Because it had nothing to do with Colend's past glories, not in that tone. Oh yes. *That* regatta, he thought, smiling into her eyes. Right before he married Ananda, the last time he'd dressed up as Matthias the Magnificent of Colend. What his partner hadn't found out was that she had been one of three dalliances that memorable night.

So. The women already knew that Ananda wasn't skipping the social duty tonight as she usually did, but was gone. *Of course* everyone knew. His worst enemy was rumor, something you couldn't fight with a sword. He'd underestimated how quickly they'd come a-courting.

The music changed, sparing him having to come up with a reply that was agreeable, but not too agreeable, friendly but not flirtatious.

How was Atanial faring? He had almost completed the circle. Atanial was maybe eight or ten men away, talking and laughing with one of his barons. He was aware of Jehan behind him, murmuring something about Sartoran tapestry weaving, and from the tittering, effusive response, he too was being courted.

Where was that daughter of Atanial's? He hoped there'd be a message from either Zhavic or Randart soon.

The dance ended.

Atanial watched how the circle broke into tiny circles, each revealing in its numbers, in who moved to whom, who collected company, who stood where.

The biggest circle formed around the king. Of course. But

Jehan's was nearly as large—moon to his father's sun—with the younger women forming most of his group. And if they were all doing their best to attract the attention of a handsome prince, who could blame them?

Father and son retreated to get something to drink.

On either side of the room, mirror images, were great carved tables set with rows of tall, fluted glasses containing punch, water, wine. Water! Atanial located the table on her side of the room and reached it in twenty swift steps, her veil fluttering behind. She took one,and lifted her veil to drink. Over the rim, glimmering with reflected fire from the chandeliers overhead, she saw father and son meet to exchange brief words before they were surrounded.

The musicians struck up a melody, and both heads turned, for a breathtaking moment poised at exactly the same angle. There was Canardan's handsome profile, in his son planed and refined, Jehan's coloring moonlight and silver instead of ruddy gold. But one thing for certain from their body language: they were fond of one another.

And she, Atanial Fatwit Blitherer, had just tipped her hand to the son. *Why, why, why? Ananda, why did you do that to me, was it revenge after all?*

Jehan chose at random a partner for the new dance. The rest of the young women drifted by, ribbons fluttering, silks glowing richly in the candlelight, no one wanting to ask him and risk being turned down in front of the others, so they eyed him and smiled.

Atanial felt a touch on her wrist and looked up into the face of one of Canardan's aristocratic working men, this one the governor of Vadnais harbor. Numb with self-loathing, she set down her empty glass, curtseyed and trod with him to the middle of the floor. He chatted with cheery ease about his racehorses until the dance ended. The seductive triple beat of a waltz—the first one of the evening—signaled, in straightened shoulders, lifted chins, laughs and shimmering fans, the electrical impulse of expectation.

So strange, Atanial thought. Not just that they had the

waltz here, but it apparently was far older than it was on Earth. Chicken/egg.

Canardan watched Atanial look around, her profile behind the veil etched against the wall as she watched—who? Jehan was busy with a very young lady dressed in a stunning gown made up of fragile silk roses of twenty graded shades of pink.

Canardan flicked his gaze back. Atanial was lost behind a long whirling knotwork of dancing couples. When they passed, she was visible again, over by the refreshments table, nibbling a cake—

"Your majesty," someone murmured behind him.

He looked down at the short, balding Chief of the Guild Council, and frowned. No use in hiding behind masquerade nonsense now. His relations with the guilds were already teetering.

"Your majesty, you have not had time to see me, despite my petitions sent each day," the man stated. "But I must and will speak. If I end up with the Scribe Sharveshin in the dungeon for my temerity, despite its being my duty—"

Canardan sighed. "It's not even remotely treason to ask questions, Guild Chief. Why are you pretending it is?"

"Why do you have a scribe in the dungeon? A scribe! May as well be a herald! And the Heralds' Guild Mistress as well as the Scribes' Master, at my office every day demanding to know why. If it's whim, who's next?"

"Asking questions is not treason," Canardan said. "But meeting in a cellar and planning overthrow of the government is."

"Who says they were planning overthrow?" the Guild Chief stated stubbornly. "There has been no public trial. We did not hear witnesses against them. As mandated in the agreement between guilds and crown."

Canardan cursed, mind working rapidly even as his gaze sought Atanial.

She paid no attention to the king. Or his heir. She finished her cake and wondered who would be mortally offended if she left. She should get away before she bumbled even more stupidly—

A flash of blue, and Jehan was suddenly before her, his partner having been relinquished to another dancer, though her glance lingered over the man's shoulder. Jehan's blue eyes were no longer as empty as the sky, but focused. Intense.

It was time, he'd decided, to trust someone. Again, that is.

"I saw her," he murmured, and passed without turning his head.

It was her turn to draw in her breath.

To the Guild Chief (having watched Jehan pass Atanial without stopping) Canardan said, "I will see you after I've had a chance to examine the prisoners myself. Everything according to treaty. But I've not yet had time."

The Chief of the Guild Council had to bow and accept that.

Three men ranged before Atanial. She put out her hand somewhat blindly, smiling her social smile, and triple-stepped, neat and light, with the owner of the first warm fingers that gripped hers.

She did not come within speaking distance of Jehan until the evening was nearly over. That dance was the Khanerenth version of a quadrille—that is, a complicated line dance that broke into whirling and braiding twos, fours, twos, eights, twos, fours, and twos as they slowly moved down the line. One always coming back to one's original partner for hands across.

The dance, she had already discovered, had changed only in one regard. There were two dips where there had been two hops, otherwise it was the same one she and Math had drilled down the long royal portrait gallery on those soft spring nights, as they talked and laughed about every subject in the universe.

Jehan was suddenly before her, bowing, holding out a hand so they could step past one another.

"You saw Sasha?" she asked.

They parted. Round, round, step, step, smile, dip, twirl, hold up one's hand, traipse in another circle, dip, bow, turn, step step step, and there he was again.

"She's gone. I assume she's seeking Math."

Twirl. Step. Atanial fought impatience. She could feel Canardan watching. A quick look showed benign pleasure, but if he saw them talk, saw them even look serious, that expression could change fast.

*I must protect Jehan too.* She glanced at the white-haired prince's vacant smile in the next group over, all four with their hands together in the center as they tripped in a circle.

He was thinking the same thing. He couldn't quite see her eyes, but her manner, the way she'd drawn in a breath—the absence of that giggle—had convinced him that he'd done at least this much right. So far. But hurry or furtiveness or even too much said would catch idle eyes, raise questions. They could only speak for that brief time when they met in the center of the square, changing places with hands across.

"She trusted you, then?" Atanial asked, and they parted.

*Three*, he thought. *We only have five chances left.*

Instinct prompted him to lie, as he always had. But the relief he'd felt on telling her the truth overrode the mere protective instinct, and so when they met again, he said, "No."

Another indrawn breath. Her hand trembled under his fingers, as though she tightened her muscles against betraying expression, and once again he felt relief and alarm.

On the next, when she looked her question as she reached for hands across, he murmured, "Kissed me, yes. No trust."

And he was gone, not seeing her face.

No one could see her face, except behind the mysterious shimmer of her veil, so they could not see the sting of tears. *My fault, my fault*, she was thinking. No use in trying to excuse herself. They'd returned to Earth all those years ago grief-stricken and angry; sunshine dancingstar, she who had left her world a hippie idealist, had come back bitter and afraid. She'd told her daughter over and over, in infinite variation, *Men are pretty and fun to be with, but never. Ever. Trust them.*

*Think. Do not make things worse.* They had three more exchanges ahead, and the dance would be over.

When they met, both uttered a word at the same time, he blanked his face and she said again, "Is she safe?"

*Two more,* they each thought as they parted, the pretty melody tripping through the silver flutes and reed horns and harp strings. *We have to talk.*

He trod his stately pace, smiling at the two young heiresses who cast him languishing (and watchful) glances over their fans as he circled them and mentally reviewed the palace. Her rooms, warded. His rooms, warded, and spies in the stable, kitchen and the government rooms—

There she was again, and he could feel her question, but he had no answer, and so number seven passed in silence.

When she neared for number eight, he saw in the rigid line of her shoulders, the tension outlining her veiled head and neck, that the question still stood.

He said, "So far, yes." Knowing that she'd figure out what it meant: that he was having Sasha followed.

# Chapter Six

I learned two things the first week of my journey.

The first occurred two days to the northwest, on the meandering trade road alongside the Lembesca River. I did not risk any gallop in that withering, humid heat, shade too seldom a relief, and then only briefly under hardy trees with long thin leaves through which the brilliant sun shone in a lacework of glare.

I arrived at an inn early in the afternoon. I would have liked to push on farther. I'd been careful to walk the horse and to offer water at the two streams we'd passed, but she was looking dangerously droopy as we plodded along the road under what seemed to be a permanent dust pall. Since I had no idea how long I'd ride before finding another village, I thought I'd better stop.

So did a harvest party. And the friends of a journeyman who'd been made master joiner that day, after they'd been working on a building somewhere over the dry, golden hills.

The two parties converged almost at the same time. I had gone in to arrange for a hammock when the harassed innkeeper, who had deployed his entire family for the first party, paused at the door in dismay. From outside came the merry sounds of a crowd turning off the road to the stables as, behind us, the harvesters flowed downstairs into the common room, singing out for food and drink!

Mr. Innkeeper reminded me of my father. Mrs. Innkeeper was a round-faced woman my mother's age who bustled anxiously to the door of the kitchen. Their expressions were a mixture of stun and a kind of helpless horror.

I swerved away from the door, moved to the shelf behind the counter and took one of the aprons I saw folded there.

The man ran out to the stable to commandeer bodies for cook's helpers. The woman turned her head, her braid half coming down, and stared from the apron to me. Brows rising, she glanced at my arms.

"Experience?" she asked, obviously trying not to hope.

"Four years."

Relief made her face redden. "Here are the choices," she said rapidly. "Broiled cabbage rolls, fresh-water fish, rice, onion, cooked in pressed olive. Rice with melted cheese and chicken with lemon glaze. Lentil soup with yesterday's chicken, and cheese over it if they like. Bread until it runs out, and green-apple tarts."

"Got it. Drink?"

"Don't fret over the drink, my daughters can see to that." She indicated two light-haired girls of about ten and twelve who'd appeared from the storeroom door, both in aprons, one dusty with flour, the other setting down a mending basket behind the bar. "But they are too small to carry more than one plate at a time."

"I can carry six." I flexed my biceps. "On one arm."

She laughed. "You shall have a royal meal when we finish, and our best wine."

"Innkeeper! Wake up!" a man roared, and that was the last time we spoke to one another for many hours.

It was about midnight when I thumped down onto a bench, weary, my arms feeling like string. I had just enough energy to appreciate it. A good workout is a good workout, however one gets it.

The woman entered from the kitchen (from which every scrap of food had been emptied), took one look around the empty room where the two daughters and I had finished cleaning the tabletops. The younger daughter had fallen asleep on a bench in about two breaths, head on her crossed arms, washcloth still gripped in her fingers. The other girl stood at a window, staring out at the pinpoints of dancing lights as the harvesters wove, singing, back to their homes.

"A bed is waiting." The woman touched my arm. "Follow my daughter."

The older girl led me upstairs. She was stumbling in exhaustion. I'd expected a hammock but found myself in a narrow but comfortable bed, the linen sheets smelling of a recent drying in sunlight. Heaven.

When I woke, there was hot water steaming on a table.

I went downstairs to a massive breakfast, which ended as the footsteps of the celebrants overhead began thumping about. The family, still tired, seemed cheered by the father's grin. He'd made enough, he said, to refurbish the stable against winter. Then one by one they turned to me.

So, my two discoveries. One, in a world without the level of bureaucracy that binds the US of A, you can do things like pick up an apron and there's no worry about contracts, the IRS, etc. That was the good thing. The not-so-good thing I learned is that it's really difficult to make up believable lies when you are a stranger in a strange land.

"Were you inn-raised?" the mother asked me, and as I opened my mouth to lie, the father said, "Where? We know most of the inn families up the coast and a good ways along both rivers."

They were so friendly, and eager for news and gossip. There I was, struggling to come up with lies.

Well, they were not supposed to know I was lying, I told myself sternly. This was the only way I'd get to Dad, which meant a few harmless lies. Therefore my answers had to be short, and boring.

"Stables, mostly." At the surprise in the older daughter's face, I vaguely remembered leaving my mare to be curried, and I said quickly, "Supplies. Cleaning. Helped with the tables, when I was little, down south. Then I became a sailor." I ventured that shot on reflecting how far inland we were. Hopefully they knew nothing of the sea.

"Where did you sail to?" The daughter leaned forward. "I love stories about other places!"

"Why are you so far north?" The mother also leaned forward, ready to be sympathetic if there'd been some disaster.

"Maybe we could get you to run a message, if you're passing toward some of our folks?" the father put in. "Even with things being bad, handing off letters still always nets a free bed for a night, among our folk."

I dealt with all these as best as I could, accepting the message finally, figuring I would pay in the next town I could for a messenger. And I took my leave, feeling isolated, uncertain, afraid my lies would explode behind me.

The route I'd chosen was, I hoped, random enough to keep me anonymous and not make my destination clear to anyone who knew magic. Ivory Mountain lay to the west of Ellir, at the far end of the Bar Larsca Valley, inside of the border mountains. The road to Locan Jora was alongside the river that divided Ivory Mountain from some of the other high peaks. I knew from childhood Ivory Mountain had a mysterious rep, having to do with magic. I didn't want to risk going straight to it, so I chose the trade route between the two biggest rivers, where, yes, the most traffic was constantly moving to and fro. I hoped there'd be safety in numbers. The idea was to cruise as unobtrusively as possible to the big trade city, Zhavlir, which lay at the fork of the great rivers. Hang a left to the west. After crossing the Northsca, zap south into the valley.

That was my plan.

I'd also planned to reach Zhavlir in a week—Southern California freeway flyer optimism!

My reeducation began with a high-pressure front squatted over the sweating countryside, forcing all traffic to a crawl except maybe on the military roads, which were beautifully maintained by mages paid out of the king's coffers.

When at last the weather broke I was scarcely halfway to the city, still angling up to the northwest, my butt sore, my clothes soggy, the mare slow. I wished I had my old junkmobile, which (when it was working) at least had air conditioning. Better, I could rev the thing up to sixty miles per hour instead of the two to five I was sort of making now. I'd been on the road a week and a day. That last morning dawned hotter than ever. The sultry stillness began with a peculiar sheen to the light that gradually oranged and blended into shadow as overhead a massive storm boiled up, ready to rock and roll.

And rock and roll it did.

The rain felt good for about the first thirty seconds, until the wind rose. A sudden, cold wind drove stinging hailstones directly into my face and hands. The hail peppered my poor mare, who snorted, skittish with ill temper, and who could blame her? The blackish green clouds barely cleared the lashing treetops. The light vanished, and my mare now plodded, head low, directly into the oncoming storm sweeping down from the northwest.

The road soon turned to muddy slosh, caking her hooves and slowing her so much we seemed to be squelching in one place.

After a couple of ice ages, I realized I was not hallucinating, there really were lights somewhere beyond. I threw back my aching head, peering blearily. Yes. Real lights, glimmering through the downpour. At least the hail had given over to real rain, but so much, so quick, it was like a hose turned onto my head, and I had to breathe behind my hand.

The mare picked up her pace. The lights appeared to recede and I wondered miserably if mirages also came with cold and wet, but then the wind brought the warm scent of horse and hay. A stable! And between one shower and the next, I glimpsed the silhouette of a long, rambling building. Inn? Farmhouse?

Whatever it was, I vowed, they were going to take me as a guest, or discover my frozen corpse on their doorstep come morning, seriously lowering their property values.

Someone called out. The words blurred in the hissing roar. With my waning strength I kept my gaze on that square of golden light, which resolved into a broad, open door, like the gates to heaven.

Silhouettes emerged, one bearing a swinging lantern. I rode past them into the barn, and stopped. Warmth gradually dissolved the grip of cold, and sound returned, the flutter of wings and fretful murmling of birds in the rafters overhead, refugees, like me, from the storm. Around me, the quiet voice of command, and response of obedience.

Gradually I regained sight. Lantern flames flickered in the eddies of wind, reaching into the warm stable, their light stippling with gold the edges of a pile of hay, gleaming along neatly hung lengths of horse harnesses, and on people dressed in uniform color.

I had yet to dismount, though someone held my horse's bridle, waiting patiently. I stared uncomprehending into the faces of a group of young men and a couple of young women. In brown. With little silver cups stitched over the heart.

Sound, sight, and finally sense.

I had fumbled my way into a military outpost.

# Chapter Seven

The drought-breaking storm was a major weather front, catching the entire east end of the continent.

All over the kingdom people reacted, either running out to celebrate, or rushing about trying to save things that wet would ruin. Most snugged up inside of castles or cottages, barns or shops, and those on the road sought the shelter of trees or cliffsides.

Out on the sea, traders, navy, smugglers, fishers and pirates alike lay up under mostly bare poles with a scrap of sail to keep them pointed into the wind, and rode it out.

War Commander Randart, having kicked the captain out of his cabin on the ship he'd declared as his flag, sat with his meal uneaten, fighting against rage. The king had done *what*?

The report lay on the table, the words mocking him: ...*promised a treason trial for the prisoners taken along with Princess Atanial.*

Randart shook his head in disgust. Canardan was getting weaker every year. Why not just line them all up and have them shot, in as public an execution as possible? That would end his dilemma with rumors.

At least there was one possibility. Randart could show him how it could be done. Soon as he finished this pirate mission, he'd have those old guardsmen of Prince Math's, Silvag and Folgothan, taken out and shot in a public execution, under military law. That would demonstrate effectively how Canardan ought to handle those fools, and Randart would not have to say a word. It would all be in accordance with military regulations—the ones Randart himself had designed, and Canardan had signed into law.

He balled up the paper and tossed it out one of the stern windows into the storm.

Some welcomed the rain as a chance to escape snooping eyes.

Just outside of Ellir two columns of cadets, riding inland toward the siege war game they'd all been looking forward to, heard the horns call for camp setup, and they gladly broke ranks. Cursing, laughing, calling out insults, they dismounted and stumbled through the furious rain toward their places.

Camp setup was something you began in your first year. The senior cadets under the command of Damedran Randart oversaw the younger students. In good weather, watched by the critical eyes of the adult captains, they were fast, quiet and bored. The storm freed them from constraint, and though everyone knew what to do, setting up tents in that splashing downpour was an adventure. As the adults were as busy, there were surreptitious mud fights (the evidence, they knew, would soon rinse off) and some running around. It was fun and also a relief, so strict had been discipline in the temper-exasperating heat of the past three days.

Ban found his arm gripped as he struggled with his team to get the picket line set up. He whipped around, violently flinging off the hand. But he saw Damedran's face reflected in the ruddy glow of a torch.

Damedran jerked his chin over his shoulder. Ban followed. Not to the command tent, which was a misshapen giant mushroom full of snickering, cursing bumps and lumps as the setup crew tried to raise it from inside. Damedran led him to a clump of hardy trees a ways away. They stopped under the foliage, rain rattling the tossing leaves overhead.

"What," Ban shouted.

Damedran put his mouth near Ban's ear. "I think the sheep knows about the invasion."

"What?" Same word, but entirely different intonation.

"I've been thinking. What he said. On that yacht. Not outright. Mostly about what we ought to be doing in training next spring. You know. The hide-and-attack games."

"You told us that. I already told you it's a great idea. Bowsprit, even your cousin thinks so. Everybody does. Except your uncle. Won't let us change the training. So what can *we* do about it?"

"Not that." Damedran shook his head again. "Right before we got off the yacht, the sheep said something about those outsiders who pinched the prizes at the games and scragged my cousin Wolfie and Red. One said something about Norsunder going to war soon."

Warning tightened Ban's shoulders. The wind shifted, bringing a whiff of hot olive oil from the direction of the cook tent, then the cold wind snapped it away. "And?"

"Told Father, who told Uncle Dannath. Before we left. But he just laughed."

Ban shoved his fingers into his armpits. The storm had caught them too fast for them to fetch their gloves from the baggage train. "If the warning came from Prince Jehan, of course your uncle and your father won't listen."

"But I didn't tell that part. I told Father I'd heard it. Gossip. That's one reason why I waited all week. Father reported it to my uncle, then told me Uncle Dannath says I'll hear that all my life from cowards. Slackers. Fools."

Ban shook his head, thinking, *Why am I hearing this instead of Red or even Wolfie?* "Who were those fellows? I mean, how could a nine-year-old have the strength to dust four of us?"

Damedran shook his head. "I asked Wolfie that first thing. I thought the brat snuck up, brained them from behind one by one. Wolfie said they all four tried to take him on, teach him a lesson. Said it wasn't strength, it was that he always seemed to know what they were going to do before they did it, and then he knew exactly where to hit that hurt the most. Wolfie said he could have killed them all if he'd wanted to. The brat didn't even break a sweat. What kind of training teaches an undersized brat to do that?"

Ban shook his head. "I dunno. So why were they even here?"

"And why did they single out the sheep to give their warning to?"

"I think the sheep isn't a sheep at all," Ban said, voicing an inner conviction he'd never thought he'd share.

But Damedran did not scoff. They fell silent, neither quite looking at the other.

Damedran said, "I don't know what to do."

"Nothing."

Damedran frowned at Ban, meeting his gaze at last.

Ban relented. Damedran had been different since that day. He could be setting Ban up, but his instinct was against it. "There's nothing we can do. We're under orders, at the very bottom of the chain of command."

Damedran scowled. Ban was right. What was the good of being senior in rank above all the cadets if the only orders you could give were how many paces apart the tents had to be pitched?

"The real captains don't listen to us," Ban went on. "Your father listens only to your uncle. The king, too. They have their plans. We aren't going to change those." When Damedran ducked his head and grimaced in agreement, he added, "I think it's better to wait. Keep our ears open. Because one of these days we'll find someone who does listen."

Damedran frowned at the runnel of muddy water flowing over his boots, carrying twigs and yellow-edged leaves. The storm was lifting enough to permit some light.

Light. They'd be seen.

Damedran said, "All right. Then we'll wait."

They ran off to resume their duties.

At the same time, not far to the southwest, the proximity of the western mountains caused the air to roil and boil, sending lightning and thunder smashing across the sky.

Under cover of it, Devli Eban and his cousin Nad sped from the mage house where they were staying, circling around and climbing up onto the roof.

There they huddled under the eave of the servants' dormer window, which was shut tight and shuttered.

Ever since Devli had arrived back, they'd longed for a chance to speak to one another, but hadn't dared—not after Nad read the note Devli had slipped into his hand that night:

*We have two spies among us, one for the prince and the other for the king.*

Now they looked at one another, and as soon as the thunder overhead died away, Devli said, "What is the gossip about me?"

"They told us you got captured along with Prince Math's daughter by the pirate Zathdar, but you escaped. Had to make your way cross-country on foot, as they'd taken your transfer tokens, and you were afraid you were warded by the king's mages so you couldn't use the regular Transfer Destination. How much of that is true?"

Devli looked into his cousin's round face, blotched by cold. At least the worst of the rain was hitting the other side of the building. "Only that I was with them. We were on the pirate ship. When I was let go, I transferred outside of town. I lied to cover how long I was gone, because the king's got at least one spy with us."

Nad pursed his lips in a soundless whistle, knowing how very dangerous it was to transfer anywhere you either hadn't a Destination made safe for transferring, or had laid a token down somewhere in preparation.

"And the prince has a spy with us," Nad prompted. "That's what your note said."

"Here's what I didn't tell anyone." Devli leaned close. "The pirate Zathdar is none other than Prince Jehan."

Nad's jaw dropped.

"I swore on my honor not to tell, and they let me go. They

didn't have to, but he believed me. But I've always told you everything, because we've been like brothers. I won't tell anyone else, and I haven't. So you have to promise too. And keep it."

"I swear."

Devli let out a shaky sigh. "He's on our side. I'm convinced he's telling the truth, though he's living a lie. He wouldn't tell me everything."

Nad gave a single nod. If the prince had suddenly and readily supplied answers to all Devli's questions, that would have been suspicious. "What convinced you?"

"He wants Prince Math back, and before spring."

"So he believes the invasion rumor is true?"

"Yes."

"And so he'll turn against his father?"

"Said he wants to avoid that. Wants Prince Math back, who is the only one who can stop the invasion, and find some solution with Canardan Merindar."

"If." Nad winced. "If. Two big ifs. What are we supposed to do?"

"Find out who is spying, and what they are reporting. Learn what we can of Magister Zhavic and Magister Perran's orders from the king, though I know Magister Wesec is trying to do that."

Neither had to express what they thought of adult efforts to do anything. They liked Magister Wesec. She was an excellent teacher and a fine mage, but it seemed odd that she couldn't keep out spies, or break the king's mages' wards. But then neither could the king's mages break her wards, and everyone knew they tried.

Adults were just incompetent sometimes.

"And stand ready to aid in the search for Prince Math."

Nad thought rapidly as rain poured between the warped shingles and down the back of his neck. He still wasn't convinced about the royal heir. But these two orders, they did not require any action from him that was morally reprehensible. Everyone in the resistance wanted to know what Zhavic and

Perran were doing on the king's behalf. Everybody dreaded hearing that the king's mages were no longer claiming to be neutral, but had allied with the war commander.

Devli said, "Prince Jehan said we ought to find that acceptable to conscience and vows."

Well, if that was true, it argued for a good prince, didn't it?

Nad still wasn't sure. But he could think it all through later. "What about Prince Math's daughter?"

"Zath—the pr—he took her away. I don't think she wanted to stay with him. My sister certainly didn't. And there's the other trouble. My sister."

Nad blinked rain from his eyelashes. "Elva knows?"

"She discovered the ruse on her own. But she wouldn't believe him and went back to sea."

Nad winced, thinking of his stubborn cousin. "Won't help the prince if she's blabbing his secret all over. Trouble indeed. Royal trouble."

"She won't," Devli said. "Promised. What worries me is that she hired out onto a ship that got commandeered into Randart's fleet. Which is right now chasing the pirate ships. Zathdar's pirate ships."

"Zathdar who is really Prince Jehan."

"Right."

A silvery bell chimed inside, calling the mage students to study. In silence the two young men climbed down, separated and returned to the house via different doors.

And in Vadnais, thunder rolled across the sky, cursed by the musicians, flower arrangers, cooks and servers who had been hired by the ambassador of Colend for the river-barge party she had planned as a return gesture for the lovely masquerade ball. Overlooking the bend in the river where the barges rocked—the blossoms from their ruined garlands strewn over the quay in multicolored profusion—was the old audience hall, opened up today because of the mass of petitioners who had arrived on orders of the Guild Council. Safety in numbers was the whispered word, and so they stood all round the walls in a room still slumberous with yesterday's heat as the storm flashed and rumbled, making it impossible to hear the king and the Chief of the Guild Council.

Canardan, oppressed by the heat, the smells of too many close-packed bodies in the still room, and above all by the fact that he could not get around the fool treaty, wished Randart were here to clear them all out at the point of a sword. He wished even more fervently that his son and heir would not slouch over there watching the rain beat against the windows, his profile so obviously bored.

"Yes," Canardan said heavily, before yet another guild master or mistress could belly forward and launch into a bad reading of four or five close-written pages, borrowing the most tedious phrases from old history books. "I see your point. And I promise there will be a hearing, attended by guild representatives as well as those of government, mage and military."

The Chief of the Guild Council bowed. The guild masters and mistresses bowed. Canardan nodded, bending forward to lay his seal on the hot wax of the proclamation the scribe had written.

He noticed, distracted, that Jehan had slipped out, and shook his head. If only the boy had a head for governing.

The room began to empty. Suddenly stifled beyond bearing, Canardan rose, unlatched one of the long mullioned windows and let the wind blow in to cool his face, not hearing the muffled exclamations and curses of his scribes who dashed about trying to catch the flurry of papers that had taken to the air.

# Chapter Eight

Lightning flickered and thunder rumbled like an avalanche of mountain-sized boulders across the sky as Prince Jehan ran up the backstairs, pausing long enough to note where everyone was.

Chas, as he'd hoped, had marshaled all the royal servants to straighten the king's rooms which, because the king had commanded all his windows to be opened that morning, were a welter of puddles, papers and anything else that was not too heavy for the wind to smite spinning into chaos.

Jehan paused at his own rooms long enough to motion for Kazdi, who was bent on the same task, to follow. The boy left the other servants working, shutting the door to the outer parlor on his heels.

"Guard the stairs," Jehan murmured.

Kazdi frowned. "Decoy?"

"Do it. Use the rock collection."

The boy zipped inside the room, emerging with a silver bowl of exquisite crystal stones, which he scattered all over the landing, resting the bowl inside the door. Then he took up a stance from which he could see in all directions while Jehan raced up the marble stairs four at a time and down the hall to the tower where Atanial had been isolated. He stopped at the landing of her own stairway, where he suspected the spy-wards bordered—the larger the wards, the harder they were to maintain. He whistled the calls of night birds until apparently she recognized one of them as an anomaly and came herself to investigate.

She ran forward, fists pressed together under her throat. "What is it?"

"Stop there."

She jolted to a stop, her hands flinging out wide as she pressed herself against the wall.

"It's the wards," he finished.

"I get it." Her brow cleared. "If I cross, the mage spies know. Or if you cross."

"Right. Chas is busy cleaning up the mess in the king's rooms and making sure none of the other servants get a look at his papers. We probably have a few moments to talk."

Atanial clasped her hands again. "You saw Sasha. She's really all right?"

"She's fine, as of last night. Riding west of Ellir. Listen. My father agreed to a hearing for the conspirators."

Atanial did not waste time quibbling over the term. "And?"

"And so it frees you, do you see it?"

She frowned down at her tightly clasped hands, then looked up, eyes narrowed. The expression, so much like her daughter's when she reached a conclusion, acted like a hammer inside his chest.

She said, "He can't use their lives against me, not now. Is that it?"

"Yes. I will see what I can do to get you out."

"Tell me more. Tell me what's happening."

"The cadets from Ellir Academy are on their way to their siege. Most of the harbor guards from three harbors are marching inland, ostensibly to war games."

"That much I gathered. What does it mean? It's not really war games at all?"

"Oh, they'll play their extended war game through the harvest season, right enough. But the games will go on so long that they will be caught by surprise by the first snow, in which case they'll have to winter along the border—"

She drew in a breath. "I see."

"—where supplies will be carried over the next two months, stockpiled against spring, as harvest goods are carried in all directions. They can then launch an invasion over the border at the first snowmelt." Because she not only seemed to comprehend, but was waiting for more, he said swiftly, "Leaving the harbors and coastline all but unguarded. Randart is busy making sure the coast is safe by his definition right now."

"Pirate hunting, right?"

"The excuse is pirate hunting, but what he's really going to do is clear the seas of anyone he deems inconvenient."

Atanial said, "I don't understand. So you rescued Sasha from the pirate?"

"I am the pirate."

She pressed her knuckles against her forehead.

"I've been—"

"Wait. Wait. What were you doing before we showed up in this world?"

"Raiding the coast to keep the army pinned down there. Well away from the border."

"And dropped everything to chase after my daughter?"

"I found out about Prince Math's ten-year spell at the same time as Zhavic and Perran did. I couldn't get to your world to warn you, but I got to the old castle in case they brought either of you back."

She let out a long breath. "Our timing," she said with Sasha's crooked smile, "could hardly have been worse. Though it was not our fault we're here in the first place."

"Yes," he said, because there was no time for anything but the truth.

"Does Sasha know that?"

"No."

Atanial rubbed her eyes again. "I see. She wouldn't listen."

"It was a matter of trust."

"I know. I'm afraid that's my fault—"

A soft whistle from below caused her to freeze, poised for flight.

Jehan motioned her back to her rooms. They were both frustrated that that the interruption came right then.

Voices echoed up the marble stairwell. They belonged to Chas and Kazdi. The boy was busy shuffling gap-mouthed around outside the prince's rooms, cleaning up the stones.

"...where is the royal heir?"

"Haven't seen him," Kazdi replied in his adolescent honk. "We've been here trying to restore order. The windows were open, and—"

The voices faded behind Jehan as he soft-footed down the hall in the other direction. He slipped into the dusty royal guest chambers, unused for years, and through the servants' door there, as Chas reached the landing where he'd been before—to find it empty.

Chas cursed, ran back downstairs and dispersed with a few curt words his other trusted spies, who had been ordered by Randart to know where the prince was at all times. When at last they found him, he was sitting peaceably at a table in the heralds' archive where the air was still and cool and the storm a rare low mutter. He was busy translating an old Sartoran treatise on the symbolism of flowers. He began a long, cheerful explanation of the treatise to Chas. "Do you not think this a fine gift for the Colendi ambassador when she reschedules her barge party?"

Chas bowed, effaced himself and placed a servant on watch in the outer chamber. Idiot!

Hours later Jehan finally was able to get to his rooms and grab a moment of privacy. Not that he expected any messages. Surely the entire kingdom had been grounded by the storm.

But there was one. From Owl.

*Lost her.*

# Chapter Nine

*Oh, nice going, Sasharia Disaster Zhavalieshin.* I stared in dismay at the cheerful faces surrounding me.

There was absolutely no chance of escape. The mare was finished for the day, and I was shivering so hard I was afraid I couldn't walk, much less ride.

They were waiting for an answer, and I hadn't even heard the question.

Not that it wasn't easy to guess what they wanted to know: Who are you and where are you going?

What kind of lie could I possibly tell now that wouldn't just cause more questions? Various stupid scams flitted through my mind, but it was one of the warriors that actually gave me my out.

"Maybe she's a foreigner," one muttered.

"That would explain her getting on the military roads," a woman as tall as me spoke next, tossing back her short, curly auburn hair. "A foreigner wouldn't know about the laws."

"Likely blundered over at the river bend," a fellow behind me said. "It's the only place the two roads are close. Mare probably found the better footing, and there she goes."

So far, they weren't suspicious or angry, only curious. Or resigned, as they briefly disparaged the "river-bend turn", one of them adding in a sour voice, "You know who's gonna be detailed to build a wall between the two roads."

I worked my numb lips, gesturing with my cold hands.

They all fell silent. Marshaling all my knowledge of cartoon-character fake accents, I said, "Sheep. Shiiiip?" I mimed going up and down on waves. "Sailor." I hit my tunic front with a loud, wet smack. I scowled. "Pie-rats."

"Pirates!" the tall woman exclaimed. "Wager you anything they got hit by Zathdar's gang."

The others all made noises of agreement.

She turned back to me. "But what are you doing inland?"

I stared, uncomprehending, and one of the fellows said in a loud, distinct voice, as if loudness magically translated into other languages, "Where-do-you-come-from-and-why-are-you-here?"

I dismounted, my sodden clothing slapping against my limbs. I patted the horse, and pointed outside. "Home. Road." I pointed west, waving my hand in a circle that encompassed most of the broadest continent in the world.

"Her ship must have been grounded by pirates. Or they were raided, and the crew turned off." The woman addressed me slowly and loudly. "Where you from? Not Locan Jora—"

"Naw, they talk like us," someone else said.

"Not Colendi either, I know a Colendi accent," a younger guy spoke up.

"Oh, well, your kingness," the big guy behind me retorted, and they all laughed.

"But I do! I got a cousin in service inside the—"

"Stow it. And your cousin too. She's no Colendi, or where's her coach and eight matched horses, diamonds and the like?"

"They're not *all* toffs. That's not even possible. My cousin's a cook—"

"All Colendi swank," the woman said, and the others made derisive noises of agreement.

The young guy sighed, eyes rolling up toward the ceiling.

Then they all started guessing, naming kingdoms—Devrea, Arland, Sarendan, Gyrn, Deshlen. Recalling some of the names I'd seen on that exquisite map aboard the ship while practicing the Khanerenth alphabet, I waited until they reached a couple of countries a bit farther west, and when one said, "Melia!" and another, "Couldn't be Tser Mearsies?" I nodded violently, pointing somewhere between the two.

Triumph turned into a sick hiccup when the big guy came round front. He was a full head taller than I, broad face like granite, and a pleasant, helpful expression as he said, "Doesn't Farhan speak Mearsies?"

I tried to hide my dismay.

The woman thumped him on the arm with her fist. I was surprised she didn't break her knuckles. "Don't you remember? Farhan got orders to run with one of the siege attack teams."

They expressed sympathetic disappointment on my behalf. I beamed, unable to hide my relief, and they took it as a complete lack of comprehension.

"Never mind," the youngest one declared to me, loudly and distinctly. "Come. We show you. Eat. Dry out."

"Eeeeet. Dryyyy ouuuut." I nodded like one of those bobbing toy things some people put in the back windows of their cars.

They surrounded me, everyone using loud voices, as if I were deaf and stupid. I shrugged, smiled and hefted my pack over my shoulder.

The warriors led me through a side door into a long hall that smelled of old cabbage, the oil they use on their weapons and wet wood. When we reached a big office, they all straightened up. The woman seemed to be taking a silent vote with her eyes—she was chosen—so she motioned me into the big room, where we found an older man seated behind a desk, a woman maybe ten years older than I at the wall, in the process of sticking pins in a big map. They turned around. After a quick exchange, the commander gave permission to house me until morning in the women's barracks, adding, "Make certain she gets to the civ road at first light."

"Yes, Captain."

Next upstairs, where ten or twelve bunks lined the walls of a steep-roofed room. "Here's where you sleep." My guide pointed to the single bed with no gear hanging next to it and no chest neatly stored beneath it. As I hesitated, thinking of my wet pack, she took it out of my hands, which were beginning to tingle as they warmed, and yanked it open. "Here, let's spread your things out. See? Spread. Out. Make sure dry." She gestured with one hand, as she pulled things out with the other, hesitating when she saw the rolled firebird coverlet. She whistled. "Where did you get *that*?"

I grinned, rubbing my fingers with my thumb. "Buy. Much gold!"

"Oh yes, I'd say. You must have used half a year's pay, unless sailors make ten times what we do. Phew, either you really love your family or you've got one handsome fellow waiting at home. Marda, come here, see this."

"What? You got the foreigner in there?"

Three women entered, all of them exclaiming. "That's a Zhavalieshin firebird! Aren't those against the law?"

"Naw, only banners."

"That is a banner."

"And someone who knows it's against the law obviously sold it off. Very sensible. She probably got it for a fraction of the real value. Hey! What's this?"

As they spread the firebird coverlet out with careful fingers the innkeeper's letter slid out and landed on the clean-swept wooden floor.

Another woman picked it up and looked at the address. "Three Falls Inn. Zhavlir. She must be running as a courier, to save the scribe-runner cost."

"I would," someone else spoke up. "You run letters, especially for inns, they almost always give you at least a meal, sometimes a free bed."

"Wonder how they got the idea across."

My auburn companion grinned. "They probably do the same in Tser Mearsies. Just because she lacks our language doesn't mean she's ignorant about regular life." She turned to me. "What's your name?" She thumbed the front of her tunic, saying, "Britki. That's Marda." She poked one of her friends. "Name! Britki. Marda."

I was ready for that one. "Lasva." I patted my soggy clothes, which made a wet smacking sound.

"Poor thing, she's got to be icy in that stuff. Let's get her before the fire."

"Cleaning frame first." Marda laid my coverlet out on the bed.

The third one put the letter next to it and they led me to the cleaning frame, which zapped away sweat and mud. The women took me downstairs, chattering past me as they decided between them that because of the wicked Zathdar my ship had been raided and the sailors set ashore.

As we gathered round a long plank table, they happily cursed Zathdar, whose raids had kept a lot of their friends on double-duty patrolling along the coast all during the summer, until the fleet recently set sail.

Then out came dinner, fresh cornbread, a thick pepper soup with cheese crumbled on top, and three kinds of layered fruit tarts. They got tired of shouting questions at me while I shrugged and smiled. Gradually they fell into their own conversations.

They reminded me of armed-services people at home—most of them big and buff, cheerful, neat either by inclination or by habit after years of inspections, full of jokes told in their own particular slang, jokes aimed at one another as well as their daily routine. The atmosphere was one of friendly rivalry, but the really creative commentary was reserved for the upper command.

"Didn't I say? Didn't I say?" one guy demanded, waving his fork, after someone commented about the storm. "We're going to end up way out in the field up to our butt cheeks in snow before the rankers wake up and notice winter's here."

"No they won't," a woman retorted, arms crossed. "Because *they'll* be kipped out inside the castle, whooping it up in disgusting luxury. It's only *us* who'll be frozen."

Everyone laughed except the big guy, who shook his head. "Too late in the season for a big war game. Autumn's gonna be short this year. You can smell it in the air. Crazy. Why not in spring, like it used to be? We're gonna end up stuck in the snow."

Bets were exchanged with brisk efficiency while others griped. Not revolutionary stuff. Nobody as much as looked over a shoulder. If anyone questioned the right of the Randarts to order what sounded like a massive siege war game involving nearly the entire army, they didn't do it here. The griping was entirely confined to what seemed foolish timing, and what it would mean down at grunt level.

After the meal most of them vanished on various night duties; those off duty did the usual things people do when there is no television. They talked, mended uniforms, played card games. A couple of people played instruments—a kind of flute-recorder that did not need a reed and a stringed instrument—and one fellow with a good voice sang either love songs or funny marching songs with jokes I did not understand.

Their cards are all hand painted, and though I could see a kind of relation to our deck, it was different. Six suits, for one thing. The most popular game was with cards and markers, reminding me of bridge and chess at the same time. They did invite me in. From their manner, they believed a sailor would know this game so it had to be universal. I hunkered down by the fire, indicating I would sit there and dry out my clothes as I watched them play.

I was forgotten. I meant to listen more, hoping to find out something useful, but as a spy I was worthless. If anything of import was discussed, I wouldn't know how to identify it. Canardan's name had never come up, much less Jehan's or my mother's, or even anything about me. All I got glimpses of were their personal lives.

When I was dry, I was so tired I gave up the spy game and retreated upstairs to sleep. I didn't even waken when the midnight watch changed.

I woke with the others at the dawn bell. After breakfast, two of the women led me to the stable, where my mare had obviously had a good night. She was freshly curried, fed and ready to go. Even my weapon in the saddle sheath, which I'd stupidly left to rust forgotten, had been taken out, cleaned and oiled for me. I thanked everyone in sight.

We rode out into the cool morning air, frost lying lightly on grass and stippling the edges of leaves, drifts of vapor rendering the farmland countryside into a kind of etching. The military road was hard-packed dirt kept by magic as smooth as asphalt. It cut straight through property. But military roads were forbidden to civilians, and so we crossed a couple of meadows, riding under dripping trees, to the regular road—pot-holed, soggy and winding.

The women pointed to the northwest, saying loudly, "Zhavlir that way." I nodded, thanked them, they wished me well in words of one syllable, and I departed, delighted that I'd managed to get out of what could have been major danger. It had not only been easy, it hadn't cost anything!

While behind me, as part of the routine, my hosts wrote me into the daily watch report: *Civilian sailor strayed off the civilian road during storm, female, tall, blond, hazel eyes, name Lasva, from Tser Mearsies. Carrying only personal gear plus a letter from one inn to another, the only item of interest a silken banner in the old Zhavalieshin style.*

# Chapter Ten

The next few weeks brought bands of rain, nothing as spectacular as the storm that broke the summer. The air was much cooler, and all over the kingdom, harvesters were anxious to get the crops in before another storm came, maybe a worse one, to destroy everything.

So while people concentrated on harvest and storage, and the military were converging on the castle chosen for the siege game, out on the ocean, War Commander Randart's navy chased elusive ships while the war commander cursed.

For several days he'd mostly caught up on his sleep. But after that, time seemed to wear with excruciating slowness. Though he had his magical message case, he hated using it because he was convinced the mages read his messages, though they swore they didn't. It was, after all, what he'd do if he possibly could. Including lie.

That was the worst of it. He didn't really know what magic could and could not do. Even if he asked, he wouldn't believe the answer. Yet Canardan insisted he cooperate with the mages, and even include one on the flagship. "Show good faith," the king had written in a final order. "Who knows? They might even be useful. By whatever means it takes, I want that pirate hanged!"

Randart had obeyed because he must, privately resolving that he would call upon the mage only if there was no other way around it.

That was before several weeks of frustration and

incompetence from everyone around him. The merchant ship he'd chosen as the flag seemed incapable of running with proper military order, and the second fleet was always reporting sightings of possible pirates, but no catches. If Bragail wasn't lying, that had to mean the pirates were playing catch-me-if-you-can.

Finally Randart issued the order for the entire fleet to converge. He would stretch the fleet in a net and sweep the entire coast of Khanerenth, as far out into the sea as they could reach, and burn *everything* that had no proper papers.

At dawn a few days later, a scout craft appeared with crowded sail, signals flying. The pirate was on the horizon. Not one of his many underlings, but the *Zathdar*, bold as the sun, riding just within view of the spyglass.

The pirate matched the fleet's speed, keeping the same distance between them.

Randart summoned the merchant captain and ordered him to catch the *Zathdar*, packing on as many sails as needed.

The captain said shortly, "He has the wind. Sir."

"Which means what?"

"Which means he can sheer off any time he wants to, or he can sail down and engage us. He's faster. We can only catch him if the wind shifts."

"Is it likely to do that?"

A shrug was the answer. Irritated, Randart waved him off of his own captain's deck as he stared through his glass at the pirate vessel etched against the morning sky. At last he said without losing sight of the ship, "Get the mage."

Rapid footsteps thumped down the stairs to the companionway and below. Randart watched sailors form a line along the companionway, holding long ropes in order to do something with the sails. He listened to the patter of bare feet around him, the creak of rope and wood, and the whappita-whap of sails being lowered or raised or changed. Somewhere on the other side of the ship, the sailors talked incomprehensible slang as they prepared for an approaching boat. His orders were to chase and close. The sailors were doing the best they could, he could see it, but ships were so *slow*. With a horse under you, you at least moved, and even better was...

A quiet step behind and he looked down at the short, stout woman the mages had sent him. She was probably thirty or forty, her expertise was in preserving wood (useful on a ship) and if she'd ever expressed the slightest interest in political power, no one within Randart's extensive spy net had heard it.

He had forgotten her name. "Do you see the pirate?"

She narrowed her gray eyes, pursed her lips so her double chin tripled, and gazed out to sea. He did not offer his glass, nor did she ask for it. They stood there in silence for a moment as the ship rose on a swell, then thumped down, and behind, the thumps, cries and knocks indicated the approaching boat was hooking on.

The mage finally said, "Just barely."

"Tell me in plain language why I cannot transfer my force to it by magic, since we can see it. I know that magic requires a clear destination. That ship seems clear enough to me."

"First, we can only transfer one or two at most, and the transfer spells must be prepared for. Second, yon ship is not clear enough for transfer," she said.

"Then I'll give you my glass, which I assure you brings details close. I can make out the damned pirates doing whatever it is they do to sails. I can see the planking along the side of the pirate ship. I can see the ropes at either side of each mast."

"But that does not constitute a proper Destination."

"Plain language," he snapped. "I want a concise field report. And if you don't know what that is, I am going to suggest that Perran and Zhavic include basic skills in whatever it is they teach you people before they let you out in the world."

Her cheeks flushed, but her tone was steady, and her gaze stayed on the pirate ship. "You can see the details of the sides of the ship. You can see sails. You can see masts. Is that correct?"

"Yes."

"But you cannot see the details of the deck."

"No."

"If you wish to be transferred"—her tone totally devoid of irony—"you would wish to appear on the deck. And not halfway through a mast, a sail or the side."

Randart thought of the tiled Destination chambers, and nodded. Now he remembered something of an explanation Mathias Zhavalieshin had given him many years ago. Mages memorized the pattern of the tiles, or you could get lost in whatever-it-was between physical spaces. Forever.

"So either you need Destination tiles, or the equivalent on that deck, or you need transfer tokens. And I remember what transfer tokens do: act as a beacon."

"We call it a focus, but yes. However, there is another very important consideration. Destinations must be kept empty. If someone, or something, is already in the space where you transfer, bad things happen. Two objects cannot occupy the same space at the same time."

Randart grimaced. He'd never been able to bring himself to ask Zhavic these questions, and give Zhavic the pleasure of exposing his ignorance. "They don't...melt together, do they?"

"No. That would call for a very strange magic indeed. Transfers are just that, but between spaces, so the newly arrived thing impels itself into the new space. It is the impact with air that hurts so much. If the arrival collides with any object it is thrown aside at violent speed. Things break, people are killed."

"It's the same with transfer tokens?"

"Yes, pretty much. They must always be left on floors or open spaces, or on tables next to open spaces."

*So much for salting ships with transfer tokens and sending a force by surprise*, Randart thought. And, with a brief spurt of self-mockery, *I wonder how many kings thought they invented that idea first, to find themselves at this same impasse.*

He collapsed the glass with a smack. "Back to the crawling pace of the chase." And, because he had to work with the woman and she'd been prompt and informative, "Thank you, Magister." He still couldn't remember her name.

She bowed and withdrew; at once the aide-de-camp on duty stepped to his side. "Commander, Patrol Leader Samdan is here to report."

Samdan. Randart remembered that name. Samdan was the idiot whose entire patrol couldn't stop a pirate, a girl and a couple of brats belonging to that traitor Kreki Eban. Randart had wanted Samdan and his fools put up against a wall and shot as an example of what to expect for incompetence, but the king himself had pardoned them, reminding Randart that they were a scratch troop, scarcely trained, culled from road-patrol duty when the best warriors had all been shifted to the coast against pirate raids.

Randart remembered quite clearly that he'd concurred on the orders to reinforce Prince Jehan's small honor guard when he was sent to the old World Gate tower. Randart had also agreed to send the prince to the old castle as he himself was busy hunting the pirate, and hadn't those two fool mages made the world transfer once before, to return empty handed?

But that did not excuse the sheer incompetence of an entire troop, however badly trained, defeated or driven off by four people.

By two, really: the pirate Zathdar and the Zhavalieshin girl.

Randart turned back to glare at that distant ship, now a silhouette against the rising sun. On that thing Zathdar now stood, presumably with Atanial's girl. He also knew Bragail of the *Skate*'s secrets, all of them on Randart's orders. Why hadn't the pirate brandished either the girl or the threat of Bragail's exposure yet? No one could accuse him of lacking in arrogant boldness. What did he want, this pirate bestirring himself in the matters of kings? The very idea of pirates and politics did not make sense.

Randart became aware of the aide still standing there. "Well? Cannot Samdan report to his captain on his own ship?"

The aide lowered his voice slightly. "Said he ought to speak directly to you."

Sharpened interest caused him to nod. "Very well."

Samdan, meanwhile, stood against the rail on the weather side of the ship, watching Randart's back. He'd been living with disgrace for weeks, all the more telling because it was unspoken since the king himself had ordered pardons all round. The looks and whispers and avoidances resulting were, he'd decided bleakly, far worse than the floggings War Commander Randart handed out. At least those, if you lived through them, were then over. And people didn't hold your mistake against you.

Now he limped forward. His knee where the pirate had stabbed him still hurt. As it should.

Maybe he could retrieve some of his old standing, so easily taken for granted before most of his old cronies began turning their backs or not being around when he slipped away from his mother's place in Ellir, where he'd been sent to convalesce. Ever since the king's pardon, he didn't feel welcome in any of the guards' regular haunts.

That lack of welcome as well as the wish to retrieve his honor had caused him to volunteer when the word went out for supply duty on this pirate expedition.

Now the war commander's dark eyes flicked from his bound knee to his face, his lips curled in contempt. "You had a report you thought I should hear?"

Samdan's heart thudded against his ribs. This was it. He licked his lips. "The navigator. On our boat. I've seen her before. She was one of those with the pirate and the princess, in the old tower."

And watched the contempt in Randart's face clear to surprise, then question. "Are you certain of that?"

Samdan licked his lips again. "I made sure of it. They've had her on night duty, see, or I'd have noticed before. But yesterday she had to do a day rotation, I don't know why. And so when Captain Dembic had us out on deck doing our morning drill, well, there she was behind the wheel, and I knew I'd seen her before. It wasn't until I heard her speak to one of the sailors

I got it. She was in the court that day, along with the mage-boy who transferred 'em out."

"Did you say anything to anyone?"

"Only Captain Dembic. She said by rights I should report to you myself."

Randart turned around. Captain Dembic stood at the rail. He beckoned her over, and watched the sturdy, gray-haired woman tromp across the deck. She was his head of supply on the coast. She'd been trustworthy for decades and also close lipped.

With marked approval, he said, "Does anyone on your ship know about this matter?"

Dembic shook her head. "No, War Commander. Patrol Leader Samdan reported to me, and I gave orders for a boat to the ship captain, but told him it was to make my regular report on your orders."

Randart nodded, recognizing the implication: the use of his name guaranteed no questions, even if the explanation was not strictly true.

"Well done," he said, to both of them. What the king had said about Samdan—*It's our fault, not his, that his training has been so slapdash. If they're lazy, it's because we've let them become that way*—now sounded different. Good material, slapdash training. Yes. The words were different, the morning light looked different, the cold air felt different—full of promise. Randart felt his sour mood lift for the first time in weeks.

He almost smiled as he began issuing a rapid stream of orders.

On board the *Clam Dancer*, the mess bell had rung. Elva yawned as she gladly handed off navigation to the afternoon watch. Two yawns punctuated her repetition of the standing orders; the man taking her place grinned in sympathy, but said nothing. Everyone knew what a middle-of-the-night-till-noon watch was like.

She followed the slumping, shuffling sail crews down to the

galley, where, according to universal ship rule, the off-coming watch had first serve on food. She loaded her plate, thumped down at a table and picked up the square-bottomed mug full of soup. Holding it in tired hands, she sipped, so intent on drinking without slopping as the ship swayed around her she didn't quite notice the sudden silence until the fast tramp of booted feet caused her to frown. Sailors never wore shoes unless it was freezing outside—

Hard hands gripped her arms, yanking her to her feet. Her soup went flying. She tried to twist and fight but was shoved violently face-first onto the table. Her arms were wrenched behind her back and rope bound around them while she struggled to breathe.

The brown uniformed guards muscled her past her astonished mates. At first she was stunned. It wasn't until she was flung down into the boat that it occurred to her that she'd been betrayed. By who? All she could think was, *Prince Jehan.*

Anger replaced the sick horror, fury so hot she could hardly wait until she saw the enemy. And could tell her side of the story.

No one spoke on the trip to the flagship, either to one another or to her. The sound of the oars, the jerking rhythm, the wind and the choppy sea, all of it she noted with a remote part of her mind while righteous anger streamed and streamed, helping her shape what she'd say about the Pirate Prince of Liars.

Everyone aboard the flagship watched their approach, the sailors from the relative safety of the upper yards. Randart had told them nothing, but no one could miss the way he'd suddenly ordered up a patrol of heavily armed warriors from his own personal guard and sent them to the *Clam Dancer* as fast as the rowers could pull them.

No use asking questions. The army didn't talk to anyone except one another, and no one wanted to approach Randart, who during the first day out to sea had had four sailors rope-flogged at the foremast for not taking orders from the warriors, or not getting out of their way, even if the sailors were on duty and the warriors not. It had been made abundantly clear that sailors and ships existed to serve, were in no way equals, had no rights. Even aboard their own ship. The captain had reminded them in a private meeting down in the hold that they were getting a year's pay if the pirate was apprehended, and to think on that if they didn't want to end up dead.

So the sailors invented reasons to be watching from above, and the warriors from the deck as the boat came back, and what they saw instead of a slinking spy or a glowering traitor among their own kind was a slip of a young woman barely out of girlhood, blood trickling down into one eye from a cut on her scalp, the other side of her face bruising fast from where she'd landed after being thrown into the boat with her hands tied.

Samdan's good mood ended the moment he saw that pale face with the obscene trickle of red dripping down.

Randart clapped him on the back, laughing. "Excellent work, excellent. You shall be in at the kill."

The *kill?*

Samdan watched from his place of honor behind the war commander as the girl was summarily hauled to the deck, and muscled into the spacious cabin that Randart had taken for his own. He was thinking, *I don't want to see any more,* when the war commander gestured for him somewhat impatiently. He'd regained his honor. He'd done his duty. Hadn't he?

Yes. So it was probably fair for him to see the results. Grimly he limped after the war commander, the rest of the guard falling in behind. His knee was throbbing by now; he leaned against a bulkhead as the men found room to stand.

The Eban girl was thrust into a chair.

Randart said, "Don't even bother lying to me." He gestured toward Samdan. "He positively identified you as having been in the courtyard with the pirate the day Atanial Zhavalieshin's daughter appeared through the World Gate, attacked the king's guards sent to meet her, and vanished. Using, I understand, magic done by your renegade brother."

Samdan saw the girl's eyes widen and her lips part in surprise. Then a flush of—relief? No, it couldn't be.

Relief it was, followed by sorrow, and anger. Elva, her head aching, her muscles trembling over watery bones, recognized how close she'd come to betrayal. *It wasn't Prince Jehan. He kept his word.*

She hated his guts, but he had kept his word.

So she had to keep hers.

"I don't know anything," she said shortly.

Randart stepped forward and struck her across the face so hard he knocked her out of the chair. He gestured for the guard to pluck her off the floor and plunk her back onto the chair.

She blinked, her cheek now smeared with blood.

"Let's begin again," Randart said pleasantly. For the first time in weeks, he was enjoying himself very much. "Where were you transferred, and where, exactly, did the pirate take the Zhavalieshin girl? What was your part in all that?"

"He dumped my brother and me as soon as we transferred," she said through rapidly swelling lips. "Didn't want us. Only her. For ransom, he said."

"She went willingly?"

"No."

"What happened next?"

"Left us behind. Took her away. Pirate escort."

Randart leaned forward. "You mean I am supposed to believe that the pirate Zathdar happened, without any previous communication with you or your brother, to pop up at the tower the very day your brother crossed to the other world, and you had no idea he'd be there?"

"He had spies. Following Devli."

"Spies, is it? But you fought alongside him anyway, against the king's own? Did the pirate have a knife at your back?"

Elva flushed. "We wanted to save her from *you*. You already know we're fighting to restore Prince Math to the throne—"

Randart struck her again, so hard she lay stunned, gazing up at the bulkhead above.

"Prince Math," he stated in a soft, deadly voice, "is dead. Or gone, living it up somewhere far away. There is, you may have noticed, a legally crowned king."

Randart was aware of stirrings and shufflings around him. He would have loved to beat some sense into this arrogant scrub, but not here, not now. Some of these fools were young enough to be sentimental, obviously.

"Get the mage. Tell her to bring kinthus. We'll get the truth without any further exertion. After that you may take this traitor out and hang her. I think our friends working the sails need a reminder of who the lawful king is, and what upholding the law means."

Below, Magister Lorat was expecting some sort of summons. Randart's voice had carried through the scuttle quite clearly, and she had been writing his words as they were spoken. She had enough time to twist the tiny paper up, drop it into her magical transfer case and send it to Magister Zhavic by the time the banging came on her door.

She slid the case into the pocket in her robe and turned to fetch her herbs, including her vial of the powder made from the kinthus plant, carefully dried and ground into a concentrate of dangerous power that could so easily part spirit from body.

There was no time to wait for orders from the king's mage, but then he could not countermand the king's war commander. She would have to do as she was told.

She trod up to the captain's cabin, and said nothing when she found her victim lying on the deck where she'd fallen. She said nothing when she saw the look in the girl's eyes, not dazzlement, but a single-minded concentration.

*Her brother is a mage student*, Lorat thought. Her own observations had not been commanded and would not be offered. She would do as she was told.

While she slowly and steadily poured water into a waiting cup, and then measured out the fine powder whose smell was so strong she had to hold her breath—and every man in the room moved back an inadvertent step—she gave the girl as much time as she dared.

On the third ship out, Captain Tham watched his boat return from the *Dancing Clam* and his trusted first mate clamber up.

Closed in the cabin, the young men stared at one another in dismay—both big, strong, smart and very loyal to Zathdar. Tham knew his secret identity. The mate hadn't been told, but suspected enough *not* to ask questions.

The first mate said, "Word is, they arrested the daughter of old Steward Eban. Randart is putting her to the question right now."

Tham was writing as the first mate spoke. He sent the message off, and sat back to wait, case in hand. Either the prince got it now, or he wasn't there to get it.

An answer came back almost immediately.

*Send notice to Robin: attack, full force. I am on my way.*

# Chapter Eleven

Elva lay on the deck, grateful not to be moved. The commander and all his men stood around, looking like brown, frowning statues from this vantage, and maybe it was supposed to be humiliating, and it did hurt with her arms doubled so unnaturally behind her, but lying flat she could fight better against pain, nausea and fear.

Kinthus. *Focus on the present.*

She stared up at the wood curving overhead. Devli's face, long ago, when he came home on a visit. Took her to the woods, said, *Did you know there's a trick to getting round green kinthus? The mages taught us, but not all of us can do it.*

Her own voice. *A trick? Teach me.*

She never thought she'd need it, or maybe she did, the way her mother worried every time a messenger came and went. But it seemed fun, it seemed a way to fool *them*, the king's people, and they practiced keeping their thoughts strictly on the present.

*Don't think of the past*, Devli had said, *or it opens the door to memory. The trick they showed me is to run through all the senses, what you're seeing, hearing, smelling. Right now. If you do it and keep doing it, memory stays locked away. Your mind runs along in the present, and there's nothing they can do.*

She concentrated on the present moment, each sense in turn. When a mage appeared, kneeling down beside her, Elva kept her thoughts on the now. *She's my mother's age, maybe, moving slow—light on the glass—oh, that was a good wave, the lamp swinging, is the wind north by northwest—what grain of wood is that?*

The woman finally slid her hand firmly under the back of Elva's neck and lifted her head enough for her to drink. And she did, because she knew there was no other choice, *Taste—it's actually like chidder-weed and mint, but it makes my nose feel like a sneeze, ugh, ugh, cold, I'm thirsty—*

A blanket seemed to settle over her mind, but she did not examine it, she kept on looking, listening, sniffing, taste, touch, the touch of her fingers bunched behind her, the grit on the deck boards—

"Can you speak?" the mage murmured.

"...the grit of the deck boards feels like sand. Sand at sea, I can't smell it past this kinthus nobody told me it smells like chid-weed. We call chidder-weed chid or..." Elva whispered.

The mage looked up at Randart. "The kinthus has taken hold."


On board the *Zathdar*, Robin, temporary captain, received Tham's note. She carefully slid her magic case deep into a pocket. None of her current crew knew the captain's real identity, though they knew he sometimes had access to transfer magic. Anyone who had enough money could buy transfer tokens.

She placed the one Owl had given her on the table in the captain's cabin, then backed hastily out, closing the door and staring upward, ostensibly watching the set of the sail.

She was wondering how long she'd have to stand there looking stupid when she heard a muffled thump and thud in the cabin behind her. She opened to door to find Prince Jehan getting up from the deck, his complexion the familiar greenish-tinged mask of nausea and pain.

She waited while he leaned on the table, hands gripping the edge of it, as he recovered his balance. Two deep, shuddering breaths, his face flushed red, and he gave the sheen on his forehead a swipe with an exquisitely made cambric shirt sleeve.

That and his white hair were proof he was really a prince in disguise. She always had trouble believing it. She'd always known him as a privateer, until very recently.

"I'm here," he said. "And awake. Status?"

"Fleet downwind, on station in two columns. The *Skate* had been leading the Aloca fleet. They're tacking straight out to sea. They have to be trying to get upwind and close on us, so we've hauled east to keep the wind."

While she spoke, he flung off his clothes, rolling up the expensive linen and cambric. She glimpsed his long, muscular back and shifted her gaze out the stern windows, where she could see the *Jumping Bug* rising on the swell, sails taut. Funny, how when she was small the older men changed in front of everyone, as did the women. You didn't get much privacy on a ship. But when you were little you didn't pay any attention, and Zathdar had always seemed one of the grownups, Owl's generation. Then suddenly—she hadn't really noticed when—he was closer to *her* generation, and, well, you couldn't help *looking*.

So she scowled at the *Jumping Bug*, forcing her mind to shift to the crisis. Attack. Bad enough of a crisis, yes. There's the *Bug* with fighting sail ready, and probably passing out weapons to the fire crews. Ready, waiting for orders to... Could even Zathdar take three ships in against half the entire navy?

She swung around, forgetting irrelevancies like personal privacy.

"We're really going to attack Randart's whole *fleet?*"

"Are you ready?" He was pulling on a shirt, brilliant pink, she noted, a flicker of laughter appearing and vanishing back in her mind like a stray sunbeam during a rainstorm. Brilliant pink except for the orange peonies embroidered all over it. The trousers were striped blue and white. "I signaled to prepare for action before I got out the transfer coin. You know how many of them there are?" Strange, how when he was Prince Jehan his eyes were so blue under that white hair. Blue and vague. When he put on the pirate clothes, his face changed. Intense, it became.

"Are we really going to rescue Elva Eban?" Robin asked. "She acted like a worse snot than you'd have expected of the princess. And *she* wasn't a snot at all."

"Elva Eban was crew."

The subject was ended, Robin knew. Even if Elva only actually helped serve a day or so, he'd decided she was crew, and they all knew his first rule: *We never abandon crew to the enemy.*

He yanked a green-striped bandana from the chest, flung his old clothes in, slammed the lid. A few quick, practiced twists and his hair was bound up, the yellow fringes dancing against the horrible pink shirt. Last, he unfastened the diamond in his ear, moved to the little carved box on the shelf above the bed, and she heard the clatter as he tossed it in. "Let's take a look." He grabbed his spyglass with one hand and snapped the clasp on his gold hoop with the other.

Together they strode out on deck, she aware of the waiting tension, the watching eyes, he seemingly unaware as he tucked his glass under one arm and scrambled up to the masthead.

She was right behind him with her own glass.

No sound, no voices, only the endless wash of the sea, the creak of wood as he eyed the fleet. And then he smiled, lowered the glass. He spoke in a pitched voice. He wanted the others to overhear. "He doesn't have half the navy, he only has part of it."

Everyone was listening.

"Another thing. What we see here is not one fleet, but two. Randart thinks he has one. But one look at those ill-kept columns and it's clear to anyone used to the sea he's got his dozen or so of the Ellir Fleet, beautifully on station, plus a lot of craft that seem to be having trouble staying more or less in a line. Which one is he on? Fleet flagship doesn't seem to be flying the king's banner."

"That's because he's on the biggest merch," Robin said.

"He's what?" Zathdar looked askance, and there was some subdued laughter from the tops. "He isn't that stupid."

"According to the orders relayed among the merches via

Tham, he's been there to see that they learn their place. He *says* he's training them navy-style."

"But he doesn't know anything about the navy."

"That's the word."

Zathdar murmured so softly the wind almost took his words away, "Chain of command forged by fear." He nodded. "Then that gives us a bit more time. Even better, my rescue attempt might even work."

"Two fleets..." "Two fleets..." The whisper susurrated through the crew.

He lifted his voice. "Set sail now, right down the middle. Fire-arrow barrage from both sides. Aim for sails, no human targets. I want every single sail in that fleet on fire. As soon as we draw nigh Tham, tell him to be ready with the sugar bricks."

Randart crouched over his prisoner, who stared upward, a slight frown between her eyes. The rest of her dirty, blood-smeared face was impossible to read, but her bruised lips kept moving as she whispered.

"You were taken by the pirate Zathdar," he said clearly. "Where did he take you?"

"...and what is that smell? I smell sweat. Old sweat, some mud. Mud on a ship—you don't get mud on a ship—from the swell I'd say the wind is out of the northwest..."

Randart raised a hand, hesitated, not wanting her blood dirtying his hands. So he gripped her hair and yanked her head so she faced him.

Tears filled her eyes.

"Hurts! Pain—stab of needles, hot needles, not on the scalp but down my neck my stomach boils I might puke I don't want to puke I had nothing to eat my head aches feels like a cloth tied around it—"

Randart sighed in exasperation.

"Zathdar!" he said sharply.

"Pirate," Elva responded. "Those colors ugly colors brown, brown, brown all around am I wearing my blue tunic I need a cleaning frame don't want it ruined—"

Thumping and yells on the deck distracted Randart, who bent closer to hear the continuous stream of whispered words.

"Where. Is. Zathdar's. Land. Base?" he enunciated distinctly.

"...different pain from my arms, that's red pain, white pain is the sudden sharp one maybe it's like the glow of a dying fire..."

"Atanial! Zathdar!"

"Princess. Pirate name." Elva blinked, her eyes losing focus. "Ugly—my clothes are never ugly I don't like choosing clothes blood on my sleeve I can feel the wet against my arm it smells like sweet salt but with iron rust—"

The rumble of feet overhead caused Randart to glare at one of his aides. "Tell them to stay quiet on the ceiling. Whatever they are doing can wait until I am done."

The door whisked open. The noise from outside the cabin was briefly louder.

"Voices," Elva babbled on. "Do I know anyone I don't think I know them my head does hurt so—"

Randart cursed, irritated by the increase in noise from the sailors above. Were they possibly making it on purpose? He'd have them all flogged as mutineers. He was also irritated by this fool of a girl, who should, by rights, be spewing memory, not inanities about whatever she saw right in front of her nose.

His aide returned and took up his position beside the door as Randart glared at the mage. "I thought you people were supposed to be experts with kinthus. I can do better. Have done better my very first interrogation."

She opened her hand as if to say *Be my guest*, but said only, "I am not trained in interrogation. My expertise is wood. However, it appears she's caught in an immediate thought stream. It can happen to some, with green kinthus."

She sat back, hands folded. She had been ordered to cooperate with the war commander, and her oath to the king required that she strictly obey orders. But he made her so angry she would not offer him a single breath of aid beyond what he'd ordered.

So if he didn't know that the girl had managed to shutter off her memory, she wasn't going to offer the information.

For a time Magister Lorat watched, impassive, as he shook the girl, slapped her again, barked words at her, but all she did was talk about what she was seeing, hearing. Feeling. Especially feeling. When she started commenting on the revulsion she felt at the commander's proximity, and there was a revealing scrape somewhere behind them—probably someone trying hard not to laugh or even to breathe—he flung her down.

"Is there any use in continuing? How about giving her more?"

"She is on the verge of falling asleep as it is," the mage replied tonelessly. "Any more will probably kill her."

"Save the herb." He looked up at his aide and the day captain of his personal guard. "Take her out and hang her."

The guards were in the act of picking up Elva by the arms when there came a rap at the door.

"What," Randart shouted over his shoulder.

"Pardon, Commander," came the voice of the ship's captain. "But I felt you should be informed that we are under attack."

"Lower the cutter," Zathdar ordered.

Robin frowned. "You're not going to board the flagship?"

Zathdar paused on his way to the weapons locker, and glanced back. "Who else?"

"Anyone else. How did that fool get herself caught anyway?"

"I'm afraid it's our fault," Zathdar said.

Robin scowled, for she hadn't liked that Elva Eban, always grumping about on the deck with her sniffy attitude. As if *she* were the princess, whereas Prince Math's daughter had been instant mates with everyone, without a hint of swank. And she could have swanked, not only because she was a prince's daughter, but because she was one of the best fighters in the fleet.

Zathdar could see Robin's thoughts fairly clearly, and so he stepped close and murmured apologetically, "Owl's mistake, actually."

Leaving her nothing more to say on the matter.

That is, until he drew out a fine Colendi dueling blade, long, thin, edged but not as strong as a saber. She gasped. "Take the cavalry sword. You can't defend yourself with that!"

"It has an edge, and a point, which is all I ask. Remember, Randart has seen my fighting style with the cavalry sword. But not with this." He swung it, making it whistle. "That might be the only disguise left to me, besides these absurd clothes, so I'll take what I can."

*You shouldn't go at all.* She kept her teeth gritted as she lent a hand lowering his boat. After he called for volunteers and chose among the forest of hands that instantly shot up, she said, "Orders?"

"As much chaos as possible."

He leaped down into the cutter, which was really a one-masted pinnace, but made to his own design on the lines of larger cutters, lean and fast, its sides painted a camouflaging bluish gray.

They raised the sail, tacking directly in the lee of the *Zathdar*, hidden from view of the oncoming fleet.

Robin returned to the wheel and took over. They were nearly in bowshot. On the enemy ships, naval crews scrambled aloft to the tops, taking up their stations on the mastheads, drilled and waiting. On the merchant ships, sailors scurried about and warriors ran around, all getting in one another's way. She laughed, watching the glint of sun on swords being waved, sails jerking as their unprepared crews tried to figure out how they were going to fight and sail at the same time.

*Chaos he wants, chaos we will give him. I'll buy myself a new silk shirt if I can get two of these stinkers to crash bow over stern.* She spun the wheel and lifted her voice. "Sail crews, let's make *Zathdar* dance. Bow teams? Prepare for attack!"

The smell of rancid oil drifted down, whipping away on the

wind, as the fire crews above dipped their arrows.

Randart shoved his way to the forecastle. All the sailors scrambled back. He had his glass, but didn't need it to see the three pirates bearing down, sails taut against the wind.

"They're moving faster than we," he snapped.

The captain was an old man, weathered from years of sun and sea. "They have the wind. As we reported to you before, War Commander."

Randart gritted his teeth against snapping back a futile question. Obviously the fleet couldn't regain the wind, whatever that meant, not under strict orders to give chase.

But one question he could ask. He glared in narrow-eyed fury into the dark eyes of the waiting captain. "Why did you not report this attack at once?"

"I sent someone, but your aide said you couldn't be disturbed in the cabin. And you did say to give chase, so now we're closing." His raspy voice was devoid of expression, but Randart felt his antagonism.

"If I get even a hint," he said in a low, venomous murmur, "there was any treason in this spectacular exhibition of incompetence, I'll have you flogged to death on your own deck."

The captain's face stayed stony, his gaze steady. "Why would we do that? We were promised a year's pay for a single capture. But you said that the orders have to come from you. War Commander."

"Then your orders now are to defeat these pirates." Randart turned his head. "Signal to use ramming force and fire. I want the pirate Zathdar captured if possible, otherwise I want those ships destroyed, and no survivors."

He caught sight of Samdan limping on the companionway. Behind him his men waited, the Eban girl hanging in their grip, her lips still moving. He wanted the pirates to see her dead body hanging from one of those big pieces of wood holding up the sails. But both crews were far too busy, one dealing with sails, the other getting to their fighting stations. "She can go in the

101

brig for now. We'll hang her as soon as the pirates surrender, before we fire their ships." He stepped to the rail, glass in hand.

The captain of the ship flicked a summoning glance at his first mate, who also happened to be his wife. Together they retreated to the captain's deck. The captain took up station behind the helmsman, making certain his own crew were the only ones in earshot, "I am told that Zathdar never kills."

His wife's gray, grizzled brows rose, then her chin came down slowly. She turned away to supervise the sails and gave her own crew orders for the issuing of weapons. Around them warriors took up fighting positions along the rail as they'd drilled.

Above, signal flags rose, fluttering. Along the columns, now breaking apart to encircle the pirates, sails raised and lowered, crews ran about on decks—efficient on the navy ships, full of energy but less purpose on the merchants, for none of them knew what to do when under attack.

As the pirate drew between the first two ships in the column, fire arrows arced in glinting gold pinpricks against the blue sky. They flew in both directions, striking against the fleet's upper sails. Next, the stink of smoke reached the captain's nostrils—the distinctive stench of manure bricks mixed with sugar and set on fire, which burned messily but didn't do much else—and he chuckled softly to himself.

"Here, you, stand guard. You can't fight on deck with that knee," the patrol captain said to Samdan, motioning him to follow down into the hold. The two men dumped the girl into the tiny cupboard the commander had designated as the brig, slammed the door, slid the bar, and one turned, handing him a sword.

The lamplight shone on his grin. "My guess is, they won't get down this far, but you never know. May's well have a measure of safety." He indicated the length of the blade, and then the two vanished, their boots clattering, their curses not quite muffled as a rolling lurch of the ship slammed them back and forth in the hatchways.

Samdan sat slowly on a barrel, listening to the girl's soft whisper and wondered if he should use the blade on her. That would be better than hanging and whatever other fun and games the commander might be inspired to try first. Or maybe he should just use it on himself.

Randart was, at that moment, glowering at the mage.

"My training is in helping to help defend the integrity of the ships' wood," Magister Lorat stated. "That I can and will perform."

"Can you damage the wood of the enemy ships?"

She rubbed her lip as she stared over the water. "If I can get close enough to focus, I might enable them to waterlog, but that's only if their wood is not warded against such spells. Most well-kept ships, even pirates, are warded as a matter of regular maintenance."

Randart sighed, thinking once again that magic was basically useless for anything but housekeeping. "Do what you can. If I see evidence of your aid in defeating them, I will see to it Zhavic rewards you suitably."

Anger flashed through her, but she hid it. "I will do my best, War Commander."

He moved on, forgetting her within two steps.

She stared down at the water. *The best of nothing is nothing.*

Smoke billowed from the pirates in grayish cotton streamers, carried by the wind toward the fleet. The three in the cutter watched the navy ships tacking desperately against the wind in order to come around and close on the *Bug* and the *Mule*.

Gray, one of Zathdar's strongest and steadiest crew members, said pleasantly, "You know this madness is going to get us all killed."

Zathdar laughed. "Hinting for double pay?"

"If we're alive to spend it, might be nice." Gray gave his

captain a mocking salute.

"Ship ho," Gliss called from the tiller as she came up under the lee of the smoking vessel.

A moment later Tham dropped in, sending shudders through the craft, which was already picking up speed.

"Going to rescue the Eban girl?" Tham asked.

"That's the idea," Zathdar said.

Tham laughed. "I would rather die heroically rescuing that wheat-haired princess, if you asked me."

Zathdar said, "It might come to that. If we find her. Right now, consider. Randart, who knows nothing of fleet actions, has had plenty of time to sow resentment among all these sailors."

"You think that's gonna help us?" Tham asked, and the others looked askance.

Zathdar spread his hands. "On land, I wouldn't dare go up against him with four swords, doughty as you are. But now—whatever chance we have, we must take. As for our target, Elva Eban is crew. And you know the rule."

No one argued with that. They all knew it could have been one of them on that ship.

A grinding crash snapped everyone's eyes south as a merchant craft, half-hidden by the increasing smoke from the scattering bursts of new fires, jammed its jib over the taffrail of one of the naval ships. Faint cries of rage carried over the smoke from both ships, creaks and cracks of wood, and the beating ruddy glow of sky-reaching flames.

"Oars," Zathdar said. "There's the flagship."

# Chapter Twelve

"It's a disaster." Randart wiped his smoke-burning eyes again.

A disaster with at least one mind familiar with siege tactics employed against them. Randart knew the distinctive smell of manure-brick-and-sugar fire, called smoke screen in the military.

He watched in growing but helpless fury the slow, disastrous collapse of order at this end of the fleet. Impossible to see if the naval ships were closing in from the other side. Probably not. The smoke seemed to kill the wind, and the ships had slowed even more, wallowing as fast and furious arcs of flame hissed at them. The pirates were shooting fire arrows. He had ordered his men to kill, but they couldn't see their targets.

Randart controlled the urge to strike out at the closest target. Though he could not ride, or bugle for a troop to thunder up and encircle the enemy, he did have one last possibility. All he needed was to spot the lead pirate ship, then he could order down the boats and send his men over to take it. Wrest something from the turmoil.

But the smoke thickened, obscuring even the two ships at either side. All he could see were the tiny pricks of light of the fire arrows. The arcs now went out in both directions. His men were shooting from the topmasts above him, he was glad to see, though he had no idea who they were aiming at. Maybe a defensive measure. They certainly couldn't see any pirates to shoot.

The smoke was making his throat raw. Usually he kept his command center upwind of smoke screens, but the pirates *had the wind.*

He retreated to his cabin, and was downing his second cup of water when Jehan's cutter eased up under the stern of the flagship. Gliss, at the tiller, stayed in the vessel to fight off anyone who tried to take it. She'd come aboard if summoned as last-ditch backup. Hoping for a chance, she kept the boat as close under the stern as possible, out of sight from the rail.

The other four climbed fast, Jehan's colorful figure first.

He murmured, "No deaths if you can avoid it."

"Even army?" Tham muttered, though he knew the answer.

"Yes."

Tham sighed, not surprised. He knew that Randart would be angry enough to feel no such compunction when giving orders to his men.

Jehan leaped lightly over the rail, dueling rapier in one hand, knife in the other, the others behind as backup. And as Zathdar paced past the old captain at the helm, raked his gaze down the unarmed man and moved by, the captain flicked a glance at his wife, who promptly went about her inspection as though she hadn't even seen the intruders.

Gray, hefting his sword behind Tham, whistled softly, long and low. Zathdar had been right. Randart had made enemies of these sailors.

They might actually survive.

The breather lasted another ten heartbeats. A patrolling warrior spotted them, and yelled up at the first mate, "Hey! Who's that?" But she was coughing too hard from the smoke, and groped helplessly as she stood at the rail, whooping for breath.

The lead pirate was a slim man in garish colors. He came on fast and the warrior pulled his sword, yelling, "We're under attack!"

The ship erupted in cries, crashes and desperate fights. The warrior detachment boiled up from below, each wanting badly to bag a pirate and the promotion and reward that came with it.

The sailors all yelled "Attack!" and "Defense!" and waved their weapons, running into one another and dropping armloads of sailing gear that suddenly everyone seemed to be carrying.

Tham, backing up Zathdar, found himself pressed against the rail by three good fighters in the king's brown. He was mentally bidding farewell to a good (though short, life) when a cry from overhead startled everyone—and a sailor landed on top of two of the warriors, knocking the third spinning. Tham promptly jabbed his knee and the opposite shoulder, putting him out of action, as the sailor held up a frayed rope end and said loudly, "It broke!"

Three big blocks dropped from above, two clonking onto the heads of warriors. One warrior was knocked out, the other staggered toward the rail, a cut over one eye. Crew members leaped to help, getting in the way of Randart's men who tried to close in on the pirates.

"Get out of the way!"

"Where?"

"Help, help, the boom is about to drop!"

"I can't see!"

The first mate stood at the rail, apparently blind to the chaos as she coughed from the smoke.

A party of five sailors chose this moment to haul up a huge sail between the pirates and the advancing guards. Gray and Tham covered Zathdar, who dropped down the hatch.

He slashed his blade across the forehead of one fellow, nailed the elbow and hip of another, then jumped to the second hatchway. Now the search would begin. Where would they stash a prisoner?

Randart emerged from his cabin to discover fighting all over the deck, warriors slipping in spilled oil, smacked in the back of the head by swinging blocks of wood from the sails overhead, bumped into by groups of sailors running about, some carrying huge sails, others with long snarls of rope, everyone yelling at the tops of their voices.

"Pirates?" Randart roared. He spotted them, three around the main hatchway. On guard, it looked like.

Why? It *couldn't* be the Eban girl they were after—

A loud rattling sounded overhead, and a sail swooped down and dropped over him, knocking him flat.

"We're on fire!" someone screeched above.

"Mizzen top down! Mizzen top down! Sail crew!" the ship captain howled, and feet trampled over Randart, squashing him flat.

Randart shouted, "Get off me!" but the noise of the sailors bellowing arcane sail jargon at one another, the captain bawling orders, the noise of fighting, of sails flapping, of coughing and whooping caused by the smoke, drowned him out.

Below, Zathdar began grimly on his search, waiting for the inevitable squad to descend from the deck, each intent on winning fame and fortune by some judicious pirate killing. Take every chance to its end, he'd been taught at the academy across the continent, where dying in battle was considered the best end, far better than a quiet death after a long life.

Jehan, if offered a choice, preferred the quiet death after a long life, but that did not seem to be the chance coming his way.

Then a cough caught his attention, and he whirled, blades up.

A man's head popped up from the deck below, barely lit by the single swinging lantern. "She's here."

It was one of Randart's warriors.

Expecting a trap, Zathdar hefted his weapon and dropped down to the dim, low third level, which was usually used for storage, to find himself alone with a man with a bound knee. The face was vaguely familiar.

"He's going to hang her." Samdan looked at the pirate dressed in ridiculous clothes, like a traveling player. But there was nothing silly about the narrowed eyes, twin gleams from the lamp flame reflecting in his steady gaze, or the way he held those red-tipped weapons. "Did you kill anyone?"

A shake of the fringed bandana.

"Yes. Well, she's there." A point.

A step, a kick to the wooden bar, and indeed, there she was, on her knees, arms bound. One slash and her hands dropped to her sides, her mouth moving as she chattered a stream of nonsense observations in a low, monotonous whisper.

"You'd best thump me." Samdan turned his back. *And if you kill me, well, it's only just.*

The pirate nodded once, and didn't make the man wait. Tossing his knife up, he caught it by the blade, brought the handle down behind Samdan's ear.

Samdan dropped to the deck, his weapon clattering out of his hands. Zathdar stared at Samdan's knee, remembering where he'd seen the man last—lying wounded in the transfer-tower courtyard. Bending, he lightly nicked Samdan where it would hurt least but bleed most, the better to make it seem he'd put up a good fight, and cut the rest of Elva's bonds.

"Can't use hands," she murmured, in the slurry voice of someone who was under the influence of kinthus.

"Stop talking." The kinthus would make her obey, and thus she would also be able to halt the weird chatter.

He slid his arm under hers and supported her up one ladder—propping her against a bulkhead to step out and look round. There was only one sailor, with the galley and the officers' wardroom blocked off by barrels. The man looked at them, turned his back and dropped another barrel onto its side.

"I'm trying to get you out, but someone upset all the food stores," he bellowed to the officers shouting and trying to batter the blocked wardroom cabin door.

Zathdar helped Elva up the last ladder, where they found the deck in chaos, sails hanging loose or dropped altogether, fires being busily put out with water splashing everywhere. And what were these impossible tangles of ropes?

A rush of warriors toward them turned into a mass skid as

someone fell over a barrel of oil that had gotten spilled all over the deck.

There were Gray, Tham and Vestar, bloody but alive.

They closed around him, Gray pressing up on Elva's other side. Together they lifted her as they mounted to the captain's deck, where the first mate was busy yelling at a disaster with the mizzen topsails. A web of tangle rope jerked upward, blocking off the scrambling warriors who'd gotten past the oil.

A boom swung out from the other direction, lifting the rest of the pursuit off their feet, to crash onto the mizzen sail still being trampled and splashed with buckets of water.

Zathdar thought he heard Randart's voice adding to the noise somewhere around that mizzen sail, and laughed as they passed Elva down to Gliss.

Then they were in the boat, whooping for breath, weapons dropping from hands, minds trying to grapple with the amazing fact that they were alive after all.

Elva struggled up, her bruised, blood-smeared face lit by the ship fires.

They rowed out, and Gliss ran up the sail, sheeting it home.

On the journey back through the smoky ruin in the fleet, the kinthus wore off, and with it the numbing effect of all those bruises. But Elva didn't care. She had survived. She was alive.

She said nothing, unsure who knew what, until they reached the *Zathdar*. It was the pirate himself who offered his shoulder for her to lean on. She couldn't resist one more test, murmuring into his bandana-covered ear, "Didn't want me talking, huh?"

His quick look of surprise was revealing, but all he said was, "And ruin my reputation as the best-dressed prince on the east coast?" The smile Zathdar gave her was his rare, sudden one, a real smile full of fun.

She contemplated that surprise. He thought she'd talked, but came after her anyway. And though her heart was not fashioned to respond to him, or to any man, what she did feel budding under the miasma of weariness, shock, pain and unhoped-for reprieve was the green shoot of insight: this was what loyalty was all about. Prince Jehan had no reason to like her, he didn't even know her, but he'd obviously found her worthy of rescue. A prince who could be loyal to people was worth allegiance.

Randart rubbed his throbbing forehead, but that didn't even begin to assuage the merciless slam of his headache. The day had begun so well, emphasizing all the more strongly the catastrophic results.

He faced the captain of the ship, and his own officers, and the mage, who all waited, eyes steady, some weary, some afraid, most of them with the closed faces of unexpressed anger.

Nothing he could ask was going to reveal the true cause of that sullen fury he saw all around him. How was he to determine if the catastrophe was due to incompetence or to treachery? At home, on land, with the king at his side and the circumstances of well-understood military action at his back, he could probably force out the truth.

The king. He was finally answerable to the king.

He drew a deep breath of the stale air, for the cabin was closed tight against listening ears and the rattle and thud of cleanup. "It is very apparent to me, and I am sure it is to you as well, that this pirate attack and the rescue of the Eban girl are not coincidence."

His words were met with profound silence, except for the shifting of one officer easing a broken arm, and the captain twisting slightly as he cocked his ear upward at some incomprehensible shout up on deck.

"Someone," Randart enunciated clearly, "sent the pirate a message. It has to have been by magic, and it has to have been someone on this ship. Maybe in this room."

The captain cleared his throat. "Begging your pardon, War Commander. But there were more witnesses seeing that girl brought over than just your people. Supply boats were coming and going. Any of them would be carrying word of what they saw. It's the way of the sea, everyone will tell you that. Even your captains, if they are honest." He indicated the Fleet Captain, a thin, morose man sitting opposite Randart, whose ships had accidentally attacked merches, what with the smoke and noise and general chaos. *That* disaster had enabled the three pirates to slip between the ragged, uncontrolled line of merches and sail downwind, hidden by the smoke and the embrace of night.

Everyone turned attention to the unhappy Fleet Captain, who lifted a hand. "It's notoriously hard to keep ears from hearing things on a ship, yes," he said heavily.

Randart knew his Fleet Captain was loyal. That crash had occurred in the smoke and chaos that Randart himself had made no sense of, though he'd tried, once he got free of that cursed sail that had fallen on top of him.

The sail, yes.

He turned on the merchant captain. "Very well. Then the way of the sea will work *for* us." Randart breathed deeply, feeling the slight ease of decision. "*You* will discover who betrayed us. And when that happens—only when that happens, I emphasize—you will be paid for repairs and the month's wages. But until then, you are on your own." Lifting a hand, he added sardonically, "Let that word get out according to the ways of the sea."

He rose. Thus released, the ship captain opened the cabin door and sweet, cool air rushed in as they filed out, defeat and tiredness shaping everyone's countenance, lagging their steps.

Randart caught the mage's eye and raised a hand to halt her.

When the others were gone, he said, "Prepare to transfer back with me to Ellir. We can leave whenever you are ready."

She nodded and left.

He walked up onto the deck, staring at the snarl of ropes and wooden implements whose use he could only guess at, but which probably had something to do with sails. The big sail that had landed on him still lay where it had been kicked, with the jagged cut he'd made by his knife in releasing himself.

Bloodstains on it where his knife had caught someone or other who, either accidentally or on purpose, had been trampling the sail while doing something or other to the upper reaches of the ship. He could not know if that had been deliberate or another consequence of the chaos of sea battles. Fleet action, he had learned to his cost, lay too far outside his realm of experience.

Undeniably the sailors were hacked up, several, like his own warriors, with broken limbs, cuts rudely bound. When he asked, they all seemed not to know if pirates or his own men had caused the wounds. Yet the fact was, no more than four pirates had boarded the ship, made it down to the hold, released the prisoner and retreated again. Samdan was yet unconscious, but Randart was not going to wait for him to waken. He probably didn't know anything. From the look of him he'd fought his best, hampered by the knee and having only a single lamp to see by in the dark hold.

None of them seemed to know anything useful, except that one of the pirates wore garish clothing like Zathdar was reputed to favor. That would mean the pirate captain himself had been here, and Randart flat on his back under a sail as heavy as a horse.

There was no evidence of collusion, but he sensed it everywhere he looked. The sailors were too somber, too weary for the obvious signs of collusion. But the quality of the silence formed a wall between him and these mariners.

Randart let out his breath. Defeat, on unfamiliar territory. But he'd learned something. The pirate had spies everywhere. And he had land ties. Therefore he'd inevitably return to land, and that was Randart's territory. There would be no defeat next time.

But first Randart had to get back, and they were at least a week, probably more, from land. It was time for magic transfer, something he not only detested but distrusted. What was to stop the mages from making him vanish conveniently? He didn't trust Zhavic or Perran for a heartbeat. So he would force the mage to transfer with him. He would never use a magic token himself, though he kept them to expedite those under his orders.

Magister Lorat presented herself with her bag of belongings, and he wondered if she could have been the traitor. No, that was ridiculous. She probably was reporting to Zhavic, but she'd come with a solid reputation, he'd checked that out first thing. She was a wood mage, which meant she would not be a brilliant thinker in the chaos of battle. She'd done what she was told with the stolidity of the wood she worked with.

So he braced himself for the wrench which was no easier to endure than it ever was. He'd avoided eating dinner once he'd made his decision, so the nausea, at least, was easier to fend off if his stomach was not full.

When he recovered, the mage was already gone, and around him was the comforting familiarity of stone, the Destination room of Ellir Castle. As soon as he could get his legs to carry him, he forced himself to climb up to Orthan's tower, which was empty.

The entire academy was pretty much empty against the war game soon to commence. Randart clapped on the glowglobe and sat down at his brother's desk to look through the reports stacked there, some annotated in Orthan's neat hand.

Everything looked as it should. Randart was having trouble forcing his increasingly aching head to concentrate. That defeat rankled, the more because he knew, he *knew*, there was deliberate treachery behind it. So he forced himself to be thorough.

He read one report three times without comprehension before he finally found the sense. Zathdar's sometime ally, Tharlif, had swooped down onto his secret shipment of weapons meant for spring, and captured them all.

Fury blinded Randart, leaving him gasping, until he remembered he'd protected himself with a double order, one overland, one by sea. He had planned for this possibility.

His focus sharpened again. There was no report about the overland wagons being molested. All was well. All was well. He would stay on land in future.

He forced himself to get through the rest of the reports,

then set the pile down. It was time to eat. Sleep. Forget asking Magister Zhavic for news. The mage would just lie or leave out crucial details. No more magic. Randart would take the extra day or so to ride back to the king, and compose his report on the way—that and his strategy for dealing with kingdom matters as they stood.

But that plan vanished like the sky after the sail dropped on him when he saw the neatly tied pile at the bottom of the reports, a scrap of paper on top written in his brother's hand: *Save for Dannath.*

He pulled up that pile and leafed through it. Most of these would take concentration for it seemed there were some anomalies in supply reports, people where they should not be or missing where they should be. All of that promised painstaking checking, and by trusted aides.

But that third one down, beginning with the note in Orthan's hand. *I don't know if this is important. Looked strange.*

Randart glanced at the heading. It was a weekly report from one of the more remote outposts along the northern river.

He scanned rapidly down to where his brother had made a neat question mark.

*Civilian sailor strayed off the civilian road during storm, female, tall, blond, hazel eyes, name Lasva, from Tser Mearsies. Carrying only personal gear plus a letter from one inn to another, the only item of interest a silken banner in the old Zhavalieshin style.*

It could be any woman, on the most innocuous of journeys. Except why did the mind immediately leap to the missing daughter of Atanial Zhavalieshin? It was the banner. Randart was willing to swear an oath he had seen it or one just like it, in Prince Mathias's rooms during the old days when he was royal castle commander. The banner had been stitched by Math's grandmother and her ladies for the prince's birth: queensblossom vines around rising firebirds, all in gold and scarlet.

He'd seen it recently, hadn't he? If only his head did not ache so. Banner...and he had it. A silken banner, covered with queensblossom vines all around rising firebirds.

It had lain over the bed on the *Dolphin*, the prince's yacht. Were there two of those banners? Because if not, *Jehan had had her after all*. And lied? No. Randart had not told him why he was searching, or for what. The Fool could have been keeping her in order to bring her to his father himself, for badly needed prestige...and, being the fool he was, had lost her. No matter which, she was alone, on the road. And no one seemed to know who she was.

That is, no one *else* seemed to know who she was.

# Chapter Thirteen

Sharp voices echoed up the marble stairs from Prince Jehan's rooms. Atanial knew from the tone that there was trouble, but she could not hear the words.

Something had to be wrong in a big way. She sensed tension when the servants came to get her, as had become habit, to invite her to breakfast with the king.

She was already dressed, her hair braided up with pearls to distract from the startling gray roots and her blond hair. The number of guards at the stairways had increased. Of course no one had told her anything of what was going on since her brief conversation with Jehan. She couldn't even ask, because she knew the servants were questioned by that oily Chas every single time they came up to her tower.

As she walked down to breakfast, she wondered if she'd see the usual scene, the prince sitting there staring out the window, Canardan wearily pleasant and sometimes wry as they verbally fenced.

The first surprise of the day was when she found Canardan alone.

"Sent Jehan off somewhere?" she asked as she sat down.

Since the weather had cooled, they'd begun eating in the king's conservatory, a room facing east, mostly windows, filled with potted plants. Atanial had expressed delight the first time she saw it, and had made the mistake of asking if it had been Ananda's chamber. Canardan had talked right over her— pleasant, even funny—as if she hadn't spoken. Oh. Ananda had become one of *those* subjects.

Now she wondered if Jehan had suddenly become another one, as Canardan reached for the fresh bread, offering her some first. Then he sighed. "He slipped away to visit another female, apparently. No, he didn't tell me. He never does. But a letter was found in his chambers. Perfume. Written in purple ink, if you can imagine. Do these so-called artists really think they will actually marry him? It cannot be his company—" Canardan shut his mouth, a gesture so determined Atanial, watching in fascination, saw his jaw clench.

*A letter was found.* So the prince was not exempt from searches either. *Cannot be his company.* Definitely signs of trouble in paradise.

"Up all night worrying, eh?" she asked, and when he gave her a narrow-eyed glance, she deflected the flash of anger by shifting from specifics to general. "The price of parenthood on all worlds, I suspect."

"Your girl left you up all night worrying, I gather?"

"Oh yes." That was only fair, since she'd asked first. But to ward any more questions she added, "I was always afraid she might lose her temper with some villain, and the police would come to arrest her for ridding the world of one more slimebag."

He did not ask if that was a subtle hint. He knew it was. Therefore he knew how unsubtle. But he also knew she was being irritating in order to sting him into revealing more, and though he felt the usual surge of laughter and attraction that her ripostes inevitably caused, he was too tired to keep his guard up. He fell silent, only answering when, in desperation, she turned to the weather and the harvest.

Such a limping conversation couldn't end fast enough for either of them. Once she'd turned down his offer of a ride—a picnic—a tour (in other words, another public display of his prize prisoner), she excused herself.

That left her to another boring day. Later she barely remembered it. What she did remember was the faint but persistent tapping at the window long after she'd finally dropped into troubled dreams.

She sat up, disoriented. The tapping had sounded like the brush of barren twigs against a window, the way the bitter, dry desert winds of Southern California blew the tree branches all during the months that elsewhere were called winter. But she was in a tower, not in Los Angeles.

She sat up, and once again heard the faint tapping.

She threw off the covers and ran across the floor of the bedroom, and started violently when she saw a pale face peering in through a dark window.

She stumbled back, then halted when the pale starlight revealed the oval of a young female. Atanial unlocked the casement, swung it open and stared down into vaguely familiar eyes. A hand extended up in mute appeal. Atanial gripped it and pulled. The girl shifted her weight, there was a rustle, a heave, and the young woman tumbled inside the window.

"Sh, sh," she hissed softly, though Atanial had neither spoken or made a sound. The girl looked around fearfully and whispered, "You have to come now. Tam can only vouch for his sentry watch."

"Tam?"

She blushed. "Sharveshin."

Tam...one of Kreki Eban's conspirators.

"Marka?" Atanial peered down. Yes, the starlight glimmered softly on short reddish curls ruffling all round the girl's head.

"It is I. Come. Did you know they are getting a trial? The king cannot kill them now. So I'm here to get you out of the castle. Tam and, well, some others, they are all covering your exit. But you have to climb down outside the window, which isn't warded like the doors are."

Obviously young love had managed to overcome political differences. "Climb down the stones of the tower?"

"There's ivy."

Atanial gritted her teeth. The idea of climbing down a hundred feet of ivy did not appeal, but neither did staying here in this jewel-box prison one second more, now that she no longer had to.

She swung around, dug through her clothes with shaking hands, and dressed in layers of dark, sensible clothing. Into her bra she shoved her magic tokens, and the few bits of jewelry she'd been given. She would probably need it to trade for food.

Marka slipped out the window. "Put your hands and feet where I do."

It felt like four hours later she was maybe ten feet below the window, her hands aching from the death grip on the branches, her muscles trembling, when she felt a familiar nauseous ache behind her sternum that spread outward as heat.

She stopped, leaning her forehead against her arm, and nearly sobbed. *Great. Climbing down a tower wall, and here comes a hot flash.*

"Princess?"

"I'm on my way," she muttered, her voice shaky.

She wiped her sweaty hands on her clothes one at a time, placed a foot, a hand, and eased herself down a few inches. Ivy tickled her nose, but she held her breath against a sneeze. Hand. Foot. Hand. Foot.

Later that journey seemed longer than all the weeks of her imprisonment. But at last, oh, at last her foot encountered stone, and she stepped onto the sentry wall.

Marka took her hand, sweaty and gritty as it was, and pulled her unresisting inside a dank accessway. They flitted down some mossy steps, across a dripping hall that smelled of mold and old wood. Then they continued down, this time to a stable.

"Here she is," Marka breathed, running toward a shadowy corner.

Tam Sharveshin emerged, sword in hand. "Ride out."

A tall, skinny teenage boy with a prominent Adam's apple and tousled cinnamon hair silently handed to Atanial a folded cape, the plain brown of a runner.

"Don't tell us where," Tam added.

She shook her head. "I won't. But I'd like to know whom to

thank for this rescue."

Tam and the teen glanced up at the tower where Prince Jehan's rooms were lit, even though he was gone.

"Ah." *Jehan Merindar.*

The teen said in an unprepossessing nasal honk, "He told us to arrange it. Not to say when. So he officially won't know when or how. His fellows in the guard helped. They're all busy looking elsewhere."

"I understand." Atanial suspected the cost of being caught. They were so young to be in such danger, but she knew better than to mention it. From the looks of him, that teen would on Earth be a computer geek, the type who loved logistical challenges. "What will you say?"

"Nothing, if I get back to my patrol. They know you have some magical device." Tam mimed holding a disc. "I overheard the orders for the search of your rooms when you were with the king, under Magister Zhavic's direction. Rumor was, the magister thinks you carry a token around, but the king wouldn't let him search you. So we figured if there were no signs left behind—and they won't think to check the ivy—they'll figure on magical transfer. And no one on wall duty right now will see anything at all."

Atanial nodded, then the boy gave her a hasty lesson in horse care, indicating the feed bag, rolled blanket and curry comb in the saddle pack. "Most people will help with a horse if asked," he finished.

Atanial thanked him as she shook out the cape and pulled up the hood. The soft, sturdy woolen garment smelled sun fresh. "All of you—I mean all including those outside this space. Thank you, my dears." She kissed Marka and Tam, laughing silently when they blushed like children.

She hesitated before the teen, whose shoulders had come up to his jug-handle ears. She knew from his agonized face, his defensive posture, that however he felt about kisses from young ladies, he was definitely at that age when teenage boys would rather be tortured by fire and sword than kissed by old ones. So she patted him kindly on the arm, and laughed to herself at the way Marka and Tam's hands came together, gripping tightly.

She mounted up and left at a sedate pace, riding along the military trail they'd pointed out only until she was out of sight of the city gates. Then she turned off the road.

Before long the low gray clouds began to drizzle, and she discovered that the runner cloak was warded against wet. The cool, sweet air smelled the better for the sense of freedom.

During the days and days she'd had time to think, she'd decided if she ever won free, she would begin her search at the abandoned morvende geliath Math had talked about, where mysterious mages had once taught him some mysterious magic: Ivory Mountain. Oh, not ivory from animals. They didn't kill mammals for fur, meat, or anything else on this world. "Ivory" was far weirder, a stone that was more like metal, and in ancient histories—so Math had told her once, his eyes wide with wonder—it *sang.*

But before she found her way to Ivory Mountain, she needed allies. Alone, she couldn't do anything. But one thing people in Los Angeles knew was the sheer weight of a crowd.

An inward image of a smart girl with capable hands, jug ears framed uncompromisingly by braids: What better person to go to first than Lark Silvag?

# Chapter Fourteen

Because she was riding to the northwest, she and Jehan were on the opposite sides of the city, one departing, one arriving. Though they would have loved to have the leisure for a talk, they were unaware of the other's movements.

Jehan's mood was sober. Triumph after a successful escapade didn't last long any more, not before the impending storm of trouble threatening the kingdom. At least this time he was spared the necessity that—it was becoming more obvious every day—only he insisted on, the swearing of a new partisan not to himself but to King Math. Elva Eban was already sworn to Math.

Even thinking about it brought Owl's voice back a year or two ago. "What are you going to do if he's dead?"

"I can't think of that," Jehan had responded. "I have to go on as if he's alive."

Owl, who had never known Math, shook his head with some sympathy. "You'd better think of it. Because you can be sure Randart is. Every single day."

Owl's voice echoed in Jehan's ears as he rode through the south gate, waving in response to the salute from the sentries on the wall. He was going to be facing Randart soon, maybe now, more likely later. Jehan had hoped to get back before the war commander, who detested magic as much as he distrusted it. But that couldn't be counted on.

The covert glances sent Jehan's way when he reached the royal castle's stable served as his weather vane. From the silence, the furtive glances, and the tension in hands and shoulders, it seemed his father was in far more of a temper than Jehan had expected. Maybe they hadn't found the fake letter, or maybe they had and had figured out at last that those letters were indeed fake.

He handed over the reins of his mount and walked inside. He was met almost at once by a runner who said, with scared eyes, "The king would like you to come straightaway in, your highness."

"All right. Thank you." Tension gripped him.

His father was in his workroom. As soon as Jehan walked in, Canardan threw down his pen so hard it clattered to the floor. "Why," he began in a tired voice, "did you see fit to ride out without a word to anyone, not even your own servants?" He flicked the letter. "Was her desire for your company really all that much more alluring than duty?"

"I thought so." Jehan kept his voice even. "But then my duty is surpassing tedious. Not that I find Princess Atanial tedious, but trying to get her to go on rides, or even a walk in the garden, is not much of a duty when she refuses every single day, leaving me little to do."

Regarding his son with a strange mixture of relief and anger, Canardan said abruptly, "Atanial vanished."

Jehan had not expected that so soon. Mentally saluting Kazdi and the other guards, he exclaimed, "What?"

Canardan saw that unfeigned surprise and let out a slow breath.

Jehan comprehended then that his father had feared he'd been involved.

The king said in a far milder voice, "Atanial. Is gone. Missing. Probably used that thrice-damned magic token the mages said she had on her, but which I, being a fool, insisted they not take off her because she assuredly kept it next to her person. She would never have forgiven that."

What that revealed: the king had had her rooms searched, and she knew it. She hadn't trusted him, and he knew it.

Jehan sat down as Canardan walked round the desk, stooped, picked up the pen. "I don't know where she went. Maybe back to her world, as Zhavic insisted the token was a World Gate one. Maybe she had a transfer spell for this world over it, and went straight to the tower, and then out. Perran, who is there, might not have even seen her. At least he hasn't been here to report anything untoward at the tower. I hope that's the case."

Jehan rubbed his jaw. "Is it a problem to have her here?"

"No. Yes. Everything is a problem," Canardan said angrily.

Jehan's neck tightened. Was his father, at last, going to admit to the secret plans for the spring invasion?

For weeks Jehan had wrestled inwardly about that question—whether it would be better or worse to be told. Either way was going to mean endless trouble, but he had finally decided that if his father kept it secret, it was because the king truly knew that breaking the treaty with Locan Jora was wrong. Whatever excuses would subsequently be offered.

If the king had talked himself into speaking openly about it before Jehan, that brought its own troubles. An invasion of what was legally if not historically another country was royal treachery on a scale that could only be dealt with by a king. Like Math. Otherwise the kingdom would be plunged into the sort of bloody civil war that had happened far too often over Khanerenth's long history.

And none of Jehan's own intensely loyal, dedicated, brave, smart, risk-taking and innovative followers knew about the invasion, except for Owl. He couldn't tell them until he knew for certain it was true.

"...so you see, though I know what it's like to be young—and I loved assignations as much as the next young man, when I was your age—I need you to stay here. You can grace various occasions, especially those given by foreigners with their constant spies, when my time demands I be elsewhere. We have too many problems. I cannot risk angering the least of the ambassadors or envoys by avoiding their social foolishness, and with winter coming, there will be even more of it."

Jehan signified assent. A runner entered and bowed. "War Commander Randart rode into the stable, your majesty. Requests an immediate interview."

Canardan lifted a hand and she dashed out.

"Let's not say anything about this, shall we?" Canardan murmured, picking up the fake letter and tossing it onto the fire. "I'm certain that Randart has enough on his mind, and we understand one another, do we not?"

Jehan bowed. "I'm certain he will wish to keep his interview private."

Canardan was on the verge of acknowledging the truth of this, then he paused, regarding his son with a puzzled frown. Duty. The boy did seem to be slightly less wool-minded than usual. Was it possible he was waking up to his responsibilities?

"Stay," he said, coming to a sudden decision. "Zhavic sent me a report. There was trouble with the fleet, and the pirate apparently got away. Whatever Randart has to say, you may as well hear it."

The war commander was there moments later, a tall, husky man whose strong arms strained against the sleeves of his sturdy brown cotton-wool tunic. He scorned velvet. The tunic was also unmarked as any warrior's, except for the silver crown stitched over the golden cup—the device of the king's own man. He didn't need to wear rank markers, because in his own view, his rank was the highest in the kingdom, above mere dukes. Except of course for the king himself.

Randart's face hardened even more than usual when he saw who was sitting with the king. He hesitated, and Jehan knew that the war commander was waiting for the king to dismiss his son like an errant lap dog.

"Your report?" Canardan asked, with the smiling irony that signaled to Jehan his father was quite aware of Randart's attitude.

Randart clawed his shaggy, gray-streaked hair back, a rare, entirely human gesture. Both father and son recognized how upset Randart had been by his defeat. "The pirate tangled the merchants with my naval ships, under cover of smoke screen.

126

I'd captured one of the Eban brats, and was in the middle of questioning her when the attack commenced. The pirates boarded my flagship, a merchant, and got her away while my own guard and the sailors ran around getting in the way of one another's blades. The smoke did not help. In short, a disaster."

He dropped a sheaf of papers onto the king's desk. "Here are the details, if you want them, on the top report. The rest are my brother's reports on guard and academy matters."

Canardan did not even glance at the papers. "Why did you make a flagship of a merchant? Did they know naval maneuvers?"

"No. I intended to train them into a fighting fleet."

"In a matter of weeks? I thought our navy trained for longer. Well, never mind, I can appreciate your thinking, but it might be better in the future to set up your flag on the fastest ship."

Randart saluted, lips tight.

"I take it Zathdar himself was present?"

"Description of the leader of the rescue party fits, but I did not see him myself."

Canardan frowned. "Yet you say this happened aboard your flagship. Where were you?"

"Buried underneath an enormous sail which apparently fell due to fires in the upper masts. The pirates kept up a steady barrage of fire arrows. By the time I cut my way out, the pirates were gone, with my prisoner."

Canardan sighed. "And so we have it to do again."

Randart hesitated, looked at the vacant blue eyes of the idiot son, and shut his teeth. His subsequent discoveries and surmises would wait until he could be alone with the king. It made him angry enough to have to admit to defeat before the Fool. But he deemed it just retribution.

Except, what did the sheep know? Prompted by the sudden, unpleasant conviction that the king had told the sheep about the invasion, he tested, saying, "So as for the future—"

The king waved a hand. "All that can wait. I can see from

the mud you've been riding all day. Go get something to eat. Get some rest. I can read through the reports while you do those things."

Randart stood up. "I'll give the orders for the execution. We can do that at noon tomorrow, before I—"

"Execution?" Canardan repeated.

"Of course. The traitor guardsmen. Silvag, and I forget the other's name. If we put crossbolts through them, that should solve your civilian-trial problem—"

Canardan was just irritated enough with Randart to resent this summary disposition of his time. "Not tomorrow. I have three interviews, two of those with envoys. Nothing is more awkward than executions, especially when you're trying to smooth things over. It can wait."

Randart had been considering whether or not to tell Canardan about the report and his theory on Atanial's missing daughter. Telling the king would have eased some of the bitterness of his defeat. On the other hand, nailing that girl down first would go even further in removing the bitterness of defeat.

Then there was the matter of Canardan's wavering.

Maybe it would be better to secure her first, and...

And see.

Smiling with grim anticipation, Randart withdrew.

# Chapter Fifteen

Bored and hot, the two guards on patrol rode at an idle pace along the established perimeter. You didn't question orders, you just obeyed, but there wasn't much chance of action guarding a bunch of old people, half of whom were in jail.

Atanial watched them from the shade of an ancient, gnarled willow. Through its hanging green curtain, still in the late-summer air, she peered after the patrol, timing them as she waited for the cover of darkness.

She was tired and hungry and thirsty, despite having had a long drink at the last stream. She knew she'd be a lot worse off if she had to let the horse go. That might happen. It's difficult to hide a horse.

So far, she was all right. The animal stood patiently in the shade with her, tail twitching. When at last the shadows fused into darkness, she decided to move after the next patrol. It came right on time, roughly an hour after the last round. She waited until the pair had safely ridden by, then tied the reins of her horse loosely to a low branch, pulled out the feedbag, filled it and put it on the horse.

This took longer than she'd thought it would, as she and the horse were unfamiliar with one another. The movements were also unfamiliar.

When she was done, she took off running with her head low. She zipped across the road and over a gentle hill toward the Silvags' orchard. She was just thinking of cover, but she almost ran Lark down, who was out picking peaches now that the sun was gone.

They both gasped, Lark almost dropping her basket. The girl poised to flee.

Atanial whispered, "It's me, Sun—er, Atanial."

Lark whistled. "You better leave, your highness, before my mother—"

"Before your mother what?" Plir Silvag rounded an old peach tree, a basket on her arm. She was only a silhouette in the deepening gloom, but Atanial saw the tension in her movements. "Who are you? You can't be—"

"Sun. Atanial. Whatever—"

"Get. Out."

Atanial sighed, the inner vision of water, food, a bath vanishing. "Please. Just listen to me."

"Last time I listened to you, my husband got taken. He may even be dead for all I know—"

"He's not."

"So you say—"

"He's not. Tam would have told me. They're all safe. The king won't do anything to them because he agreed to hold a trial."

"She's right," Lark said. "Tam said so. So did my cousin in the stable."

"You hold your tongue."

"Ma, Tam keeps telling us—"

"He'll say anything," Plir retorted. "To protect that little traitor Marka."

Atanial winced. How sickening civil war was, the conflict and division from regions right down to the personal level.

Plir's basket whisked against her skirt, a scratchy sound, as she shifted it. "All right. I'll listen. But if that patrol catches you, I'll just stand by and watch. I'm not losing my home too."

"I'll be quick, I promise. I spied on the patrol all day, and I know when they'll come round again. I promise to be long gone before they do."

"Speak, then."

"First, I'm sorry about your husband, and I know they got Folgothan too."

"He couldn't run," Plir Silvag said bitterly. "Because *someone* stabbed him in the leg. And my husband wouldn't just leave him."

"Is Haxin all right?" Atanial remembered the name of the ferret-faced fellow.

"He is," Lark spoke up. "But Kenda—his daughter, my age, well, Kenda was dismissed from the service. She just got promoted to signal flag officer on *Adamant*. But the war commander turfed her out. On account of her dad."

"They went over the mountain back to Locan Jora, where his cousins live," Plir said.

"Oh no." Atanial hadn't meant it to slip out, but both the Silvags exclaimed, "What?" Their voices were hoarse with the effort to keep from yelling.

"That's why I came. Word is, the king plans an invasion of Locan Jora in the spring. No, no, please don't talk. I promised you I'd speak my piece and be gone, so let me speak it. I know you don't want any fighting, not with friends and cousins and so forth over there. I don't either. You saw what happened when I took up the sword. One fight, and Folgothan got hurt and arrested. Even small wounds can have bad consequences."

Lark and Plir gave similar short nods.

"So what I want to do is gather all the women, those who have family in the military. The military have to follow orders, I understand that. And we can't do much against trained fighters, not alone. But what if we were a great number? What if, just imagine it, we had half the kingdom raised, all peaceful, no swords among us, and we begged the king not to invade?"

Plir went very still. Atanial scarcely breathed.

"Randart would cut us down without compunction," Plir stated.

"But Canardan won't. He'd hate even the suggestion. I don't have a lot to say in his favor, but I know he wouldn't do that."

Plir shifted the basket again. "Yes, we've heard a lot about you and Canardan."

Atanial sighed. "My prison was a beautiful suite. He gave me clothes, and he even gave me jewels." *And how many times am I going to have this conversation? With every single woman, no doubt.* "He wanted everyone seeing me in those clothes and jewels. He wanted people to see me dancing at that masquerade, because he knew what people would think."

"Queen Ananda's servants swore you and he were not lovers," Plir said unexpectedly. "But he could have forced them to say that before he pensioned them off." She turned away. "I have to think."

Atanial backed up a step or two. "I said I'd be going. I'll be gathering at Ivory Mountain," she added deliberately and walked away, her heart thumping hard.

The stars were just emerging, weak glimmers overhead. It was close timing, but there was no sound of hoof beats on the still air.

She mistook four trees for her willow and had to backtrack to the road before she found the right one. Freezing into place under its sheltering curtain, she watched the riders amble into view, each carrying a bobbing lantern.

Their noise smothered the quiet, steady munch of the horse. Atanial leaned against the animal's neck, arms pressed across her front. She knew she was going to face that same conversation every time she tried to build her protest march.

Or maybe she wouldn't after all, if some angry woman reported her.

No self-pity. She would simply go until she either had her peace marchers a la 1968 or was caught. *At least,* she thought, trying for humor, *if Canardan catches me again I'll get another soak in that wonderful tub.*

She'd just mounted up when a furtive step caused her to whirl around.

"It's me. Lark. Ma sent me. I'll show you who's important. She's going to stay here and spread the word."

Atanial's eyelids burned with grateful tears. She wiped her eyes, then helped Lark up onto the horse's back. She mounted, and they vanished into the night, Lark pointing the way.

&

Mindful of his promise, Jehan agreed to attend a ball that evening, freeing up his father for his private interview with Randart.

Attending a ball was not exactly torture. In fact, one of the duchesses had brought a daughter, newly arrived home from Colend, who was bright, beautiful, witty, fun to dance with.

A year ago he would have lingered and found a way to visit her again. But now he discovered there was just no spark. Her trenchant observations on the shortcomings of last season's plays in Colend made him want to take Sasha to Alsais to see how she liked Colendi theater. Though she employed all her arts to attract, Jehan did not really notice her tiny waist, her exquisite sense of style in gown and hair. The image that compelled him most came from memory, a tall woman with a swinging stride and hawk's beak nose, her braids dancing around her shoulders, her grin rakish and not the least coy.

After two or three dances, the duchess's daughter sensed his indifference to her arts of attraction. Her laughter gradually lilted less and became a lot more wry. At the end of a long night of waltzing and scintillating talk on the subject of art, he gracefully saluted her hand, expressing a friendly wish they would meet again to continue their conversation.

Presently she left with her mother, saying, "Conversation is all he means. I think there's someone else."

"Nonsense." The duchess snorted. "He's notoriously cloud-brained. You'll have to work harder to catch his attention."

The daughter did not argue. She never did. But mentally she resolved to return to Colend, and when she came back again to Khanerenth she would be married. Next time he saw her, this Prince Jehan—who *wasn't* cloud-brained, by the way—would probably want to introduce his wife.

As for Jehan, he was glad to drop wearily into bed at last. Too tired to plan much beyond avoiding Randart the next day, he slid into slumber in the last watch before dawn.

And woke with Kazdi at his bedside, holding a tray of aromatic coffee. "Randart rode out after the sun came up."

Jehan sipped, burned his lips and tongue, and sighed. "Any idea where?"

"Bar Larsca Valley. The guards were joking about the siege site, and how Randart can't seem to stay away from the game."

Jehan frowned. "Riding off the morning after arriving? There has to be something else."

Kazdi shrugged. He never even tried to understand Randart, much less out-think him. That was the prince's job. His job was to try to deflect Chas and other spies.

"He's suspicious."

"Of us?" Kazdi's voice cracked on the word *us*, but Jehan didn't smile, and Kazdi was too anxious to blush.

"I don't know," Jehan said finally. "Let's accept that as a given and go from there."

# Chapter Sixteen

The rest of the academy and the guards finally joined Damedran and the academy cadets at Cheslan Castle.

By then the senior cadets had a camp set up at the site the baron had designated with planted flags, a stretch of land recently harvested. In the fields beyond the campsite, the work of harvest went on as the newly arrived cadets finished helping set up the permanent camp.

Damedran, as senior cadet, accompanied his father to the castle for the first meeting with the baron. It was a meeting of surpassing tedium, but Damedran didn't care. His mood was a happy blend of anticipation and triumph. After weeks and weeks of stony looks and avoidance, Lesi Valleg had finally spoken to him. It was short and gruff—about watch assignments—but that was far better than being scowled at.

As the baron and Orthan Randart settled what the army could and could not do with the castle, outbuildings and grounds, Damedran brooded.

He loved war games, he loved commanding and, well, some said Lesi had ears like open clam shells and buckteeth, but he'd liked her ever since they were little. She was tough, smart, and no one in the entire academy shot better than she did.

She was also the leader of the cadets that didn't like him, Damedran knew. When he was younger, that was the perfect excuse for scrapping whenever there was an opportunity. But this year thrashing them had gotten less fun, somehow. He much preferred things when the seniors were all together as a unit. With him at the top, of course.

It was especially clear after this boring ride that having the senior class divided was no good. When half weren't talking to the other half, opportunities for some great practical jokes and some well-earned and entirely fair swank in front of the younger brats went right by.

What was it the sheep had said? Prince Jehan, he reminded himself. They'd have to be unified if Norsunder attacked. And, much as he'd love to believe how tough they were, he and his gang, the midsummer games had sure proved *that* wrong.

Reminded of that mysterious nine-year-old boy, Damedran shrugged inwardly. Rumors had been flying around since the games disaster, most insisting that boy was really the son of the hated Siamis of Norsunder, who had commanded two world-wide wars in the previous decade. Either his son or the son of the far worse villain, Detlev, about whom the stories were amazing and chilling. But Damedran scoffed at such gassing. Even if those enigmatic villains, who commanded vast armies and had their eyes set on world conquering, had children, wouldn't those children be busy in some hidden lair learning whatever it was you learned for world conquering, and not wandering around shooting in stupid contests like the yearly games in Khanerenth?

That much he said out loud when the others brought up the games and rumors. But alone at night, thinking and, well, go ahead and admit it. Worrying. He couldn't help wonder about what Wolfie had said about that fight. And that amazing training.

"All right then, that covers it, Orthan. We're done. I look forward to watching, heh heh."

"I hope we'll show you something worth seeing."

The men stood, breaking Damedran's reverie. He was glad to be interrupted.

Orthan Randart started out, pleased with his son's quiet, even agreeable demeanor, unlike his accustomed slouch and scowl. Not realizing that Damedran had not heard a single word spoken, Orthan rubbed his hands as they descended the main stairway and clattered through the old hall to the front gate, their heels ringing loudly, their mail and gear jingling. On either side of them, servants were busy taking down and rolling tapestries, or carrying off carved chairs, some of them heavy square jobs with gold inlay, the style of three generations previous. Windows were being removed, leaving the castle a bare shell, suitable for a satisfactory siege game.

"It's good to deal with one who understands the military," Orthan said. "Here's the boundaries, here's the rules, point, point, point, and we're done. Civs, they argue about every piece of porcelain, every bush, yowling, 'But what if?' until your head aches, and then they've got their hands out. The king's purse might be deep, but it's not a bottomless pit. As they ought to be the first to know, they argue so much about taxes. Heh. Looks like we've got everyone in at last."

They had passed through the courtyard, smelling of stable, to see dust hanging in the air above the meadow where they had set up camp. The swarms of youth in brown had been obscured entirely by strings of horses, wagons and a mass of warriors moving about with various duties, most of them casting glances skyward at the gathering clouds. The smell of horse and human, of cooking food, hit them with a similar sense of sharp anticipation.

As they got closer, the mass became identifiable as discrete patrols, each with a task. Most talked, laughed and joked with the geniality that father and son associated with the commencement of a massive war game, the prospect of fun not only for a day or a week, but for an extended period.

Orthan veered to search for the newly arrived captains. Damedran lagged, hoping to slip away to his own crowd to find out who had gotten what done, and what practical jokes might be possible.

Then a bugle's exciting challenge ripped the air from a distance: the king's signal, but just blown once.

"It's the war commander. Riding at the gallop!"

Heads turned, voices sharpened, and that enormous crowd

of people—everyone at different chores—parted like the waters of a great river. Down the cleared, trampled grass rode Randart at the head of an honor guard of six.

Damedran's first reaction was the old excitement. That's what command did for you, it parted the way better than magic ever could.

Orthan laughed at his son's avid expression. "Dannath does so love scattering us like chickens in a fowl yard. Always has."

Damedran looked up skeptically. "Uncle Dannath? He doesn't love anything. Except work."

Orthan shook his head, watching the riders rein to a halt. His uncle was immediately surrounded by officers, who faded back again when Randart waved his hand. He was obviously giving some order, after which he disappeared into the command tent. Two of his guard took up position at the flap. "He loves power," Orthan murmured.

Damedran grinned. "And we don't?"

Orthan grinned back. "I like my power circumscribed. I wouldn't take a crown if it fell in the dust at my feet. Too much work. Think about it. I was upstairs watching my old cadet friend, Trevan Hazhan, now the Baron Cheslan. He was with Dannath and me and the king in the academy. The king handed out titles as he'd promised. We got ours. But are we ever *at* our castle?"

Damedran's lips parted. It was true. He was technically heir to a barony now, but that title had never seemed real. He'd only been in the castle for a few brief visits since he was eight, and old enough for the academy. Wolfie's mother helped Damedran's mother govern it, and Damedran had gradually gotten used to the idea that Wolfie would inherit. Because *he* was going to have a much higher rank.

"Would you leave the academy if you could? Go live in the castle?" Damedran asked his father. "I know Uncle Dannath wouldn't. He'd hate that, being stuck inland at some poking-small castle. He's used to being the king's right hand."

Orthan chuckled, muttering under his breath.

Damedran thought he heard the words—*he's used to being king*—but wasn't sure he'd heard right. Wasn't sure he could even ask. Anyway they were nearly at the command tent, and Uncle Dannath appeared at the flap, beckoning impatiently.

The jumble of belongings, maps, papers, swords wooden and real, had been thrust into the far corner of the tent, the folding camp table swept bare. Randart looked up at his brother and nephew, his eyes red-rimmed with tiredness and road dust. "Report."

"We were finishing up with Trevan. Everything laid out, all in order. First thing—"

Randart waved his gloved hand. "You see to the logistics, Orthan. Where are the other wings?"

"Probably on the road. I haven't had any scouts, but we just got here ourselves," Orthan replied.

Randart nodded once, staring down at the list Orthan had laid on the empty table. It was apparent that he was preoccupied, that he didn't see it. The silence in the tent seemed to sharpen the sounds from outside: horses' hooves clopping, shouted exchanges, the thrump of marching feet on the cobblestone road, wagons creaking, grunts and laughs and curses as barrels and baskets and boxes were unloaded at the cook tent an arrow shot away.

After a long pause, during which Damedran tried not to fidget or to look a question at his father, Randart said abruptly, "We'll ride the perimeter." And strode out, leaving father and son to follow.

As Randart barked orders for three saddled horses to be brought at once, Damedran sighed. More interminable talk about logistics, had to be. He longed to get back to the cadets' side of the camp.

He turned his attention that way and immediately caught sight of shoulder-length ruddy curls. Lesi. Talking to Ban! What were they talking about? Lesi lifted a saddle, turned, her gaze meeting his. Her expression changed to the remote one he hated.

"Damedran."

The sharp tone whirled him around. His uncle gave him an impatient look, and Damedran loped to close the distance between himself and the two men.

The war commander glared at the senior cadets, then mounted up. They rode out, again everyone backing out of the way, no matter what they were doing.

On the way out of the camp, Orthan talked about the baron's dispositions. Randart and Damedran only appeared to be listening.

As soon as they were beyond the camp far enough to be out of earshot even of the first perimeter sentries, Randart cut him off with an abrupt gesture. "No one can hear us. And no one is to know what we three discuss. Orthan, you are to be commended for your excellent attention to detail. I have had a chance to think over what you flagged, and I have the same suspicion as you do. That female with the firebird banner who fumbled onto the military road is probably Atanial's missing daughter. It would explain why the pirate Zathdar never tried to ransom her, or use her as a threat or lever in any way. She got free of him, then was, I believe, briefly held by the prince. Escaped him too, which argues she knows magic."

"What?" Damedran demanded. "Princess Atanial's daughter?"

"I think so. The descriptions are very brief, but what we do have all seems to fit. It's that banner, mostly." Randart snapped his fingers. "There is another matter. Increasingly I find that reports are indicating unexplained lags in messages or messages not being delivered at all. Anomalies between what was sent and what was received. I believe we have moles in our own information relay, and possibly traitors in important places or close to important people. It will be my immediate job to investigate the most flagrant of these. In the meantime." Randart turned in the saddle to face Damedran. "You are to pick six of your most loyal cadets, and the strongest, and track down the Zhavalieshin girl." He pulled from his pouch a much-folded paper and handed it to Damedran. "Here's the best description we have."

"But—a princess? I don't understand. I want to stay here with the war game—we planned this all summer—"

Randart said softly, "Are you by any chance arguing with an order?"

That voice, terrifying since early childhood, chilled the back of Damedran's neck. He was too old to be beaten, he knew that. So the punishment would only be worse. "No, War Commander."

"You aren't cavorting with that Valleg girl, are you? I thought you'd gotten past that foolishness."

Damedran suppressed a surge of anger. "No."

"The Vallegs are a good service family. Always have been. For generations. I envisioned that girl holding one of the castles in Jora, once we retake it. But if," Randart said in that voice again, soft with threat, "I thought she was suborning you from your duty, I'll have her given a dishonorable dismissal."

Damedran thought wildly. "Oh, it's only that we had a wager. About who'd get their patrol flag to the castle wall first. I hate losing. You know how the seniors gloat. We do that a lot, Ban and Wolfie and the rest of us. Wagers, I mean." That much was true. But Damedran knew he was babbling, as if to cover over his lie. He'd never dared to lie to his uncle before.

Randart's forehead cleared. "Well. I made such wagers too, when I was a boy, but you know, it is time to grow up. Face your adult responsibilities..."

Damedran had guessed right. His uncle, launched down that familiar path, could be safely ignored for a breathing space.

He had to think. These new orders were a disaster! He remembered vividly the lie he'd carelessly tossed off about that stupid princess. And how Ban Kender had reacted. Maybe he'd forgotten, but no, Ban never forgot anything. Damedran scowled. If only Wolfie's leg was healed. Ban was definitely second strongest after Wolfie, and far smarter. Well, as for the lie, he'd say he'd been told it. Yes, that should work. Damn lies anyway, they were too much trouble.

"...so I want you and your six mounted and ready to ride by

the watch change," Uncle Dannath said, his tone sharp with finality. "You'll have to begin at this Three Falls Inn, where she is apparently taking a letter, to discover her trail. If you find nothing there, you'll ride the road all the way back to Ellir until someone responds to her description. But you will not halt for more than a single watch until you have her in hand. Got that?"

Damedran gave a stiff nod.

"You'll have the king's sigil, which will get you horses wherever you need them, and supplies. Once you find her, you will bind her against her performing magic. You will contact me, and I will tell you where to meet me. Because she is to be brought directly to me. Only to me. I will be giving you a magical case and the code to use to report, in case those damned mages are intercepting our messages. You are to reveal her identity to no one."

Damedran saluted. "It shall be done, War Commander."

"Questions?"

Damedran did not dare, not when the word was barked in that tone, but Orthan said, "I take it this is the king's personal errand?"

Randart hesitated. "I deemed it better, after a night of rest, not to tell the king. It will be far better in a number of ways if I have her first. Once I know what manner of person we are dealing with, she can be surrendered to the king."

No one spoke. But Orthan pursed his lips when his brother turned to survey the camp, and sent a glance at his son.

*He's used to being king.*

# Chapter Seventeen

Whammo! Back a few weeks, to me.

When I left off, I was gloating over the ease with which I had gotten away from the military people, who had not only housed and fed me for free, but who had checked the shoes on my mare as well as curried her. They'd even cleaned and oiled my sword.

My gloat lasted, oh, about two hours, as I recall. Long enough for the next rainstorm to move in.

The civilian roads were soon quagmires at every dip. Once again the horse was up to her knees in muck, but this time there was a wagon to follow, and follow we did, until the wagon got stuck in the mud. I helped, the horse helped, but the big, strong workhorses pulling could not get those wheels out of the mud.

The owners, a pair of sisters, offered space under the wagon to me. I took it while my mare joined the two big workhorses, all three of them apparently too wet to bicker. There was as much mud under the wagon as there was outside, but we were out of the rain.

I will pass quickly over that long, miserable night, everyone gritty and shivering, sharing soggy bits of food, while one of the women worried almost constantly about their baskets of fruit— until her sister begged her, eyes closed, to *please* stop asking what they were going to do.

We all finally fell asleep in a kind of exhausted dogpile, waking stiff, creaking, in vile tempers. I rode on, promising to send anyone I saw to help; they perforce had to stay until the mud hardened enough to roll out.

That week there was a series of rainstorms coming through, nothing ever as spectacular as the first, but definitely enough to keep the road soggy and impossible to travel on, unless you're a frog. I got lost not once, not twice, but several times, ending up in fields, in a forest and once in a bog. Then I'd have to laboriously retrace my steps, always watching for signs of a road. I looked for the muddiest, most puddle-washed stretches and was usually right.

I tried to keep my temper. I did not look skyward and demand *what can be worse than this*, because my mother had trained me well. Ask the universe that, and it will happily show you just how many ways things can get a whole lot worse.

I said once, "What about asking 'What can be better than this?'"

She smiled and patted my knee. "That you have to do on your own."

As a philosophy it probably left much to be desired, but as a rule to go by, it worked. I hunkered over my horse and endured, glad when at last I reached a village with an inn.

They had a map on the wall as decoration, with all the nobles' castles and flags drawn in. Ignoring those, I did some mental math and discovered my slogging had probably advanced me all of a couple hundred miles. The key word there, you notice, is *advanced*. I probably covered three times that in false trails and backtracking.

But I finally reached Zhavlir, and asking around got me to the Three Falls Inn, the sight of which cheered me immediately. Barliman Butterbur couldn't have run a cozier-looking place, opened in a V, at one side a stable, at the other a garden, big windows, the entire bottom floor golden-lit, the sign a big painting of three waterfalls.

The owners, a tall beanpole of a man and a tiny woman with wispy hair, were delighted to receive the letter, waterlogged as it was. I explained that I'd done my best—carrying it next to my skin, along with the remains of my journey food—but they hardly stayed to listen, the man was so anxious to read his letter, and the woman to get me to a bath, to hot food and to bed. I cooperated fully.

Trying to recall the lies I'd told at the first inn, I deflected their friendly questions as best I could. I departed the next day, armed with a carefully hand-drawn map with all kinds of landmarks on it to help me get across the mountains and through the dangers of Locan Jora to Tser Mearsies. Lovingly made—and quite useless. I did try, ever so casually, to ask about landmarks leading to the Bar Larsca Valley, inventing a shipmate from there, but no one seemed to know much beyond the fact that the lands south of the Northsca River were reputed to be wild.

Great.

I tried to remind myself that the worst of the journey, distance-wise, was over. I had to cross a river, pass the city of Barlir to the southwest, and there I'd be.

Well, the day's ride out of the city to the great bridge over the Northsca was about as pleasant as I'd had yet. Cool, clear, the autumn colors stippling the hills to the west with glorious reds, russets and about ten shades of gold. Even the neon orange leaves were beautiful, like little tongues of flame, highlighting the autumn shades with brilliant color. In the distance jutted up purple dragon-toothed mountains—the border dividing Khanerenth from Locan Jora. I was riding into my favorite kind of scenery, mountain forest, and my spirits soared.

The road was crowded the last half of the day, as it narrowed toward a massive bridge. I found myself near a small group of early high-school-aged kids training to be minstrels. I kept hearing their voices rising and falling over the sounds of talk and laughter and the snufflings, whinnies and brays of animals. The voices were high and sweet, the songs complicated rounds and interlocked rhythms that I could have listened to for days without ever getting tired.

I crossed the bridge sedately behind the singers, looking at the rushing river below, and the sturdy, magic-protected bridge around me. Bridge structure wasn't much different from Earth, only the materials varied. But those mighty braided chains, the iron-banded timber supports, were all reinforced by magic spells, the wood hardened into something that almost looked like stone, the chains glowing with a dull metallic gleam and no speck of rust. The bridge was maybe twenty feet wide, ten feet for traffic in each direction. No one rode over, everyone walked their horses. Bored warriors in brown waited at either end, on the one side with wheat stalks sewn onto their tunics, and at the far end roses: ducal sigils.

When I neared the last of the bridge, I followed the motions of people ahead of me, thinking *I'm nearly there.*

That lasted, oh, thirty seconds?

A woman my age and height in brown with a rose waved me over to one side.

Surprised, I went. I was not about to call attention to myself, not without good cause. I joined the group of people waiting for questioning. Behind me, people showed papers to the woman and passed. Those were all people with wagons or people dressed as runners.

My crowd moved briskly; the young singers barely spoke to the guards. They waved, laughed, said something or other I couldn't catch, and ran down the hill to join the crowd of people at the foot of a well-kept road, most of them climbing into a long wagon waiting there.

It was my turn. "Business?" asked an older fellow, stout, with a ducal coronet stitched over his rose.

"Travel," I said.

"Join," the man replied, pointing.

"Join what?"

His eyes narrowed from boredom to mild interest.

I said, quickly, "I'm a sailor. This is my first journey inland."

"Oh." He shrugged. "The Duke of Larsca's law states that anyone on the road during harvest time not on king's business or delivering goods puts in a week of harvest duty for ducal lands."

A week! Annoyance flushed through me, and I gauged the situation with a quick glance. Maybe ten of them in various jobs all over the bridge foot. Then I turned back to the man, who was now regarding me with more wariness than curiosity.

"Oh." I swallowed, my throat tight. "What do I do next?"

His expression cleared. "Go down there. Wagon will take you to wherever they need. You get housing and food during the week, and extra over quota gets pay. Your horse gets stabled free of charge."

I bobbed the way I'd seen people salute the warriors and followed the young singers, who had jumped into a wagon and were now singing a splendid round. A brown-liveried stablehand took charge of the mare, leading her to a string of animals. I climbed into the wagon thinking sternly: *Lie low, go along. Let's not get search parties and arrests and descriptions going out, shall we? If you need to, you can always run off.* People clambered in behind me, their ages roughly from about fourteen or fifteen, like the minstrels, to maybe early thirties or so. When the wagon was full, someone up front yelled, "Here we go!" and the team of six big plough horses started moving—an empty wagon almost immediately being guided into our place.

When a rainstorm boiled up over those hills to the northwest and bore down on us, everyone in the wagon helped put up a canopy, laughing and joking, and we rode dry while rain drummed the canvas overhead, cascading in silvery fringes all around. The minstrels sang rain songs, many joined in, and I sat there safe and smiling.

There's no use in going into the daily details of my career as a farm worker. I decided by the end of the first day to dutifully put in my week without drawing attention to myself. The place was comfortable, the food was plain and plentiful, the work easy. Here was my chance to hear gossip that would be useful. Or at least learn how people were feeling about the government, so I could tell Dad when I saw him again.

Human nature being what it is, mild fun—though we live

for such moments—is really boring to read about.

The ducal farm we were taken to was a series of long, low buildings, sturdily built. The crop we'd been chosen for was olive picking. I was surprised there were olives growing here at all. The single thing I knew about them was that a Mediterranean climate was needed. But these olives had adapted over the countless centuries since being brought over. The hot southern sun during the summer ripened the olives, the way the hills were sheltered by the mountain ridge looming to the west apparently kept off the worst ice storms in winter, and so these gnarled, rough-barked trees had been steadily producing olives for centuries, while all around Khanerenth's crazy history raveled and unraveled itself.

I learned about olives' growing cycle and that the right time to pick them is an exact science. I also learned that for maximum value they have to be pressed within a day or so, depending on the outside temps.

The work was mostly a lot of reaching overhead, as I was tall. I did my picking as far from the others as I could, carrying on long mental conversations in English.

When I was done picking, I entertained myself watching the girls watch the guys who watched the girls as we carried our bucket loads down to be washed and pressed. Big guys mostly handled the presses, which is why the more flirtatious girls were really enthusiastic about filling their buckets in order to make the trip down the hill. In fact, I am pretty certain that our work boss, a tough grandmotherly woman, deliberately put the cutest guy on the first press, a tall, buff hottie with long curling reddish gold hair and a wickedly flirtatious manner. He *always* had a crowd around him, after fast, enthusiastic picking.

As soon as the sun went down, we were off work. After dinner there was equipment to ready for the next day, then we were pretty much on our own. Every night people who had learned some sort of instrument (some good, some not so, but they could all more or less follow a tune) and the singers got up some sort of concert or dance, and tired as we were, we found energy for dancing.

So did I get a romance going?

Either I tell the truth or toss this thing in the fire.

Easy answer first. Tavan, the cute guy, took no notice of me. He seemed to prefer the shorter girls. But there were other guys, nice ones, cute ones, who seemed to like my looks as much as I liked theirs.

Did I flirt? Jokes and comments, yeah. The easy stuff. But ardent eyes, the narrowed gaze of interest, personal questions, that subtle shift from general interest to individual—whenever I sensed those things, I found somewhere else to be. My favorite retreat was the women's baths, which were a long room with a hot spring diverted to run through, carrying endless clean water in a natural Jacuzzi. Wow, did that feel good.

Anyway, back to the guys. Why didn't I respond? I'll get there in a sec.

At the end of the first week, which was all I owed as a traveler, the work boss called me over and asked me if I'd put in a second week as the crop was ripening fast, and I'd be paid. They didn't have enough tall women.

I thought, why not? I was having fun, I didn't feel any hurry, except a vague sense of unease when occasional bits of gossip radiated out from Vadnais's royal castle. When my mother's name came up, the rumors were all about how the king and Princess Atanial were constantly giving parties and balls. Sifting that, I figured my mother was at least safe. She'd been guarding herself a lot longer than I had been guarding me, after all.

In fact, there is one conversation I'll report. We were all sitting on the plain plank porch outside our dorm, the evening cool but still, the air faintly blue everywhere but the forest, which was a vast black silhouette. Insects chirruped peacefully, and in the distance a couple of the horses whinnied at one another.

They'd passed out letters brought in by a runner, and someone had mentioned the king and Princess Atanial.

One woman said, "So is she gonna marry him? I mean, she must be after him."

"She's a prisoner," I said, but under my breath.

The woman next to me, who was sewing a hole in the armpit of her shirt, glanced over. "She is?"

"Ribbons for chains. But she can't leave. Remember whose wife she is." I was somewhat desperate, wishing I'd kept my mouth shut. I'd gotten into the habit of talking under my breath while picking.

A thoughtful silence settled, and one of the younger women, sitting on the ground leaning against the rail, murmured slowly, "I never thought about it before, but what does a princess *do*?" At the laughs and expressions of scorn, she added hastily, "I know! Balls, gowns, flirt with princes. But, is that it?"

"Practice to be queens?" said the sewing woman. "You would have to know how to read, for example."

The younger woman stirred at this sarcasm, so I said hastily, "I never thought about it either, but you're watched all the time, I expect. Everyone wants a piece of you. I don't mean that necessarily in a good way."

"'Piece of you'," the sewer repeated. "A strange way to put it. Yet it seems right, from anything I've ever heard."

The younger one laughed. "You can't be serious. How much work is going to a ball?"

They broke into chattering groups, but at least the subject of Princess Atanial was forgotten.

So now the subject I've been avoiding. The real reason I didn't flirt was because of Jehan.

I worked hard to shove him out of my mind. Even after bits of gossip that mentioned him. I worked so hard that one afternoon I accidentally broke a branch by yanking too hard, but luckily the olives on it were all ripe and I hastily stripped them off and stowed them in my bucket. I took my three-quarters-filled bucket away so I wouldn't hear the chatter about Prince Jehan and the Sartoran ambassador's beautiful cousin dancing all night in some marble hall. I didn't care about his flirts, no, not me. He could double-talk anyone he wanted, yessiree-Bob.

Despite my determined efforts Not To Think About Him, I always ended up in those long, exasperating imagined conversations with him. They were exasperating because I didn't know the truth. So when I was mad at him, I imagined him admitting to being a liar, traitor and all the rest of it, lower than the lowest slug...and I'd think, why fool yourself? You were a total IDIOT to have dusted out without finding out the truth.

But how was I to find out the truth while his prisoner and surrounded by his people?

No, I had to stick to my plan. Find my father. Dump the entire mess into his lap. He'd know what to do about Prince Jehan Jervaes Merindar.

I wished—oh, you have no idea how hard I wished—that I hadn't kissed Jehan.

Because my subconscious, who is about as stubborn as a corral full of hungry mules, didn't care about politics, promises, power, princes or princesses. Her needs were direct. Despite how hard I fought during the day, every night when I had to surrender to her realm she adored pressing the backtrack button over and over to replay in my dreams every moment of that sweet, breathlessly intense, absolutely glorious experience.

Me: *Subconscious, please don't do that.*

Her: *I want that one.*

Me: *You're being a total cow. I mean, anybody with half a brain does not mistake lust for love.*

Her: *I want that one.*

Me: *He's a liar. He cheats his own father! He says what he wants me to hear, just like dear old dad.*

Her: *Oooookay, you wanna be like that? Just wait for your dreams tonight, girlfriend.*

Despite the fact that in this culture, as long as you have not married with the ring ceremony, it's expected you'll shop around before finding a mate, I couldn't head for the sweet-smelling shadowy glades where insects softly chirruped and autumn leaves rustled, to enjoy some recreational kissy-face with one of the nice, cute, pleasant young men I met there, who had no possible interest in politics or power or any of the rest of it, only in me. Because my subconscious promised stubbornly that if I did, I'd have about as much fun as kissing a fence post.

There I was, almost three weeks later, when the last of the olive crop was pretty much down and we were doing a second run for gleanings.

I was a day from finishing the job, so I put in some time that morning asking easy questions here and there about the main landmarks that would lead me to Ivory Mountain.

We were about to break for the midday meal when the entire camp was surprised by new arrivals.

We Got Males.

# Chapter Eighteen

Once they were actually on the road, Damedran and his princess-hunting posse enjoyed the ride. The second morning, as they relaxed around the campfire in their bedrolls while the two servants saw to the horses and cooking, they gloatingly counted up the toilsome chores they *weren't* doing, unlike the other senior cadets.

When breakfast was ready they climbed out of their bedrolls, and after the servants cleaned up, they took to horse. Through the remainder of the day's ride, they wondered aloud from time to time what their own group was doing right at that moment, but Damedran and Ban both noticed that once you were actually out of sight of the game, most of the fun was gone. You had to be there.

Adjusting to what they were missing was a whole lot easier when they remembered that they had the king's sigil. They could change horses whenever they wanted, and could eat anywhere they wanted, what they wanted, and that included drink. And no one made a peep. The shot would be sent back to Vadnais to be paid by Uncle Dannath's paymaster.

Ban Kender and Bowsprit Lanarg hadn't much liked being pulled from the war game, but that was because Damedran hadn't told them why until Castle Cheslan was far behind them. Their first reaction to *We're going to intercept Princess Atanial's daughter* was surprise. Then both of them thought philosophically of the fact that success meant early promotion. Their families counted on their doing well in the military, and if finding and escorting a princess's daughter to the royal city got them made patrol leaders way ahead of the other seniors, well, see the tears?

Except for one bump, the good mood lasted until they reached the outskirts of Zhavlir a few days later. The bump happened midway through the ride, when they reached Barlir and visited an inn. There they were, with no glowering captains, masters or war-commanding uncles to order them around. They didn't have to spend, or account for, a copper dunket of their own. And the dark ale here was famed throughout the army. What a perfect opportunity to get snockered!

...except they had to ride the next day.

Well, all right, so you learn something about how unfun it is to get drunk anywhere but at home, and not with duty the next day.

After that never-too-soon-forgotten ride, things went right back to first rank. Even the weather cooperated, turning from cold with occasional bands of rain to a stretch of sunny, warm days.

The moment finally came when they cleared the last hill above Zhavlir and saw the fine, smooth military road curving gently down between hedgerows toward the city gates.

Damedran cleared his throat. "Getting sick?" Red asked.

"No." Damedran did not look at any of them. Of his six companions, Ban, Red and Bowsprit rode close. The others had formed in a row behind, and could only hear the murmur of voices ahead. Behind them rode the two servants with the equipment packed on the remounts, talking quietly to one another; they didn't even try to listen in on the toff cadets.

Damedran said quickly, "Our orders are, we grab her, and report to my uncle. Then we take her back to him, wherever he is."

Red shrugged. "Sounds easy to me."

Bowsprit turned to Ban, who sent him a grimace.

Ban eyed Damedran. Something was wrong. "We're not taking her to the king?"

"No."

Bowsprit whistled.

Damedran flushed. "My uncle is the war commander. He's the king's voice, his right hand—"

"This isn't a military matter," Ban cut in. "It's a royal one. Why aren't we taking her straight to the king? Or at least contacting him?"

Damedran snarled, "Shut up. Just shut up. You want to be reported for insubordination? In case you have forgotten, *I* am patrol captain for this mission, and it's *I* who has the communication relay." He dug the gold case out of the pouch at his belt and brandished it.

Ban's jaw tightened, his eyes narrowed and he faced forward.

Bowsprit sent Damedran one last, unhappy glance, then he too faced resolutely forward.

Red jerked his good shoulder up in agreement. When the three behind started in with variations on "What did he say? We can't hear!" he explained in a few terse words.

Two of them shrugged. They were used to Damedran's ways. But the third burst out, "I don't like this."

Ban drawled over his shoulder, "*Lord Damedran Randart* is the *patrol leader*. Oh, I beg your pardon. Patrol *captain*. Haven't you heard? *He* has the communication relay. *He* can snitch, I mean, *report*, us for insubordination. Just for asking honest questions."

"Shut up, Ban."

Ban lifted his voice. "But we're not to think. We are here as muscle. Our next order will probably be to beat her up. That doesn't take any thinking. Six of us! Six and no thinking allowed—"

"*Shut up, Ban!*"

"Is that an order, *Lord High Patrol Captain*?"

Damedran burned with fury, and his fists bunched. He longed to fling himself on Ban and pound his face into the dirt. But they weren't behind the stable where cadet fights were carried out with friends on watch. They were here, they were supposedly on their first mission as men, and not cadets.

First mission. As men.

He groaned, remembering his uncle's softly uttered threat, and his anger doused like water on flames. "*My uncle* ordered this secret mission. Want to know what he said when I dared one single question?"

Instantly sobered, Ban shook his head. He'd only seen the war commander lose his temper once, but he'd seen the results of it many times. Not only terrible floggings before the entire assembled academy and garrison, but he'd heard of people vanishing altogether.

As for Damedran, Ban had never actually envied him his exalted position, not after the first time he watched his fellow ten-year-old leave his uncle's chamber after a thrashing. Though Damedran's father was the head of the academy, everyone knew he obeyed his older brother in everything, including how to raise his son.

Red said in a make-peace voice, "King or war commander, what's the problem?"

Bowsprit slewed round in his saddle, studying Ban's long face, then he slewed back. "When Red puts it that way, what *is* the problem?"

Ban hunched his shoulders, glowering between his horse's flicking ears. She was aware of the animals on the civilian road on the other side of the hill, though none of the humans were.

Ban said slowly, working it out as he spoke, "I think it's the secret part of the mission. And the fact that it's *us*. And not any of the guard. Think of it. Your uncle could send any of the top scouts, any of his honor guard, who are all picked for skill and speed and all that. I mean we're about the best in the academy, with one or two exceptions—"

He paused for the hoots and scornful comments to die down, then continued. "—but we're still academy. Why isn't he sending any of them, when they are so much better?"

"Yeah." Bowsprit slewed around again. "Yeah!"

"We don't have orders to, ah, kill her, or anything?" Ban asked in his most surly voice in an effort to hide his anxiety.

Not that it worked, because Damedran felt the same way. "No! No. We're to capture her in secret. No one to find out who she is. Tie her up so she can't do magic. Report to my uncle via message box. And then take her to wherever he says. Only to him, he kept repeating. Not to anyone else, and not a word to anyone, either."

Silence fell between them as they reached the bottom of the hill. They were in arrow shot of the city gates, and the military road was about to blend with the crowded civ road.

"I don't like it," Ban said as the two roads converged, and Damedran made a short gesture meaning *shut up!*

This time Ban obeyed, and they fell in just behind a wagon full of bushels of vegetables, driven by a very shapely girl who kept looking round in a pretense of checking her cargo.

Bowsprit and Red sat up straighter, sneaking peeks at the girl, who scoped them out pretty thoroughly from under drifting black curls. The boys tried to catch her eye when she looked their way. The rest of the time they were checking out her figure instead of watching the road, until Damedran caught them at it. He pulled his riding gloves from his belt and whapped Red.

"Pay attention," he snarled. "What if that pirate has spies tracking us?"

They all looked around, radiating furtiveness.

Satisfied that the passing farmers and merchants were not secret spies, Damedran said in a low voice. "Now, here's what we'll do..."

None of them gave a second look to the scruffy, scrawny red-haired man slouched on the back of a tired horse, who plodded two wagons behind them. The kingdom seemed to be filled with plain, wiry red-haired men who served in stables or at table or sewed or cobbled or did masonry.

The same was not true of this scruffy red-haired man—known at this end of the continent only as Owl—who was finally close enough to identify them.

He'd first spotted them as the military and civilian roads topped separate hills and started down toward the fork. He always watched for military roads and who might be on them, going where.

His glimpse of a patrol of cadets had taken him by surprise. The boys looked familiar. He'd ridden along in frustration, peering as they vanished and reappeared again, hidden by hedgerows and the last hill, and then never-to-be-cursed-enough wild ferns growing alongside the roads.

He dared not gallop or in any wise call attention to himself. If that really was Damedran Randart and some of his pack of rats, they might possibly recognize him from his menial labors around the academy. Unlikely, but he wasn't going to take the chance. It was too strange to encounter them here, so far from Castle Cheslan and the rest of the army. Surely they should be at the center of the war game.

Everything seemed to conspire against him, including the angle of the bright sun turning them into silhouettes, until at last the two roads merged. A few moments later the one riding point turned his head, long blue-black hair swinging, as he whapped the red-haired boy with gloves—and Owl stared in amazement. That was indeed Damedran Randart.

Why? The only thing Owl was sure of was that Randart was behind it, for some purpose sinister and sneaky. Surprise inspection for the local garrison, maybe?

The urge to write a note to Jehan gripped him, to be fought off. One thing that would call attention to him would be scrawling a note on horseback, and whipping out a golden case to put it into. Owl knew that he'd be seen. Circumstances were lamentably predictable that way.

So once they were through the city gates, he deliberately turned his horse up a different street than the main street, which led straight to the garrison. He dismounted when he found a quirk between two old alleyways, moss growing between the bricks. He slid off the horse and kept it between him and the alleyway intersection as he pulled out his chalk and a scrap of paper from his pack, and wrote:

*Damedran here. Know why? Should I do anything?*

He tucked it into the notecase and leaned tiredly against the horse to wait. Jehan might answer right away, if he was alone. But if he wasn't, it could be half a day. Or longer. So he'd give himself a breather. If nothing came, it meant Jehan was away from his rooms.

As he stood there absently running his hands over the neck of the drooping animal, he thought back over the exercise in frustration the past weeks had been. Like losing the princess during the very first storm that ended the summer and discovering she'd vanished. He'd ridden as hard as he could along the river road, pausing only to arrange for changes of mount, until he reached the foothills below the border mountains. Here the road narrowed, leading directly to Moonsky Lake at the border. He'd asked at the inn where absolutely everyone stopped, and despite coins and exhaustive questioning, discovered no trace of any tall woman fitting the description of Sasharia Zhavalieshin.

So he'd ridden all the way back to the last inn he'd seen her at, wishing he'd dared sleep inside the first time. But that enormous wedding party and all those harvesters had convinced him to ride on to the next inn and wait for her to catch up. That was before the big storm.

He hoped that the inn folk remembered her. A description, some added coin, and the innkeeping pair told him they did indeed remember her. She'd helped that night, and further she'd carried a letter for them to the Three Falls Inn in Zhavlir...

Zhavlir? On the other side of the river?

Owl got a room, sat down, wrote a bitter letter, tore it up. Wrote another saying only that he'd found the right road. Sure enough Jehan wrote back: *Waste no time. Find her.*

So here he was again, after another mad dashing ride. Now he only had to locate the inn.

He yawned, leaning against the horse. "Just one more ride, old friend," he murmured, making a mental promise of bran mash as he himself thought longingly of a good pull on some fine dark ale...

While he was trying to find the energy to get himself back in the saddle and seek the inn, Damedran and his posse had ridden straight to the garrison in the middle of the town, sent a servant in to get directions to the Three Falls, and rode the few blocks to reach it.

They dismounted in the stable yard, Damedran saying, "The trail is at least a week old, so she can't still be here. But in case, I want a perimeter. Make certain you can all see one another. No yelling, no attention."

The others obeyed while Damedran walked into the inn. A teenaged girl clearing a table took in his long stride, his swinging black hair, the sword at his side, blushed and ran into the kitchen. He never gave her a glance, but made directly for the tall man at the counter.

He said, "Master Innkeeper? I'm looking for an old friend I was supposed to meet on the road. A woman with honey-colored hair, one of her names being Lasva. Very tall. Carried a letter for you."

Until the mention of the last, the innkeeper had looked puzzled, for he'd served plenty of tall women with honey-colored hair, and Lasva was a very common name. But the letter?

"Ah, the sailor! Very nice person. You come from the west, then? Your accent is good. Are those not guard colors?" He indicated the brown tunic.

"West?" Damedran repeated, as confused as the innkeeper.

"Yes. What was it...somewhere west of Colend...Bermund? Hanbria? No, I think it might have been Tser Mearsies. Yes. My wife made her a map, see. She can draw a mighty fine map. She puts things like rivers and forests and mountains in it, little tiny ones. Not like real ones, if you get my drift, but to represent—"

Damedran waved a hand. "I comprehend. So she rode west, did she?"

The man shrugged. "One can only assume so, if she asked for the map to help her get home again."

Damedran bit his lip against letting out any curses, turned

away, then turned back. He pulled out his coin purse and laid several heavy golden six-sided coins on the counter, but kept his hand on them. "Did she happen to mention any other places?"

He shrugged again, but his wife appeared, drying her hands, glanced from the coins to Damedran. Her tired face took on a wary look. "Is there a problem? She was a very nice young woman. Even neatened her room when she left. They don't always, the young."

"I think someone we know sent her wrong," Damedran invented desperately. He'd never been good at lying on the spot, he always had to think them out first. "But she was going to meet me, and I was east, see, not west."

"You don't look anything like her." The wife smoothed stray hairs off her forehead and narrowed her eyes. "Family, you say?"

"Friends. Ah, my older sister is a sailor too, see, and they got to know each other. And, well, I'm trying to find her." Running out of ideas, Damedran fought against losing his temper again.

The wife looked up at her tall spouse, he gazed down with an air of helpless question, and when a customer yelled out, "Innkeep! Is that ale ready, or must I fetch it myself?" the man whirled away and the woman gave a tiny shrug. "Well. Not my business, I guess you could say. She did ask a bit about Bar Larsca Valley. Said she was looking for a friend. I think she might even have said a sailor, come to think on it."

Damedran grinned. "Ah. Listen, I don't want any more mixed messages. It's not likely anyone else would ask. But if they do. You've forgotten, yes?" He took his hand off the coins.

She smiled, sweeping them into her apron. "I'm always happy to help a nice young woman like that. Indeed, sir."

Damedran almost ran out, signaling to Ban as he did. Ban waved at the next cadet down, and they soon assembled in the courtyard.

"Bar Larsca Valley," Damedran said. "Right back where we started out!"

"Unless she's at the other end," Ban put in. "You know, at the mountains."

"Why would anyone go to the mountains?" Red asked.

Damedran ignored them. "Or she went to Tser Mearsies. But why would she go there?"

"Escape us," Ban said dryly.

"Not in Bar Larsca." Damedran shook his head, thinking of Castle Cheslan sitting at the southeast end of the valley. "Anyone would tell her about the siege game. You'd think. So maybe she did go to Tser Mearsies after all."

"And leave her ma behind?" Red put in.

They all looked thoughtful at that, turning to Red with expressions very close to respect. Red blushed. "Well, I wouldn't. Leave my ma. If—" *If I knew she was a prisoner of the king.* He might get himself into trouble if he said any more, and so he flapped his hands out from his sides, looking skyward.

Damedran was done with the conversation anyway. "Back to the garrison. New mounts, and we're on the road. Remember, we're at least a week behind her."

They returned to the servants, who had been holding the reins of the horses all this time. They remounted and rode sedately out, remembering the order not to call attention to themselves.

One they reached the open road, they could loosen the reins and gallop with the wind.

They reached the garrison at the same time as Owl reached the inn. He walked up to where Mistress Innkeeper was polishing the counter, her expression distracted. The common room was empty except for a table of drunks at one corner, with whom Master Innkeeper was obviously trying to reason. In the kitchen a pair of young teens were busy frosting pastries. Both glanced at Owl, then went back to work, obviously losing interest.

Owl felt the inward tingle of magic—an answer from Jehan.

He laid a silver coin on the counter. "I was told that your relations sent a letter via a young woman, tall, wheat-colored hair probably in braids. I would like to know where she went, if you remember?"

The woman glanced from the coin to Owl's face, her jaw tight, her hands thrust into her apron pockets. "Couldn't rightly say," she finally replied.

Owl sighed. "I may as well get a room, then. Send word to the stable I'll pay for a bran mash for the mount. Name's Owl."

He sat in a corner, looking about. The man was dealing with the drunks, the woman had vanished, the teenagers were busy in the kitchen, talking and working.

He pulled out the golden case, found a rolled paper on which Jehan had written:

*I know nothing about Damedran and some mission. Will try to find out. I don't like this coincidence.*

Owl turned over the paper, took from his pouch his drawing chalk, wrote, *I'm at the inn. They say they know nothing. Do you really want me riding on, weeks behind the last sign of her?*

He put the note in the case, sent it, stowed the case, and then ate supper while one of the teens brought in his gear from the stable and carried it upstairs.

He'd expected an answer right away, but none came. One never knew when Jehan could get the freedom to visit his rooms.

At sundown four young musicians came in, bearing instruments. Mistress Innkeeper opened all the windows and set lamps on each sill. The music drifted out onto the streets and before long the place was filled with custom, drinking, eating, dancing, singing, talking. Owl sat in isolation, too tired to care when the dancers, maneuvering for space, bumped him with hip or elbow. When he caught himself falling asleep right there in the chair, he trod upstairs to the third floor and down the hall to where someone had chalk-marked "Owl" on the door.

The door shut out most of the noise. Someone had lit a lamp, which cast weak light on a bed, a small table with his saddlebag directly below it, a window opened to the cool night air below the slanting beams of the roof.

He pulled the gold case out and removed the tiny scrap of paper on which Jehan had written in careful letters that betrayed not haste but a long period of reflection:

*Return to Vadnais.*

Though he suspected Jehan was bitter with disappointment for several good reasons, Owl sighed with relief and fell into bed.

His mood was as sunny as the weather the next morning. After a long sleep, a long soak in the bath and a long breakfast, he slung his gear over his shoulder, paid his shot and sauntered out to the stable to retrieve his mount and start the journey south. This time he needn't hurry.

He was smiling to himself, mentally planning a route that would include as many good inns as possible, when he noticed the head stableman watching him in an uncertain way. A stealthy way, even.

Owl checked shoes, saddle, feedbag, then mounted up, and couldn't resist a single glance back. The man shook his head slightly and turned away.

"What is it," Owl said, suspecting he would hate whatever he was about to hear.

The man turned around again, this time scanning in both directions. But all the stablehands were busy, out of earshot. He stepped to Owl's stirrup. "The mistress is a good one, few better. But she does like a gold coin, and she also is partial to a young, handsome face."

"What?" Owl knew this could not possibly refer to him, as he had offered no one gold, he was no longer young and had never been handsome.

"Boys in cadet gear here yesterday." The man looked around. "Girl told me they offered six golds for information, and for Mistress to keep quiet. But no one saw fit to pay *me.*"

At that subtle hint, Owl dug into his pouch. "Guards?" Damedran? *Here?*

A nod, then the man leaned up and muttered, "Lookin' for a

tall woman. Light hair. Named Lasva. Carried a letter from Master's cousin at an inn downriver. Girl in the kitchen overheard it all."

Owl gaped. Damedran Randart had been *here*. Not at the garrison, on some fool army task.

There was only one explanation for him being here. He was hunting Sasharia. What had happened? Owl could have sworn Randart had no suspicions when he left the *Dolphin*. Well, of course not, or he would have used that force to take her.

The man sneaked another look around. "I'd swear that boy on point was a Randart. To say no more, a certain relation o' his being one of the reasons I no longer serve in the guard," he added sourly.

Owl handed down a fistful of silver coinage, which was the highest worth he carried. "She say where she was going?"

Another look. "Mistress drew her a map to go west cross-country. They said west of Colend. But she asked about Larsca territory. And when she rode out, she didn't turn west or north, but right down the south road."

Owl slapped the rest of his silver into the man's hand. "Thank you," he murmured. "And...I'd not mention this conversation."

The man gave him a wry smile. "I never even saw you."

Owl paused once, again at a corner where he couldn't be seen, and wrote a fast note to Jehan. Without waiting for an answer he started galloping down the south road.

# Chapter Nineteen

"Lasva, there's a couple of lookers here to see you," one of the younger girls said to me, eyes wide with interest and curiosity. Probably the moreso since I hadn't been among those going off for long walks in the woods during those evenings, or dancing until past midnight.

"For me?"

My first thought was Jehan.

I scoffed at myself. How would he possibly know where I was, after all these weeks? And second, more to the point, if he was here, they wouldn't say "a couple of lookers", not with that white hair, and the inevitable outriders and hoopla. They'd be going nutso over the sudden appearance of a royal prince.

So I shrugged, hefting my bag as I'd been heading toward the stable anyway. Probably someone who wanted to hire me for my great reach. Like for apple picking or something.

When I reached the stable yard, two of the younger of my dorm mates were flirting with a pair of teenage guys. The one with the red hair was flirting back. I couldn't hear the words over the noise in the yard, what with horses coming and going, shouts of workers, conversations everywhere as our former olive-picking mates began their departures. The redhead laughed, leaned down, tugged teasingly at one of the girls' braids, to get his hand slapped away with a pretense of anger. The other one, cuter by far, was tall, with a long, serious face and thick waving brown hair worn clipped back. Both wore ill-fitting summer tunics over their shirts, and brown riding trousers tucked into blackweave riding boots much like the military wear. They each had swords at their saddles and knives at their belts.

I walked up. "Looking for me?" I asked, relieved I didn't know them.

The dark-haired one regarded me with an expression impossible to interpret, but the redhead wiggled his brows. "Oh, I do hope you are Lasva."

The girls laughed, and the shorter, blond one (the biggest flirt in our dorm) cast me a mirthful glance. "Good luck winning a kiss out of Lasva! She's far too picky. You're better off with me."

"If they're hiring for kissing, you are the expert. But if it's apple picking," I said, making a show of looking down on her, "you're hopeless."

The girls and the redhead laughed. The other boy leaned forward to pat his horse's neck, as the animal was restless, ears flicking, weight shifting from one leg to the other, head tossing. His hand was big, strong and callused across the palm.

"Apple picking?" The redheaded guy pretended surprise. "How ever did you know?"

"Because I've already worked a week over the quota on account of my size," I retorted. "What did they give you at the front, a name of all the tall ones who don't spend their time chasing after kisses?"

"Hey! I was a good presser," the blonde protested.

"Yeah. When Tavan was around," her friend retorted, rolling her eyes.

"Am I as handsome as Tavan?" The redhead smoothed back his tousled hair.

"No." All three of us women shook our heads.

Both of the guys laughed this time.

The redhead said to me, "Well, will you come apple picking?"

"Is it really apples? How amazing is that?" I said.

"How...amazing...is what?" The dark-haired one looked

puzzled.

The blonde said, "She talks funny. But she's a sailor." As if that explained everything.

"We have an orchard." The redhead waved a hand in a vague circle. "Actually, several fruits and things."

I shrugged. "How long and where? I do have somewhere to be."

"Oh," asked the redhead. "Where is that?"

The dark-haired one sent him a frown, but the redhead shrugged.

"Tser Mearsies." I gave them one of my lies, surprised a little that they would ask.

"This won't take long. Not a large orchard." The redhead grinned.

"All right." I shrugged, thinking that the fewer of those jewels I had to use on my journeys, the less attention I garnered. And anyway my father might need them back. "Let me get my mount."

The blonde grinned at me. "We'll keep them occupied. Take your time."

As I trod to the stable, the teasing, flirting and laughter promptly took up behind me.

I found my mare. She was fresh and ready to go, her head tossing, eyes alert, nostrils flaring. The stablehands had already saddled her, and my sword was intact, so all I had to do was tie on my gear and lead her out.

The short time I'd been gone, several more of the younger girls had gathered round. As I led my mare up, I was informed by the girls that my escorts were named Red and Ban.

"Call me Lasva." I mounted up. My riding muscles twinged. Weird, how quickly you lose it if you don't use it.

Everyone exchanged farewells and the fellows led the way out of the place I'd spent so pleasant a stay. My earnings jingled with satisfying weight in my little belt pouch.

We proceeded at a walking pace toward the crossroads on the other side of the hill from the farm. They did not angle toward the big main road, rutted from all those wagon runs to and from the duke's row of farms and orchards, but toward a smaller side road. We cut through all the traffic of wagons, riders and walkers. The boys had fallen silent. I was fine with that. I was wondering how I could get to a map without raising any questions—which meant lying. Which, of course, promptly threw right back at me all the self-righteous yap I'd given to Jehan about his lies.

Of course *my* cause is good, I instantly told myself.

But I could hear him insisting he wanted my dad back. If so, why didn't he just come out and say so, as Prince Jehan— why the purple pirate secret identity? Could it be for the same reasons I was lying? But he was a prince! Princes had power.

Or did he? On the yacht, Randart sure hadn't behaved like...

I sighed sharply, causing my mare to sidle.

The boys looked over at me, Ban concerned, Red confused. "Anything wrong? Uh, Lasva?"

"No. Just, next time someone tells me something, I'm going to listen," I said with fake cheer. "Instead of boring myself afterward with trying to imagine what they would have said."

Now both looked confused. I sighed again and looked around. While I'd been arguing with myself for the thousandth time, we'd gradually left the other travelers behind. We were completely alone on a road that had narrowed to something little wider than a worn footpath. "Where are the others?"

Ban said with a tight expression, "Others?"

"Hirelings." I motioned upward, as if picking an apple from a tree. "You cannot tell me I'm the only one hired from that place. I could name you at least a dozen who were faster and better than I. Taller too." I meant the last as a joke, and belatedly Red laughed, but it was a strangled sort of laugh, and Ban's smile was more of a wince.

I stopped my mare. "Um, what's going on here?" I asked. "You two look like you swallowed glass. There's nobody else around—"

I was interrupted by the thud of horse hooves from beyond a rocky outcropping.

From the other side of the scree, five guys in cadet brown emerged, followed by two more guys with a string of horses. The first rider was familiar—hawk nose a lot like my own, generous, curving lips, black eyes, long glossy black hair—

"Damedran Randart?" I squeaked.

His mouth dropped open. "How did you know that?"

I swung my horse around. "All I know is," I ripped my sword free, "I am not going *anywhere* with a Randart!"

I whapped the mare's sides. Her muscles bunched. She was very ready for a run.

The others closed round me, their faces determined.

None of them were armed. Yet. I whirled around in the saddle, swung my sword so fast it hummed. Whizz—snap—whoosh! I cut through the reins on three of their mounts. The horses panicked, and the boys couldn't control them.

That was enough to win me a gap in their circle. I gave the mare the knees again. She, rested for weeks, loved the opportunity to gallop and took off like a rocket. I bent low over her head, bushes whipped past—

A darkish blur thundered up on one side. A flash of silver—Damedran Randart brought his sword down toward me.

I slewed, whipped my blade up. I was already off-balance. I had never fought on horseback and feared my block would be weak, so I rose up in the stirrups the better to brace against his killing blow.

Which was a feint. Damedran snapped his blade to a low flat thrust under my thigh. He flexed his wrist, and whoop! I tumbled right off the horse.

Only my martial arts training in falling saved me from breaking at least an arm, if not my neck. I tucked under, rolled over what felt like 345,679 jagged boulders, and momentum propelled me to my feet. My sword had vanished when I first fell, so I shifted into kenpo mode. When Damedran flung himself down from his horse, I whipped up a foot, kicked his blade clean out of his hand, followed up with a whirl and a sidekick to the knee, and he yelped, falling right in Ban's path.

I ran.

Got about three steps before two big, brawny boys came at me, arms out. No swords. I feinted toward one, and when his hands jerked up to block, I gave him a nasty palm-heel strike to the solar plexus, blocked a reach from the other and snapped another side-sweep to the knee. He went down first, the other whooping for breath as he stumbled after me.

I whirled, dashed two steps—then two strong hands closed on my shoulders. I twisted, used an elbow strike.

A teenage-male *whoof* blew in my ear. I grabbed his arm to swing him into his partner—but he planted his feet, and his heavier weight caused me to stumble.

And so the sixth one caught me round the waist. I twisted my hip in order to shift him off-balance, but he gave a grunt and lifted me off the ground. We both fell, he landing on top of me. Crunch. Thud. Three more muscle-bound teenage-boy bodies piled on in a first-class scrimmage heap, with me at the bottom.

Now it was my turn to struggle for breath.

The dogpile shifted, and the boys scrambled up. Two or three hands grasped at my arms, knees thumped on my back and legs. Though I squirmed and struggled my mightiest, the fight was lost, and determined fingers twisted my hands behind me.

I heard a breathless, "What do I use? What do I use?"

"Who has the rope?" I recognized that voice as Red's. "Nobody brought any? You idiots, we knew we had to—"

"No rope!" The low voice was Damedran's, equally breathless. "Rope is for criminals. You have your sash?"

"We wore belts, remember?" That voice I didn't recognize. It cracked on the word "remember".

"Here. Use your handkerchief. It's besorcelled, isn't it?"

"Yes."

"Let me do it. I don't want her hurt."

I was struggling with all my might while this conversation went on, not that it did me any good. My hands were effectively bound. Damedran kept pausing to check the knots with shaking fingers.

I heard various versions of fast, heavy-guy breathing all around me as someone stuck hands into my armpits and pulled me up so I could sit.

When the dizziness subsided, I found myself looking into a football huddle of grim faces, as sweaty and dusty as I knew my own had to be. Red's grimness was slightly bemused as he wheezed, and Damedran glowered.

A couple of them exchanged uneasy glances, obviously unwilling to speak first. Damedran kept flicking dark-eyed looks up at me then down at one hand as the other rubbed at his knee.

"Your call." My heart raced. I shifted my weight, knowing I probably couldn't do much besides spring to my feet, but if this ambush was shortly to end in murder, it wouldn't be with my cooperation.

Red gave me a somewhat shaky grin as he rubbed his middle. "Hoo, princess. You really do know how to fight."

Princess. Not Lasva.

So this was a royal hunt.

"Yah. Well. Not well enough to get away."

Damedran glared at me. "How did you know who I was?"

I occupied myself for a moment in trying unsuccessfully to blow a couple of my braids out of my face. My hair knot, so easily made that morning (as the universe had neglected to hint that I should dress for abduction) had come undone.

Though I was ambivalent about Jehan, I had one sure conviction: I did not trust Dannath Randart or any part of his family for a nanosecond. Reluctant to outright lie any more, I said slowly, "You look like your uncle. And I remember him from when I was little."

True, though I would not have recognized Damedran without that introduction aboard Jehan's yacht.

But he seemed to accept it.

"If you're supposed to kill me next, I really would like the chance to fight for my life."

Ban sat back, looking revolted, and Damedran said quickly, "We are not here to kill you."

I sighed. "Nice to know, but you have to see what it looks like to me. The disguises—" I nodded at Ban and Red in their humongous tunics. "The lie about hiring me—"

"Why are you traveling under a false name?" Damedran asked abruptly.

I shrugged. "Come on. Think about it. I'm yanked to this world against my will. My mother is taken prisoner. Am I really going to tell everyone who I am? I want to be left alone."

"To go to Tser Mearsies or to Bar Larsca?" He leaned forward. "I mean, what is there?"

"Nothing except anonymity. I've been a law-abiding olive picker for the past few weeks. I was about to become an apple picker. I thought."

"But you said you had somewhere to be," Red pointed out.

I shrugged. "Conversational gambit. To find out how long I'd be hired."

They exchanged uncertain looks. I suspected they didn't know whether to believe me or not. Time to get the subject from my goals to theirs.

I wriggled my shoulders. "So what next? The noose, war-commander style, or would that be a crossbolt in the back?"

Damedran's splendid cheekbones highlighted even more splendidly with a blush.

Ban said, "Blade in the back? Why did you say that?"

"Well, isn't that the way he gets rid of inconvenient people? He certainly did to Magister Glathan. I cannot imagine he'd find me anything but inconvenient, or I wouldn't have been ambushed like this."

More uneasy glances met these words.

"Tell me where I'm wrong," I invited, trying again to sling

my braids out of my face. I needed to see. I would have expected gloating, bullying, but if anything, these boys seemed if not reluctant, at least ambivalent about their having captured me.

"He wouldn't," Ban said, but I think we all heard the unspoken *Would he?* and he shot a pained look at Damedran.

Who seemed to be totally absorbed in reading his palms. Once again quiet fell, except for the breeze through some autumn red trees, the distant chuckling of an unseen stream and the snort of a horse.

Finally I said, testing the parameters of this abduction, "Hey. If you're not really going to kill me, how about untying me? You know I can't get the drop on seven of you."

"Yes—" Ban began.

But Damedran put out a hand. "She has magic, remember?"

I sighed, wiggling my fingers. They were tingling slightly, despite Damedran's efforts not to cut off my circulation. I suspect adrenaline had not made him as accurate in safe knot tying as he'd thought he was. "I only know about three spells. Make no mistake, they are powerful, but they are also specific. If I could transfer around by magic, I would have rescued my mother and vanished long ago."

Damedran turned to Ban, who jerked his chin up, then brought his attention back to me. "So you can't use any of these powerful spells and turn us into rocks or something?"

I shook my head. "They are specific, having to do with types of healing, I guess you could say. Like that one your guys saw me do when I was first brought here by Devli Eban. That spell changes..."

I thought in English, because I did not know the magical vocabulary. The spell enabled one to "see" a poison in a person and shift what amounted to a dangerous molecule or two, so that they became neutral, and that shift propagated swiftly through the person.

I turned my attention to Damedran, who had crouched down near me, one hand absently rubbing his sore knee as he waited for my answer. It seemed plain that this situation was as important for him as it was for me.

"The spell calls a kind of fire, and not all people can hold it, but it seems I can. So you send the fire in a kind of thread into the person, and it burns out the poison, so to speak, and then is gone."

Ban nodded soberly. "My sister said something of the sort once. But she said that kind of magic is only taught when you're at a high level."

"My father was desperate," I answered, glad to speak *some* truth, anyway. "And I guess I had the aptitude. My mother doesn't. She told me once he tried to teach her, but she couldn't hold the magic up here." I tipped my head back and forth. "There wasn't time to teach me all the basics, so he taught me that healing spell in hopes it would protect Mom and me in the other world. Unfortunately, there isn't enough magic potential there for it ever to work."

Damedran rubbed his jaw. "You can't use the spell to, I dunno, change someone's mind about something?"

I laughed. "No. No mood-altering, or mind-altering. At least, I do remember someone talking about the ancient Sartorans, and how they could do that sort of thing. How the villain Detlev can kill with just his mind, without moving a finger. But whether or not that's true, or the exaggeration of rumor, I can't do anything like that."

"Well, remember that Siamis fellow, Detlev's nephew, enchanted us all by talking to leaders," Red said.

Damedran sighed. "All right, but those rotters are four thousand years old, supposedly. Enough about them. What use is magic? I mean, I know, it keeps water clean, and so forth. But—" He shrugged. "Can you use it for much of anything else?"

Ban said soberly, "If you mean for war, my sister says any new spell has to be vetted by the Mage Council. And they find out if you're doing them. Magic is like rain to them. Say you ride into a territory well after the clouds dispersed, but you can smell the wet grass, see puddles, so forth. That's what my sister has told me. There's a lot of it at high levels that can do frightening things. But the other mages always know it."

Red said, "Like Siamis spreading that spell just by talking. Of course he didn't care who knew he'd done it."

*Come on, boys, see me as a person, not an objective.* "Didn't you all pretty much lose a year? That's what I was told. Though I don't get how enchanting leaders of countries got people enchanted too."

Red pulled off the huge rough-woven tunic and threw it down, leaving him wearing his shirt and brown cadet riding trousers stuffed into his boots. He was the shortest and leanest of them, but that meant he was my size. "If you were loyal to anyone, and he enchanted that person, you fell into it too. That's what *we* were told."

Ban opened a hand. "My sister thinks time kind of stopped during that enchantment. The way they know is, babies stayed babies. You know how fast they grow. Nobody's baby started walking and talking that year."

*That's right, talk to me, boys. Don't let me be the war commander's next crossbow target.*

One of the quieter boys spoke up unexpectedly. "There's even bigger magic, in history. Like mages raised all the mountains north of Sartor. My tutor told me it affected weather for a century or more. Yet those spells didn't keep out Norsunder."

That silenced everyone.

I was trying to think of a way to shift the talk from evil mages to evil war commanders when Damedran got to his feet. He looked skyward, then around at the countryside, which was full of russet-hued trees and grass and late-flowering weeds, birds, a stream, and our horses, but no other people.

Then he sighed and faced me, though he wouldn't meet my eyes. "I'd like to untie you. Even if you give us another run." His brief grin was wry and changed his entire demeanor. His gaze touched mine for a fleeting moment. "I apologize for knocking you off the horse."

I shrugged. "Hey, you didn't use the blade on *me*, for which I'm grateful. That was a cool trick."

*Cool* puzzled them, but they seemed to get the idea.

"As for my part of the fight, well, I'm not going to apologize for anything until I am convinced I'm not on my way to a hasty execution, just because my family name happens to be Zhavalieshin."

Their easy expressions vanished as if wiped by a cloth.

Damedran looked sulky and brooding again. "I can't do anything until I report to my uncle and get orders."

"But—" Ban began.

Damedran swung around. "You know what the orders were," he snapped. Under his breath, though I heard it, "And what will happen if anything goes wrong."

I'd forgotten about fear.

In silence he wrote a note reporting my capture, put it in his magical transfer box and sent it to the war commander.

# Chapter Twenty

In a lifetime of unexpected blows and tough decisions Jehan had avoided the toughest of all. Until now.

As soon as he received Owl's note—*I think I found her, somewhere in Bar Larsca, but Damedran is ahead of me*—he sent Kazdi to dispatch one of his covert teams of guards to Owl as backup.

And then he had to wait.

Days dragged by, excruciatingly slow and meaningless. He stood next to his father to review the palace guard before the chosen wing rode off to participate in the war game. He sat in the royal box during two jaw-stiffeningly boring plays dedicated ostentatiously to the king. Canardan skipped out on the second one, but Jehan remained where all could see him. He attended balls, picnics, regattas, dancing the night away and in the morning he attended trade sessions, but only as a spectator.

Then, unexpectedly, the king said after breakfast one morning, "There's no putting off these hearings concerning this treason-trial foolery. You may as well suffer along with me. It'll look good when these Guild Council fools unload the speeches they've been scribbling for days."

On the ride over (in an open carriage, so they could be seen, but surrounded by armed guards, so they couldn't be touched) Jehan said, "Why are we here? It's hot and stuffy in those halls, Father. Are you really going to hold a treason trial for those people?"

"Of course not. Treason trials are nothing but an excuse to

riot or an excuse to kill off half the populace. I don't want either of those things."

"So why do we go?"

"Because it looks like good faith. I'll whittle 'em down, one or two at a time, while we negotiate the trial. Meantime we'll let them talk as long as they like. It makes them feel good to talk. I want them to feel good. And so they can keep on making speeches and negotiating and feeling good until there's none of the fools left in prison."

Canardan had not meant to say that much, but the question on such a hot morning was unexpected. For some reason Jehan's tone reminded him of Math in the old days, the same dreamy pretense at being reasonable, without any awareness of how kings really did things.

He sent a sharp look at his son, half expecting one of Math's idiotic replies about ideals and loyalty and oaths, but Jehan just squinted up at the sky, admiring a flight of birds flying north for winter. Canardan sat back, wondering irritably why he was thinking of Math, of all people. Maybe he shouldn't eat so many smackerberry tartlets on hot mornings.

At first things began exactly as Canardan predicted. Jehan stood behind his father's cushioned chair on a hastily made dais as guild masters and mistresses unloosed long, carefully written speeches that were almost comical, how constrained they were to be complimentary to the king and yet make their demands clear.

Another person might have laughed at how the plump, red-cheeked Wood Guild Master bowed every time he made a demand, followed by half a dozen effusive compliments. "As your majesty well knows, your loyal populace appreciates your condescension in..." hoola-loola-loo. "But." Bow. "We feel that if we are truly to move past the sad events of two decades ago, as you have often said so gracefully in your Oath Day speeches, then perhaps it might be deemed wise to forgive the, ah, assumed transgressions of these unfortunates in custody..." Bow.

Jehan did not laugh. Nor did he find the thin, tremble-voiced Hatters Guild Mistress funny when her good shoes, worn once a year, squeaked as she walked to the front. Her speech had been signed by all the people involved in hat making. As if the king cared for any of those named, but Jehan could imagine the courage it had taken to tramp the hot streets during this unconscionably hot autumn weather, collecting these names, believing that the number of them would impress the king.

Jehan sustained a brief but intense memory of Prince Math's face. He would care. He would listen. Jehan knew it. He could almost see Math listening to the frightened old woman, his head slightly tilted at an encouraging angle.

Pity conflicted with resentment for his father's faint air of endurance, of boredom, the little smile that indicated the king was far off in thought. These people with their wretched speeches so full of clumsy hyperbole were not laughable at all. They were simply out of their realm of experience, but that was evidence of their courage. Wasn't it?

That image of Prince Math nodded emphatically, frizzy hair lifting like a sun corona round his head.

When the Hatters had had their say, they were followed by the Bricklayers and Stonemasons, the Silversmiths, the Ironmongers, the Millers and Bakers and Toymakers and Brewers and Vintners.

After the Coopers' Guild Master hoarsely whispered through his speech, the sea-related guilds were yet to come. Canardan raised a hand, and the old Cooper hastened to his seat as though he feared the sword on the spot.

"Good people." Canardan smiled, lifting his voice so all could hear. "I did say that each of you would have a chance to speak, and I keep my word. Khanerenth's tradition grants that all have access to the king. In turn, the king has access to all. We will not hasten into any decision, be assured, before all you are heard. This has been our civil law..."

A flash of warning tightened along Jehan's nerves. He remembered his father's words earlier about whittling down and realized what was coming next.

A moment later Canardan said, "...as for military matters,

we all know that those are conducted separately."

*He's going to cut out Silvag and Folgothan first.* Jehan remembered his father's conversation with Randart, and his careless promise to deal with the matter "later". Apparently later meant now.

Canardan paused for the expected agreement, and of course he got it. He'd spoken no more than the truth. They could also feel the threat coming as Canardan said, "...and so we can agree that military matters can be effectively overseen by War Commander Randart—"

There was the name, and the implied judgment flitting toward the future, bearing those men's lives, impossible to retrieve.

"—who is, as we all know, a follower of the law." Jehan stood, heart hammering. His gaze slid past his astonished father, to the people.

Canardan stared at Jehan. Once again, this time more distinctly, there was the impulse to laugh. These good people looked so surprised, as if the unlit chandelier had begun to spout poetry. Or more to the point, as if a sheep had trotted in from a nearby field and raised up its voice to discourse on law. He waved a hand to invite Jehan to speak, wondering what the boy could possibly have to say.

"I admire the war commander second to none." Jehan turned in a slow circle, meeting everyone's eyes in turn. "You all will remember how well he reorganized the academy. The new regulations were strict, but all the old favoritism and slackness disappeared. He is an example to us all in how he obeys regulations from dawn to dusk, the same as the smallest cadet and the oldest guard captain."

He paused for breath, got an encouraging nod from his father and went on in his blandest voice. "So I just know he'll remind us that the two guardsmen are in fact ex-guardsmen, hmm, and though I don't always pay attention the way I should, it seems to me that they might be termed, ah—"

"Civilians, if I may beg your highness's pardon," the guild master said, rising with more haste than dignity. He bowed to

Jehan and to the king. "Former guardsmen Silvag and Folgothan are civilians." His voice was reedy with relief. Now he was on sure ground: civilian law.

"That is true," the Heralds' Guild representative said, raising a quill. "They have not been under orders for twenty years—"

"Their oaths were refused," exclaimed a voice from the back, and in the susurrus of *quiet*'s and *shhh*'s that followed, the Scribe Guild's representative said in her soft, mild voice, "If they have not received pay in twenty years, and that is easy to check in the paymaster's books, they are civilians in all points of law."

Someone in the back snarled, "I will not be silent! I'm related to the Folgothans, and I know they didn't do a thing, just talked. Are we all to be arrested for just talking, that is what I want to know!"

Everyone started asking questions and putting demands across one another, with many anxious glances sent toward the king.

Jehan sat down again, affecting boredom as his father sighed loudly. Couldn't he see how anxious people were for reassurance? Couldn't he understand how much they longed to hear the king promise that their way of life would be protected?

Canardan rose to his feet, the guard moving to flank him. The crowd fell silent, everyone there hot and tired, and despite his dismissive words, not there for pleasure. Canardan began to speak, using his humorous voice. He cracked a couple of jokes about the heat and heated comment, and then set out to soothe them.

But underneath every sentence his father uttered, Jehan heard the promise of the invasion. The kingdom would "soon" have land and wealth. There "would be" prestige "soon" for the warriors, the crown, the nobles. And that meant "prosperity" for every single artisan.

As for the promised trial, he assured them that there was no hurry, he granted more time for negotiation, and yes, the conspirators would be kept perfectly safe.

As he spoke, Jehan saw glances returning his way. Thoughtful glances. Jehan suspected his remarks would be repeated in private, maybe discussed, passed along. The quickest ones had recognized what he had done.

It would have to be enough for now. He knew that this would be his last appearance in public, and not just because his father was annoyed at what he seemed to be choosing to regard as a typically cloud-minded blunder.

The time for all guises to be ripped away was nigh. Damedran Randart was hot on Sasharia Zhavalieshin's trail, and if he caught up with her, the final confrontation would be forced on them all.

"Let's go." Canardan sat back in the carriage, arms crossed, his profile disgusted.

Once again Jehan had slipped just ahead of disaster. Not because of his own ability, he thought as the carriage rattled along the brick-patterned main street, but because his father did not want to see disaster.

As for Jehan himself, his own sense of honor required one last attempt to reach his father. Jehan was not loyal to his father's politics, and never would be, but he remained loyal to the good memories of childhood, the interest, care and kindness exhibited in their private moments, when matters of state had not divided them. He believed in the possibility of good intention underneath all the vagaries, the series of ambivalent decisions that had slowly led to worse ones.

And he would exert himself to try, even at the risk of his own life, to bridge that chasm of lies between them: to get his father to admit that he was about to break a treaty and throw the kingdom into war.

As the days dragged on, full of noisy parties with too much food, too many people and far too many empty words chattered in his ears, he became aware that his father was increasingly restless.

Though Randart reported daily via magic to the king, as far as Jehan could determine, there was no mention whatsoever of Damedran's secret mission.

Meanwhile, Atanial was gone, leaving a confusing number of rumors about where she was. At last count, she'd been seen in thirty-eight different villages around the kingdom, including a town five weeks' journey away.

# Chapter Twenty-One

The unseasonable autumn heat broke at last.

On a bleak, rainy morning, Jehan stared sightlessly out at the rainwater gushing from a waterspout beyond his window and vowed that whatever the result, if his father was honest with him, he'd drop all pretense and speak the truth in return. And take the consequences either way—but his instinct was that Canardan, once he got past his anger, would try to find a way to meet him.

That was, if Randart stayed out of it.

Not half a bell later, Jehan felt the tingle of magic. He'd taken to wearing his gold box next to his skin, waking and sleeping.

He had been about to go down to breakfast. He signaled to Kazdi to watch the other servants and took out Owl's note.

*Damedran's got her. I'm following. Orders?*

Jehan flicked the note into the fire, watched it curl and burn away, snapped the box closed, stowed it in his tunic.

Kazdi's young face was serious, his brow puckered in question.

Jehan flicked his hand out, palm down. *Wait here.*

He ran downstairs to meet his father.

*This is it.* He wasn't ready—too soon—such thoughts flitted through his mind, faster than he could move, leaving him tense and filled with regret.

And so the two Merindars sat down at the table in the

winter breakfast room for the first time this year. The room had been recently cleaned by the servants, potted plants moved in all around the edge of the room, tall ferny ones before the row of north-facing windows.

To the son's eye, the king was, as ever, big, bluff, handsome, his manner that of a king. The weak light filtering in behind the departing rain clouds shone on his long red hair, on the sides of his jaw, where jowls gradually growing more marked over the years blurred the strength there.

To the father's eye the son—so difficult to understand and so exasperating to control—appeared thinner than he remembered, his slim body tense. Not only that, but his entire manner was *present*, his blue gaze uncharacteristically acute.

Neither spoke as the servants brought in the steaming silver dishes, and so for a time the only sounds were those of clinking metal against porcelain, the whisper of feet on the floor and beyond the windows the soft, occasional hiss of diminishing bands of rain.

Finally the king lifted his chin. The servants, alert to royal gestures, filed out, and Chas took up station inside the door.

"You have something on your mind, son?" Canardan asked.

"Several things," Jehan replied, toying with a piece of hot biscuit. "Here is the first. I am tired of parties. I want to do something with purpose."

The king tapped his knife lightly against his plate, not really hearing the restless, musical clink clink clink. "But the parties are to a purpose."

"Nothing that can't wait."

The king's eyes narrowed. "Wait on what?"

"You tell me, Father. They all talk, but around me. Past me. Knots of people of high degree and low. Innuendo, questions, secrets."

Canardan started eating in a mechanical fashion, frowning at the windows.

Jehan sensed ambivalence and tried again. "What is Randart doing, Father?"

The king set down his cup. "Presiding over the war game. You know that."

"Why does a war commander need to spend weeks at a war game?" Jehan countered. "Why am I not there instead, if my place is over him?"

Canardan laughed, a forced sound. "No one is really over Dannath, you know that. To the people the king must be seen to command, and that extends to the heir as well. But Randart is far better at military matters than either of us. His eyes are the most discerning, and his report on our readiness for trouble would be more valuable than either of us riding out to camp in the mud to observe a lot of young men and women scrambling around shouting and waving wooden swords, and pretending they aren't watching us to see where we're looking. I'd sit there in boredom, no doubt thinking of all the work lying here undone, and as for your own boredom, you'd inevitably solve that by riding off in the middle of the night with the prettiest patrol leader who had gotten some liberty." Another forced laugh.

"And destroy someone's career? Acquit me of that much stupidity. We know anyone in the army I flirted with would be broken down to the bottom rank as soon as Randart heard of it."

The king lifted his shoulders. "Probably true, but if so, it does attest to his high standards for officer behavior."

Jehan let that pass. "I don't think his eyes are the most discerning. The recent fiasco with the fleet is proof enough of that. Another proof is how late the orders to ride were given, as if no one was aware of the advance of the season. A war game so close to winter? Let me ride out and observe. I promise I will have an assessment as good as anything Randart can give. And I can have them all back in their garrisons before the first snow."

The king set down his knife and fork and regarded his son, who gazed back with unblinking intensity.

Finally Canardan said, slowly, "I want them where they are."

"Why?"

The king's brows furrowed, a quick, irritated reaction. "Because Dannath wants them there. Because—we can move them in any direction if need arises."

"What need do you foresee?"

The king hesitated, then shook his head. "I think we are better discussing this matter when Dannath returns. With his report. We can make decisions much easier when we hear his evaluation."

And Jehan knew he'd lost. It was not a surprise. Dannath Randart and Canardan Merindar had been friends since their teens, their ambitions marching in parallel. Too far in parallel— Randart having his eye on kingship, if not for himself, for his family. But it was clear that only events would convince Canardan of that. Certainly not his son's talk. Until now Canardan saw only unstinting hard work and unswerving loyalty in his oldest friend, plus a conveniently unflinching ability to make problems go away.

Sharp regret tightened Jehan. He made one more attempt to part on terms of mutual good will. "Let me ride to the academy, then, and consult with Orthan Randart about reorganizing the cadet lessons next spring."

"That, too, can wait on Dannath's return. I know you want to put in some of what you were taught out west, and I do like the idea of some of it. But we cannot plan without Dannath's assessment of their skills. The games were a fluke, we decided. Our cadets got too complacent. Dannath is convinced our training is not at fault."

"Let me ride to the coast, then, and inspect the harbors before winter sets in."

The king shook his head. "Despite the defeat of the fleet, you know as well as I that Randart is familiar with shore defense. And he has adequate captains in place." The king gave an easy laugh. He was back on familiar ground. "You have enough flirts right here, you don't need to be riding around your old haunts, and I don't want to risk any gossip about possible princesses."

"I won't meet any women."

His father shrugged, his brow furrowing impatiently. "Stay here." *Under my eye.* "Those potential princesses are right here in Vadnais."

Jehan laid down his knife and fork. "There is only one princess for me. Permit me to ride out and find Sasharia Zhavalieshin."

This time Canardan's laugh was genuine. "If I thought you could do that, you could go with my good will."

Jehan was about to say *But I can.* Risk everything on a throw and gamble that he could meet his father halfway, as he so badly wanted to do, despite experience, despite reason.

Then the king leaned forward. "You did. Didn't you? Randart boarded the *Dolphin* a few weeks ago. Before he went out to hunt that pirate. He thought you had that girl, for some reason. Did you?"

Jehan's heartbeat raced. "Yes."

Canardan shook his head slowly. "I didn't believe it. I still half don't. Randart was so sure you were plotting treason. But I figured even if you had her—and I didn't believe it—you were going to bring her to me. A surprise. Show me you were doing your job. Which was it?"

Images flitted through Jehan's mind, faster than words. Between one thump of his heart and the next he remembered Randart's disappointment—and heard the import behind his father's question. He was not asking Jehan's reason. He was saying *Are you for me or against me?* There was no compromise.

Taking Sasha to free Prince Math would be seen as treason, because *there was no compromise.*

The shadow of Randart stood squarely between father and son. As always, as always.

And so, hating himself, sick with regret, Jehan said, "Bringing her to you as a surprise."

His father relaxed. "Knew it. I don't mind saying Randart was disappointed. She slipped away, eh?"

"Yes."

The king's amusement was back. "And you think you could get her now? No, no, let Randart do the dirty work. He's good at it. He *likes* it. Let him bring her here, and you can soothe her ruffled feathers and be the hero. You two marry in spring, everyone smiles, the problems are all solved."

Jehan bowed, low, and left.

He ran back up to his rooms and changed out of his embroidered velvet, pulling on his sturdiest riding gear. He paused and stared down at the gold case in his hand, knowing the next communication in it would be from his father. The temptation to leave it behind was severe. But his road had been laid down as well, the first time he put on a disguise and attacked one of Randart's strongholds.

He opened the case, took out his last transfer token, tossed it up in the air, caught it with his fingers. Looked across the room at Kazdi, who stood with his shoulders against the closed door.

"Ride out as fast as you can to the resistance mages. Tell Magister Wesec it's time to move her mages into place. There's no more hiding. And if Nadathan and Devli Eban want to help, they're in."

Kazdi bowed, his scrawny neck-knuckle bobbing as he swallowed. His bony teenage face was the last thing Jehan saw before the transfer magic wrenched him out of time and space.

# Chapter Twenty-Two

The sudden jingle of gear and clatter of many boot steps caused Mirnic Kender to straighten up from the row of buckets she was checking for diminishment of the cleaning spell.

From the siege-camp command tent an arrow shot away, a stampede of aides and cadets hustled through the opening, dispersing in all directions. She watched them shrug, make gestures of helplessness, shake heads at the flood of questions. She waited.

Moments later the cadet on duty to run food and drink to and from the command tent showed up, whistling softly. Mirnic bent over her buckets, making motions with her hands as the boy was met by one of his friends, also on cook detail for the day.

"What was that all about?" the cadet next to her asked the other boy.

"War Commander got one of those magical messages. Told us to wait, opened it, read it, then sent us out on the double. Said something about the king, and he had to answer at once, and he'd be out in a moment, but he did not want distractions."

"Huh. Was he angry?"

"No. Here's what's weird. Most were standing around the map, see, chattering about the siege, and I was collecting the coffee cups. So really I was the only one watching him—couldn't decide if I should touch his cup or not. I mean, if he was done. You know how he gets—"

"Never mind his coffee!"

"Well, so I was watching, see? He grinned. Like this."

Mirnic forced herself not to look. Sure enough the other boy let out his breath in a long whoosh. "I've only seen that grin once. Pret-ty nasty."

"Yeah. If you want to know what I think..."

*No*, Mirnic thought. *I don't.*

She slipped away without either boy paying her the least attention, and sped to the tent she shared with the single other mage student permitted on the run. Her tent mate was asleep— they traded day and night duty—so Mirnic made sure she made no sound as she knelt at her bunk and wrote:

*R. received note, said from king. Sent everyone out of tent right after.*

She folded it, put it into her case, sent it to Magister Zhavic, and then sped back to her duty at the cook tent. As she'd expected, no one noticed she'd been gone.

And far away at the harbor, Magister Zhavic read the note, and checked the log of message reports from Vadnais. No messages had been logged either way between the king and the war commander at all that morning. Unless there was an emergency, they always communicated at night, messages duly reported by the journeymages on duty at the royal castle.

Zhavic smiled his own nasty smile.

Time for a talk with the king.


So there I was, no breakfast in me, riding on my mare with my hands tied behind me, surrounded by a bunch of teenage boys who either rode in sulky, nervous or gloomy silence, or else clumped together, arguing in fierce whispers.

At least three times I heard Damedran growl versions of "His orders are to take her there and meet him. Shut up! Just shut up! Or if he doesn't kill you, I will!"

Red shifted his bad mood from Damedran to their lack of food. He got into a short argument with one of the other boys, which made it clear that he'd expected better planning from the others while he and Ban nipped those tunics off someone's clothesline and scouted around my former place of employment.

I think they might have gotten into another fight had not one of the servants spoken up to say that he had a loaf of journey bread that he'd gotten the morning before, just in case.

When we reached a chuckling stream with a fall rushing over a grass-covered rocky hillock, Ban said, "If we don't stop here for at least some water, you'll have to shoot me for mutiny. Your bow is right there at your saddle. Here's my back," he added, quite unfairly.

Damedran jerked the reins of his horse, who tossed his head up and almost sat down on his haunches. Damedran flung himself out of the saddle, and the horse stood shivering.

My head panged from hunger and thirst, my shoulders and arms ached, and the sight of that frightened horse snapped my temper. "Someone"—I swung my leg over and jumped from my horse—"has anger-management issues."

"Huh?" Red exclaimed.

Ban mouthed the words *anger management?*

I glanced meaningfully at Damedran's horse, and some of my irritation faded when I saw him soothing the animal, stroking its nose and murmuring, his forehead leaning against the long, sweaty neck.

He wasn't a complete stinker. But there was the matter of my growling stomach and my aching arms and oh yes. His uncle.

I said kind of generally, to the air, "Every world is different. And places on a single world are different. Where I have been living there are what we call *people skills*."

Damedran leaned against his horse, but from the stiffness of his shoulders I sensed he was listening. Red made no pretense. He stared at me, mouth open.

I went on as genially as possible, "For example, death threats whenever someone asks a question. That would constitute *bad* people skills. Telling people *why* something is being done, well, that would rank as *good* people skills."

Six pairs of eyes swung from me to Damedran and back

again. Red snickered, then looked up at the sky as though seeking the Winged Victory of Samothrace.

Ban's face had gone ruddy from his effort not to laugh. He mumbled, "Garik, I'll help with the journey bread."

A couple of the boys led the horses in two strings to the stream while avoiding looking my way.

Damedran and Red stalked ten or twelve paces in the other direction, facing away and arguing in fierce undertones. Behind some flowering shrubs, Ban and the boy named Garik alternated between growls and whispers.

Ban: "I thought princesses were supposed to act toff. Wear silk. Scream orders so they don't have to get their slippers dusty."

Garik: "I thought they were supposed to be delicate. She's nearly as big as Red. Makes Lesi Valleg look scrawny, and wee-yoo, can she fight!"

"Sh. Sh!"

Whisper, whisper.

Ban: "...if we don't follow orders?"

Garik: "I don't even want to think about it. Here. That's her share. You take it over there."

"Coward."

"Yep. And?" Garik retorted promptly and cheerfully.

While all this was going on, I'd spotted a broad rock near the base of the hillock and sat down, since I couldn't run with my hands tied behind my back. Ban rounded the shrubs and came toward me, carrying in both hands what looked like nutbread, each serving put on a broad, slightly waxy leaf— natural dishes, plucked from the shrub nearby.

He bent and set my share next to me.

"Do I get a feedbag?" I asked.

He had avoided my eyes, but the question startled him, and when he glanced up, I shrugged my shoulders and wiggled my fingers behind me. His face reddened, and he turned Damedran's way.

The Randart heir and Red were still arguing fiercely. "— when we get to Castle Ambais, where my uncle is supposed to meet us," Damedran snarled. "I'll ask him right out."

Ban whistled sharply, and they whirled around, hands going to their weapons. They relaxed their hands, but their faces stayed tense.

"How's she going to eat?"

"Will it make you feel better if I promise not to try to make a bolt during lunch?" I asked. "Which is also my breakfast, I might add. And probably my last meal as well. I'd really like to enjoy it."

"Stop. Saying that," Damedran muttered, pulling his knife out with a faint ringing *zing*.

"Don't cut that kerchief," Red warned. "We don't have another."

"The knots are all pulled hard," Damedran snapped over his shoulder.

"That's because my fingers were going numb." I shrugged. "Had to try to loosen the fabric, though it meant the knots tightened."

A couple of slices and my hands were free, and full of pins and needles. I wrung and flexed them, rubbing them up and down my thighs. When I could grasp again, I wolfed down my share of the journey bread. It was dense, made with about six different kinds of nuts, raisins and a hint of spices.

When I was done (and had thumb-pressed every crumb off the leaf and nibbled it up) I rose to get some water. All of the guys closed in around me, faces tense and determined.

I washed, drank, then silently held out my dripping hands.

Red offered an old sash. "Found it in my gear. Crumpled but clean."

Damedran sighed, but took it.

This time he did a better job of checking to make sure the bonds were not too tight. He helped me mount up, Ban took the reins of my horse, and in silence the boys mounted. They rode around me downstream a ways, Damedran squinting up at the sun to check direction, until a distant screeching of birds caught his attention.

Everyone's head turned. I looked as well, not comprehending what they could find interesting about a flock of birds rising above the trees, screeling and squawking, until I heard the faint rumble of horse hooves.

Damedran's face blanched. "Ride out!" he shouted, waving at Ban and me. "Ride out. You know where to go!"

Ban used the reins to whack my horse, kneed his own mount, and suddenly there I was, galloping unsteadily— gripping with my legs as best as I could.

Damedran whirled his horse round, pulling his weapons, to face the oncoming threat now raising a great dust cloud. I dared a single glance back. He sat squarely in the path of that billowing dust in which vague silhouettes of mounted warriors could be made out. The five other cadets spread out behind Damedran.

My horse jerked to a stop, and Ban flung the reins back over my leg. "Go," he muttered, not looking at me. "Just—go." Without waiting for me to speak, he whacked my mare on her hindquarter, and she took off downstream.

Ban rode back to face the danger with his mates.

Just as, behind me, Jehan and Owl led their force at a gallop straight toward the boys. The dust thinned, revealing in the lead a tall, slender rider with long white hair.

Damedran raised his sword, then lowered it. "What?" he cried. "Prince *Jehan*?"

Jehan did not halt his sweating, foam-flecked horse. In answer he rode straight at the string of remounts, and as the boys gaped, he leaped from a galloping horse onto the bare back of a fresh remount, who sprang into a gallop. White hair flying, he shot downstream after me, the boys so amazed they didn't even realize they were efficiently surrounded until it was too late.

"You'll note there are twelve of us." Owl waved a hand. "You might go ahead and sheathe the weapons, boys."

I was galloping about as gracefully as a teapot on a rocking horse alongside a rocky stream, hoping that when I fell off, which I was sure was inevitable, I would manage to hit the water and not a giant boulder.

A galloping horse thundered up behind me.

All I could think of was War Commander Randart. *He doesn't trust Damedran to bring me in. He's here to skewer me personally.* I bent down, as if that would help my poor mare increase her speed.

A hand reached out to grip the mare's reins near her head. Both horses slowed, and I braced myself, angry, fearful—

And stared up into Jehan's face. His pale, grim face. Searching my features to see if I was all right.

"Huh?" I said intelligently.

He leaped off his horse—which had no saddle, I noticed distractedly—and held up his arms. Instinctively I leaned forward, and though I'm not exactly a sylph, he lifted me down as if I were one, and set me gently on my feet. He tightened one arm around me, and laid his other hand along my cheek so I looked up, and there were his lips brushing over my nose, and my eyes, and well, despite the dust, and the pair of us being considerably sweaty and disheveled, the instinct that flared brighter than logic or even laughter locked us together in a long, lingering kiss.

# Chapter Twenty-Three

Eventually we had to breathe.

"No—" I began, standing in the circle of his arms. "Wait. You can't."

"Don't," he murmured into my filthy tangle of hair. "Say anything. Just—don't."

I drew in a very unsteady breath, and when I felt the sudden loosening of the sash round my wrists, I fought the urge to hug him back, but neither did I push him away.

I gripped his wrists instead. "Jehan, I don't know how you managed to get here. Or why. In fact I'm almost afraid to ask. But you should know that those boys are scared Dannath Randart will kill them if they don't show up with me at something called Castle Ambais."

"I guessed as much." Jehan whistled softly. "Ambais is a garrison full of handpicked Randart warriors. It's located at this end of the valley, tucked up against the border mountains. If the boys had managed to get you there, it would have been impossible to get you out. At least, without bloodshed that Randart is quite willing to spill."

"Ugh."

Jehan wiped his hair back off his damp forehead and squinted up at the sun's position. "It's one of his staging points for his and my father's war. As near as I can tell, it's also a secret stash for the weapons that are going to conveniently appear for next spring's surprise invasion of Locan Jora."

I saw in his dust-printed face a tension to match my own. I

was so full of questions I did not know where to begin, or how to handle any answers I heard. He'd lied before. And so had I. The situation was already impossibly tangled before those kisses made emotional reaction about ten times worse.

"Randart has to know approximately where you and the boys are, which is about half a day's hard ride from Castle Ambais. I figure we have until sunset." Jehan walked away to catch the reins of my mare. "Then Randart will send out rings of trackers to find Damedran. And you."

"And so?"

"And so the days of disguises are past." He handed me the reins and whistled to the other horse, who stood on the other side of the stream a ways away, cropping unconcernedly. It tossed its head and swung round our way. "My first act is to rescue you."

"Here I thought I was going for a Guinness Book of Records for abductions," I cracked. "You being my fourth. Except, does it count when the same fellow—"

Jehan laughed, flinging up a hand. "My second act is going to be to take Damedran hostage." Jehan whistled again, the whistle the stablehands use at the academy. "I think it's the only way to save his life." The horse trotted obediently back toward us.

"And then what?"

Jehan indicated the entire world. "You go wherever you like." He thrust a hand into a pocket in his tunic and brought out a richly gleaming flat gold box about the size of those beautiful cigarette cases that you see gangsters and snobs carrying in old movies. "While I wait to find out what my father says."

I was amazed and relieved almost beyond thought. "You're going to let me go?"

"Did I not say so?" he responded, not without humor.

"Just like that."

"Well, it does seem to me my time is going to be taken up with such small matters as Randart coming after me, with or without my father's orders. As for what he will say—" He opened his hand.

We began walking the horses back toward the others.

I said above that I was almost beyond thought. Actually I wasn't quite there yet.

I turned to face him. "How did you find me? I take it you are not suddenly in Randart's confidence. Damedran made it pretty clear that no one knows about his orders. Except you?"

"I was hoping you wouldn't ask that. But the truth is, I had Owl follow you," Jehan admitted. "Not that he was all that successful. He lost track of you early on and didn't catch up until Damedran appeared on your trail. He showed up at some inn or other. Where you took a letter."

I sighed. "I should be mad. But if he hadn't..." I shuddered. "I'd be going straight into Dannath Randart's waiting...noose? Sword? Prison cell? Not waiting arms, unless you mean the pointy steel ones. I don't think I'm his type. He sure isn't mine."

Jehan laughed. We rounded the hill where the others were gathered, Jehan's people sitting on horseback, hands resting on sword hilts, chatting back and forth as Damedran's group hunched disconsolately on or around the mossy rock bench where I'd so recently sat to eat my share of the food. Damedran stood a few paces away, head bent, staring at the little waterfall. Even from a distance his profile was strained.

"Busted," I breathed.

Jehan flicked a questioning glance my way.

I didn't answer, but jumped off my mount and ran up to Damedran. Jehan did not stop me, nor did he join us.

"Damedran."

The Randart boy looked my way, his face tight with misery. Then his cheeks reddened with anger, but before he could speak, I flung up a hand in the palm-out sign for peace that I'd seen people use. *Peace* here, and on Earth, *Stop Right There.*

"I wanted to thank you for making things as easy as you could," I said, not really sure what I was doing, just following instinct. It was that misery in his eyes. "Listen. I've been nabbed by Jehan. A couple of times. It won't be so bad."

"Nabbed," Damedran repeated, the anger fading from his expression.

"You're his hostage. And while I'm trying to sort out what's what, this I will say. You won't hear any death threats from him. Or, if you did, it would surprise me."

Damedran turned his head sharply, and I followed his look. Jehan was busy with the horses some twenty or thirty paces away, though he was watching us. But not in earshot, which I considered an honorable gesture. A gesture I knew Dannath Randart wouldn't make. "I am a hostage, then?" he asked, his voice lifting at the end. "Us. We? Are hostages? Or prisoners of war? Or what?"

I called out to Jehan, "Damedran has the same question I had earlier. Is he a hostage, prisoner or what?"

Jehan took that as an invitation to join us. "You can define your exact status at your leisure. All I'm going to say is that Uncle Dannath is not going to get his hands on you unless certain demands are met, and then only with your permission. I can explain on the ride. We're going to have to pick up our feet, if we want to stay outside of Randart's search perimeter, which will be dispatched by sundown, if they aren't riding already. So say your farewells to the princess, because she's presumably going off in another direction."

Jehan held out his hand toward my mare. I saw a new feedbag hooked to the saddle gear. With the other hand, he held out a folded paper. "Here is a map I made last night, to help me orient on you all. Go ahead and take it. I know where I am now. You'll see the major roads, cities, garrisons and towns marked. Castles as well. You should be able to find several routes out of the kingdom." He gave me a bland smile.

In silence I took it.

I don't know what I might have said or done if we'd been in private. Probably made things worse. But before all those watching guys—both sides in brown uniforms, which was kind of funny and kind of heartbreaking—there was only one thing to do.

I swept as flourishing a bow as I could, turning at the last to include the entire company. Then I said in English, "Gents, it's been teh bomb."

And leaving exceedingly puzzled faces behind me, I mounted up and rode away.

Yeah, I managed what I thought a suave exit, but I swore when I first took up my pen I'd tell the truth in this thing, and so I have to admit that within about thirty seconds of choosing a random direction I was snuffling into my sleeve.

Talk about confused. I was sad, scared, angry, mostly at myself for having kissed Jehan again when I knew, I *knew*, I'd feel terrible afterward. Because the kiss itself was so great. Despite everything. And oh yes, what *was* "everything"?

I didn't snivel too long. The sky was clouding. If I lost the sun, I'd lose my sense of direction, and the map would be worthless.

Map.

I unfolded it. There was Jehan's handwriting, in even, slanted letters with slashing curls. It was a dashing handwriting, and I resisted the impulse to kiss the map. Yeah, I know.

Focusing my blurred eyes (this is the last time I wipe away tears, I vowed) I saw he'd marked a place on the map below Ambais, where he wrote: *Should find D. here.* D of course had to mean Damedran.

That meant I could use that point as my orientation.

Tracing my finger straight north, I discovered that Ivory Mountain was not all that far away.

"Papa, I sure hope you are ready to rock and roll," I muttered, kneeing the mare. "Because the house is packed and the band is playing as hard as it can."

# Chapter Twenty-Four

Almost directly to the west the rain had already begun, a soft plopping of cold drops, when the single sentry at the gate of Zheliga Castle burst into the buttery, where Hilna and Pirie Famid worked alongside their servants, the sisters sharing the title of "baroness" for simplicity's sake as they shared the baroness chores. In this case, pressing butter into the molds and seeing it carried down in neatly wrapped blocks to the cold room.

"Gate," the boy said, his voice cracking.

"Army?" Hilna asked doubtfully, knowing that Orthan and his brother Dannath were somewhere on the other side of the hills to the east, busy with their big siege game. She hadn't expected Orthan and Damedran until the siege was over, and it was time to settle in for winter. The sisters had been laying in extra stores for weeks.

The boy shook his head. "Women," he said succinctly.

Pirie and Hilna exchanged puzzled looks. The sisters were not given to needless chatter. They untied their aprons, dropped them onto the table and left, one smoothing back her gray curls, the other brushing flour off her skirts left from the morning's inspection of the threshing.

Neither was prepared to see a couple hundred women either riding or walking over the bridge, which two generations ago had been a drawbridge, but had been left down for over fifty years. A couple of hundred? More than that, all strung out in a slow-moving line, as far as one could see.

Hilna gasped when she recognized the tall, tough-looking woman walking beside a horse. "Plir Silvag?"

Plir lifted a hand in greeting, and waved at the woman on the horse. Hilna blinked up at a pretty woman her own age, with pale hair done up elaborately on the top of her head. She looked vaguely familiar—

"You remember Princess Atanial?" Plir asked.

The sisters stared in mute surprise.

Hilna gave a stiff curtsey, her expression changing from blank surprise to a wary question.

Atanial looked down into those faces, seeing yet again the question, doubt, resentment that had been mirrored in variations during her long journey.

They had passed along the old paths, far from the fine military roads and the waterlogged main roads. The worst of the journey had been at first, when Atanial's conversation with Plir was repeated, sometimes with far more hostility than Plir had shown. But Atanial listened, and said the same thing over and over: *We cannot permit an invasion.* A few refused to join. Of those, half caught up later, like Plir herself. With her she brought a number of relatives and old contacts. Since then more were catching up day by day, women of all ages, from girls barely in their teens to women far older than Atanial and Plir.

Women led them to other women who they felt would embrace the cause, and so the group swelled in number every day. The strange thing was, Atanial had realized one night, by now they could hardly be secret, and yet at least so far, no one seemed to have sent word to the king. She did not know if all Canardan's spies were at the war game, or if some had quietly changed their minds about what side they were on.

Atanial returned Hilna's bow as best she could from the back of a horse, then said, "May we speak privately?"

Hilna rubbed her forehead. "I suppose. But what shall I do about all these people?"

"Most of them brought their own journey bread. And we've been buying fruit along the way." Atanial did not mention that she alone hadn't come prepared. Most of the women shared, but Atanial did not like taking too much. She was hungry.

Hilna shaded her eyes to ward drops of cold rain. Among those faces, most of them her age or older, and a very few young, were a couple of guild mistresses, a baroness who had inherited her title in her own right and at least one garrison captain's wife. "I think you all had better come inside." She cast a glance at her sister. "We can fit you into the hall out of the weather."

"And the sun room too. This way." Pirie gestured to the women accompanying Atanial. "I'll see to food and drink for those who need it."

"Princess, you come with me, if you will." Hilna waited at the door.

Atanial dismounted with a smothered *woof* and tried to be delicate about rubbing her inner thighs as she walked stiffly behind her hostesses. A smothered snicker from behind testified to her success, before the last of the women vanished into what appeared to be a parlor with plastered and whitewashed walls; they moved through that to the rest of the ground floor of the castle beyond.

But Hilna did not crack a smile as she stalked into a low entry, all of it bare swept stone, the enticing smell of baking apple tarts drifting from somewhere. Atanial's stomach rumbled.

A sharp turn, up a short stairway to a room off a landing, and the smell was cut off by a thick wooden door swinging shut. Hilna indicated a massive wing-backed chair that had to be a hundred years old at least. Atanial winced at the prospect of her aching hips dealing with that ungiving wood. She sighed in relief when she spotted a newly stuffed cushion on its seat, embroidered somewhat crookedly with tulips and bluebells. There was another such chair, both angled toward a fireplace where a good fire already burned.

Hilna perched on the edge of one and Atanial collapsed into the other, plopping her cold feet onto the fender.

"I'll try to be brief." Inwardly she resisted the strong desire to sleep here for at least a year. "You don't have to answer. I don't want to put you into a bad position. But Mistress Silvag insisted we should stop here and at least let you know what we're doing. Whatever you decide to do about it, considering who you are married to. Or rather, who your husband is brother to."

"Dannath," Hilna breathed.

"I don't know how much you know, but the evidence is clear that Dannath Randart and the king will be invading Locan Jora in the spring." Atanial braced for—anything. But oh, she did so hope she wasn't going to have to leap to her aching feet and bucket down those stone steps and back onto that horse, sword-waving women on her heels.

Hilna's mouth tightened.

"I know the reasons put forward in favor," Atanial said swiftly. "Locan Jora has been part of Khanerenth for most of recorded history. Though the outer borders have danced about quite a bit from generation to generation. I know there are people who lost their homes when the takeover happened. I know they want their ancestral homes back. I know that there is a belief that the economy will vastly improve, that there will be land and titles for the loyal, that this and that will all make things better. But. I really want you to consider the cost. The real cost. Which is lives. Not necessarily ours, but young people's, like your son's. Because he's supposed to be leading this war, isn't he?"

Hilna's eyes narrowed.

"At least, he'll be right at the front, with all the banners and so forth, but we know who will really be in command." Atanial paused, wondering if she'd gone too far.

Hilna rocked on her chair while rain tapped at the leaded glass window in the deep stone embrasure, and the fire on the hearth crackled and snapped. "If I interfere, I'll never see my son again. It's rare enough I see him now. Either Damedran or my husband, Orthan."

Atanial leaned forward. "Tell me."

Hilna brushed a strand of hair off her forehead with

trembling fingers. "What is to tell? I get to see him once a year. If that. Then he pushes me away with *Uncle Dannath says I'm too soft. Uncle Dannath says* after every visit home, always something aimed at me. My husband, too. *Dannath says* Damedran has slid back into boy habits, and requires a week of drills to toughen him back up again."

"So you disagree with their goals?"

"If I wished to be known as a traitor," she retorted. "I cannot have an opinion that differs from Dannath's. None of us can. Why do you think I never adopted into the Randart family? It was the one single thing I could keep of my own, my family. Even this barony is nothing but an air title—Orthan saying, often and often, that soon we'll live in Vadnais, we'll have a real title, and this castle, which I have spent the past fifteen years making into a home, is good enough for Pirie and Wolfie."

Atanial had used the past two or three days forming logic chains to argue against every conceivable point of view against an invasion. She had never expected this reaction.

"What would you like to do?"

Hilna dashed her wrist angrily over her eyes. "Is that meant as a jab? No, I see by your face it isn't. But how can you ask that, knowing Dannath? Oh, I knew from the very start that Orthan was loyal to his brother, but in those days the goal was rebuilding the army, which had gotten slack, with pilferage and cronyism and scandalous behavior shrugged at in the upper ranks. That's how we lost half the kingdom in the first place! But after Damedran was born, there were more and more hints about royal vision and royal gifts and..."

She wiped her eyes again, frowning down into the fire. "About five years ago, I realized they were not talking about the king. They meant Dami. And at first I conceded, with a mother's pride. I thought he'd make a fine king. I didn't consider how he might get there." She looked up, saying fiercely, "And it's as well I conceded, because I vow as sure as I sit here otherwise, Dannath would have seen to it something happened to me. He's never had any use for women—for anyone, really—unless they can fight."

Atanial nodded. "Or serve. But not think. That seems to go for men too."

"Yes. Orthan is plenty smart, and loyal, but he's no grand thinker. So what is it you are doing?"

"We are marching across the kingdom." Atanial swept her arm wide. "Where, you shall see. None of the other women know the destination, only that I strongly expect that we will meet the king there, and War Commander Randart. I knew that nothing I did on my own would ever make any difference. But if there were enough of us, maybe we could get them at least to listen?"

Hilna let out her breath in a slow, shaky sigh. "I know I sound like a coward, and perhaps I am one. If I ever cross Dannath, even in a small thing, I will lose my son altogether. And what you are suggesting is no small thing. I shall have to think."

"Fair enough."

"There are two things I will say. First, I will only discuss it with Pirie. And maybe one other friend who I think will be sympathetic. But I'm not sending any messages to Orthan." She gave a small sigh. "I could never force him to choose between his brother and—well, leave it at that. I'm mum. Best that way."

Atanial gestured her thanks.

"Second, if you can convince Starveas Kender to join you, she might bring some of the old Joran nobility over. Her husband loved marrying an old noble family with a title, even if deposed. The Kenders have their title by courtesy, as do all the old Joran nobility. You know that." She scarcely paused for Atanial to assent. "I know that he can hardly wait for the invasion to be over, so they can lord it once again on the other side of the mountains. But she's worried. Not only about Ban. Also about her daughter Mirnic, who will be sent with the mages. Who end up as targets as often as the warriors."

"I would love to, but I don't dare go back to Vadnais. It was too difficult to get past the guard on my way out. I don't believe I'd make it back in without being caught."

"The Kenders don't live in the royal city," Hilna exclaimed. "They live in Ellir. They left that several weeks ago, knowing about the siege running into winter, and how those with castles along the west will all go home, taking sizable portions of the army with them for the winter. The Kenders are staying with her cousin, the Duchess of Frazhan. They stopped here day before yesterday."

"Frazhan on the border," Atanial murmured.

"They have that wonderful old castle directly across the river valley from Ivory Mountain."

"Ahhhhh." Atanial smiled.

# Chapter Twenty-Five

Magister Zhavic watched the king rub his forehead with tense fingers, the ruby in his ring winking and glittering.

He looked up wearily. "Zhavic. I know you don't trust my war commander. Neither of you has ever even tried to comprehend the other, it seems to me. Yet you are loyal and dedicated. So why can't you see that we must work together now? We cannot afford strife among ourselves."

Zhavic struggled to suppress his annoyance. It wasn't as if this reaction of the king's was unexpected. "Write to him, your majesty," he urged, keeping his voice low, quiet. "Please. If there is a reasonable explanation, I vow I will never again bring forward any suspicions." *Not without undeniable proof, anyway.*

The king let out a long-suffering sigh, and with a spurt of ill-tempered impatience, threw aside a couple of stacks of papers in search of one of the small slips he used for the magic-transfer box.

Zhavic bent, picked up the snow of papers on the floor and returned them, glancing covertly at the top of each. Most of them were supply lists, but one was from the *Skate*'s infamous Captain Bragail, on which Zhavic glimpsed the phrase...*of the pirate absolutely no sign.*

The king extricated a small piece of paper, picked up his pen, dipped it, and frowned at the mage. "What am I asking again?"

"I do not know what questions you deem appropriate, your majesty, but the questions that occur to me are why he considered it necessary to send his nephew and several senior cadets away from the siege on a secret mission, and why he suddenly had to ride off, again without telling anyone."

The king frowned down at the pen, apparently not seeing the slow formation of a droplet of ink. It was about to splash on the paper when he threw the pen into the well and leaned back in his chair. "You know, it really *is* odd, when I think about it. He mentioned nothing of any of these things in his report last night. I thought Damedran was with the other cadets. And that Randart himself was overseeing things at Cheslan Castle."

Zhavic put his hands behind his back lest they betray him. Long years had taught him to keep his face impervious, but the surge of triumph burning through him made him almost shaky.

The king nipped up his pen. He wrote in a fast scrawl, folded the paper, shoved it into the box without waiting for the ink to dry and tapped it. He looked up, eyes narrowed. "If there is a good explanation I will hold you to your promise."

"If there is a good explanation, I shall be satisfied, that is a vow. You know I only have the good of the kingdom in mind—"

"Yes, yes, everyone always has the good of the kingdom in mind, especially when they begin arguing with me." Canardan waved a hand to cut off the flow of self-justification. He uttered a sharp laugh. "If you didn't, you would hardly be alive to argue."

The implied threat silenced the mage.

Canardan felt the inner click of the message-box magic, which was somewhat of a relief. Dannath had, so far, always responded immediately.

He flipped it open and pulled out the folded square. Randart's neat writing filled the entire paper. *For a month we have been tracking Atanial's daughter Sasharia on your orders earlier in the summer. Damedran has her now. I am in Ambais to meet him. Planned to have her in hand before sending my report.*

Canardan laughed, then flicked the paper in Zhavic's direction. He watched the master mage read it.

"What's the matter now?" Canardan demanded when the

mage handed back the paper, his lips tightly closed.

Zhavic looked out the window as rain began tapping the glass. "A month. And you didn't know. I wonder if he really was going to tell you when he did get hold of her."

Canardan threw the pen down. "Damnation, we're right back to where we were! Why not? What else would he do with her?"

"Perran believes that she might be coerced into a match with Damedran. So that he could become...the heir."

"That again."

Canardan's grim look sent a spurt of pleasure through Zhavic. The mages didn't believe any such thing. Randart's mind did not run to marriages. But the king's did. And reminding him of the Randarts' suspected plot to put Damedran on the throne was always a good idea.

Zhavic went on in a slow, ruminative voice, as if he were thinking, though he and Perran had rehearsed this interview half a dozen times. "I think Perran's wrong. I wonder if Randart means to assassinate her. The war commander's thinking appears to be of military and political advantage, not magical."

Canardan frowned at the mage. "What are you talking about?"

"Why else would he take so long to secure her and without letting you know? If he wanted to find out where she was going, why not send your trackers—"

"The cook! She was the cook!" The king snapped his fingers. "Jehan had her briefly. Randart went out to search Jehan's yacht and didn't find her. I assumed because the girl had slipped Jehan's grip before Randart showed up. But now I think Jehan was lying to Randart. And she was there all along. Which changes everything." The king drew in a slow breath. "Only which way?"

"What?" Zhavic's voice, which was far more revealing than his face, lost the smoothness of rehearsed musing and revealed genuine spontaneity. "Princess Atanial's daughter is a cook?"

The king snorted a not-quite-laugh. "You don't remember? I

do. I've always had a head for details. Which, one could argue, is what kingship is. The tall female cook on Jehan's yacht, with the flour all over her face so no one saw what she looked like—" He turned his head, spoke sharply. "Page!"

The runner on duty outside the king's study opened the door.

"Request Prince Jehan to attend me for an immediate interview." He turned back to Zhavic. "Finish your point."

Magister Zhavic had been wondering how to get back to it. He smiled. "Well. If you consider she was last known aboard the pirate ship, and presumably managed to escape somewhere along the coast—"

"Or was rescued by a very romantic prince, let us say."

Zhavic blinked, and the look he gave the king caused Canardan to laugh out loud.

"No, I have not lost my wits. Though I might be chasing down the wrong trail. We'll know in a moment. Go on. So Atanial's daughter escapes on the coast..."

"...then turns up in Bar Larsca, what kind of a vector, as the military term it, does that give you?"

The king rubbed his chin, mentally reviewing the map. "Not the siege, though she's close. That makes no sense."

"Think magic, not military," Zhavic urged. "Remember who her father was. Though you were not trained, surely your first wife told you some things about the magical part of our history—"

"Ivory Mountain?" the king asked and watched the mage's face smooth into blandness. "But why? That's an old morvende geliath, empty for centuries. Even I know that."

As usual, Zhavic's voice betrayed him. "If Mathias is alive, it could be that he is hiding there, beyond time."

Canardan rapped his knuckles on the table. "How do you get to that conclusion?"

"While guarding the old World Gate site, Perran decided to do a thorough search of the castle. He found a couple of hidden chambers, and one of them held some of Glathan's old papers.

Nothing was astoundingly revealing, or *we* would have reported instantly to you," Zhavic added quickly. "But in a chest Glathan had stored an old book on morvende geliaths. That book is well known to mages. Most of us have a copy. At first Perran didn't even look through it. But as time went on and he had finished his search, he decided to go through all the books and papers in a methodical way. In that book, the reference to Ivory Mountain had a scribble next to it, in some kind of code."

"So you think this girl might go to Ivory Mountain and free Math? But she's not a mage."

"We know she was taught at least one difficult spell."

Canardan nodded slowly. He was beginning to wish he'd listened to Dannath in those early days. His reasoning was clear, if brutal. A quick, clean death for Math, and the problem goes away. Kill the woman too, or send her back to her own world. Keep the girl and raise her to marry the heir. The popular but incompetent family Zhavalieshin sinks into memory, along with incompetent royal families of the past.

Canardan ran his thumb back and forth along Randart's note, remembering how he'd steeled himself to see it through. All those clear reasons Mathias should die: most important, his incompetence as king. Except at this remove, Canardan knew that most of Mathias's supposed incompetence had actually been attempts to cope with the mess the old king had made of things.

He gave his head a shake. The prospect of Mathias walking back in suddenly had ceased to worry him a few years ago. Now it was back.

Canardan turned in his chair, as if physical movement could shake certain other more uncomfortable memories, and he frowned at the mage, who was studying his hands. Underneath all this hinting and innuendo about Randart's secret plans lay the old question again. Why did the mages *really* want to find Mathias? The mages always seemed to have their own plans, which may or may not quite be the same as his. Mathias had been raised to magic knowledge, not to military. Maybe they thought if he returned, mages would gain the political ascendance that Randart thwarted with vigilant energy.

A tap at the door caused Canardan to lean forward. "Enter."

The page stepped inside. "Prince Jehan is not in the castle."

Chas appeared directly behind him, face slick with sweat.

The king locked his jaw hard against a surge of rage. He twiddled his fingers in dismissal, and the page ducked round Chas, obviously relieved at being able to escape.

Chas walked in and gave the mage a poisonous look. But the king did not dismiss Magister Zhavic.

So Chas said, "He's gone. So is that boy he kept as personal servant. And—"

"There's always an 'and', these days," Canardan murmured, waggling his fingers again. "Yes, get on with it."

"Certain among the guard are missing as well, all without leave."

Canardan smacked his hands down on the desk, stood, and dropped back into his chair. This time he swept everything except the inkwell off the desk in one angry motion. Papers hissed to a snowdrift on the floor as he pulled a small communication note from inside the desk, and wrote:

*Jehan, where are you and what are you doing?*

He shoved the paper inside the magic box and tapped out Jehan's signal.

No one spoke, or moved, until the king twitched. He'd received a magical signal, which meant an answer had arrived. He pulled out and read a paper, then tossed it onto the desk, the inscription toward them. "What d'you make of that?" he asked, grinning.

They leaned forward and read:

*I am here to rescue Sasharia Zhavalieshin from Dannath Randart.*

"My son might be an idiot, but he's a romantic idiot," Canardan said, almost buoyant with relief. He'd feared treachery. He couldn't even bear to think about that. Here was the real answer, even if it wasn't quite reasonable. But Jehan had always been like his mother, romantic and idealistic. "I don't know why he didn't tell me. Maybe more romantic that way. Wait. He did tell me the other day that he wanted to find her...and yes, I told him to sit tight. Well, well. Maybe he's not such an idiot after all. At least, not when it comes to romance."

Laughing, he bent over the paper, crossed out the former words and wrote below, in small letters: *So who has her?*

And the answer came back: *No one, right now.*

Canardan did not show that response to Zhavic or Chas, who tried to sneak peeks at those upside down letters, but the king kept using the same scrap of paper, as did the prince, the writings tinier and tinier.

*And if I order you to come home? Saying that I will deal with Randart as I see fit?*

This time the wait was longer. The king was aware of his own breathing sounding loud and harsh, his heartbeat thrumming in his ears as he stared down at his thumb prints on the gleaming golden box.

Zing! An answer. Jehan's print was small, the letters carefully formed. *I have to do what is right. I don't think you can protect her from Randart. I think I can.*

The king sighed, ripping the paper into tiny bits. Then he got up from behind the desk. The other two wheeled to face him as he paced the few steps to the fireplace and cast the note into the fire. But he kept his back to the two men as he sorted his reactions. Some relief, much exasperation. Jehan was a romantic, but it seemed he'd chosen to grow up at last. And typical of sons, with terrible timing and headlong foolishness.

Canardan sat down at the desk, pulled out another note, and wrote: *Dannath, whether you have the girl or not, return to the siege.* He shoved it into the case and tapped out Randart's pattern.

Silence again, the mage and the spy standing, the king neither speaking nor looking their way as he waited for an answer. Again there was a wait. Then:

*With all respect, sire, are you not losing sight of an advantage? Permit me to secure then bring to you this objective. You can then decide what to do from a position of strength.*

Canardan sat back. Another day—yesterday—before the mage came, before the note from his son, he might have shrugged and accepted that. As he always had in the past. But. He stared down at the piece of paper and Randart's strong, assured handwriting. Despite their long friendship, despite the reasonable wording, the implied service, the truth was, Dannath Randart had refused an order.

Canardan tapped his fingers on the magic box. His first impulse was to demand that Dannath return at once and face him. But even if he said he was riding back, how many of those damned transfer tokens did he possess? Unless he was directly under Canardan's eye, he could go anywhere in an eyeblink, do anything, while saying he was on his way back.

Canardan swung round, glaring at the fire. Did he distrust Dannath, after all these years?

Tap, tap, tap.

Randart had made no mention of Ivory Mountain. If he did capture that wretched girl and promptly ride either for the siege or for the royal city, Canardan would know everything was as it should be. Least said, the better.

The king looked up at the waiting men. "Have my guard saddle up. Say nothing of the destination, only that the king wishes to ride on inspection." His smile was unpleasant. "We're riding for Ivory Mountain, but as yet only the three of us know that. It will be interesting to see who else shows up, eh?"

# Chapter Twenty-Six

War Commander Randart counted out his paces. Fifty...a hundred. Still no answer.

Relief. If the king was going to answer, he would have by now. Why had he suddenly took it into his head to interfere at this moment, when matters were the busiest? But wasn't it always that way? You are presented with a crisis of events, and that's when one and all choose to interrupt.

Randart looked out through the tower window at the rain, already receding eastward. Rain. Another disruption. If Damedran hadn't managed to reach one of the military roads, he was no doubt bogged down on some civilian mud track, and that would slow him down.

Randart threw his gold case with a clatter onto the desk, then remembered he was at Ambais. This was a loyal garrison, but they were not used to his ways, and he didn't want to have to shoot someone who touched his things.

So he picked up the case again, thrust it into his pouch and began pacing, glaring periodically out the window at the courtyard as if he could mentally pull Damedran and those boys in by force of will.

Elsewhere in the castle he could hear the orderly march of events—sentries at their duty, some noise from the mess hall at the bottom of the stone stairway. This was an old fortress, small, inconvenient, but easy to defend and tough to attack. Not that he expected an attack.

Pace, pace, glance out the window. Was that a speck on the

road? More than one speck?

He wrenched open the ill-fitting glass, which was befogged with steam. Cold air blew in drops of rain as he peered down the gentle slope below the castle. Sharp disappointment. Yes, two riders galloping up the military road.

Not Damedran, only the trackers he'd sent out to meet the boys and reinforce them for the last leg of their journey. He'd known Damedran would be disgusted with any reinforcement on his first mission, especially a successful mission. Randart would have been at his age as well. But this vile female was far too important for any prudent commander to consider mere boyish emotions.

He resisted the impulse to run downstairs to the court—as if hearing the trackers' bad news that little measure faster would make much difference.

Instead he sat, forcing himself to review the pile of reports he'd thrust into the dispatch bag before riding away from the siege, until the sound of footsteps caused him to look up.

His trackers dashed in, muddy to the waist. "War Commander, they were intercepted."

Fury flared through Randart. He kept his lips tight for one breath. Two. "Report."

The older, more experienced tracker said, "We are reasonably sure we located their trail. Valgan here rode back down it to make certain, and said it definitely led to the farm where the cadets had tracked the target. We even found the place they had to have ambushed the target." Faint question infused the man's face and voice on the word "target". Randart had not told them who the target was, only that Damedran had been sent to this specific olive farm belonging to the local duke in order to arrest a traitor.

"Looked like a pretty good fight," he added, obviously hoping to provoke some information. "At least, as far as we could tell, as the rain was already beginning to obliterate the tracks."

He paused. When Randart did not respond, he shrugged and went on. "There was another ambush say half a watch's ride from here, twice as many hoof prints. They all rode northwest, cross-country."

"Where did the ambushers come from, could you tell?"

"Their prints began at the military road," was the answer.

Military road? Who could possibly have betrayed him? Who even knew where he was? Not the king. Not even Orthan. Only Damedran—

Randart jammed the reports back into the dispatch bag. "You two. Ride ahead, find their trail. Get a communication box from your commander, Valgan, and report the signal to me before you depart. I am going to follow you with my entire force. So you had better ride at the gallop."

Damedran did not know what to think.

Jehan, the sheep who had quite suddenly changed into a wolf, did not ask for parole, nor did he bind up his prisoners. In fact, he said nothing at all about who would ride where, he didn't even take their weapons.

And so Damedran rode next to him, silent at first as they put in a gallop. His knee throbbed where the princess had kicked him, but he could ignore that. He could wait. You don't gallop horses for long unless you have a lot of posting houses or garrisons with ready mounts. Well, the garrisons did, but the prince seemed to be avoiding them.

They galloped on the flat, smooth, well-maintained military road, and once their trail was thus thoroughly obliterated, they took a side trail over a hard-packed road, one of Jehan's people being detailed to smooth their tracks after them. Then they slowed, walking the horses until they'd cooled, and stopping at a trickling stream to water them.

Jehan squinted at the western sky above the mountaintops. The sun's limb was sinking behind a uniformly dense gray bar of cloud that covered the entire western horizon, the upper edge of which was lit with fiery oranges and reds and yellows, colors that warmed the sky and echoed in the vanguard of cloud patches overhead. It was a spectacular sunset, but it meant heavy rain on the way.

Red snickered. "They'll be up to their armpits in mud at the siege," he muttered.

"Wonder who's got the night run?" Bowsprit whispered back. "They may's well take boats."

The boys' laughter was subdued, all the clearer because Prince Jehan's men—all of them wearing warrior brown, but not a one known by sight to Damedran—worked in silence, switching gear to the remounts.

A last ochre ray of sun shone on Jehan's white hair, making him easy to pick out from the others. Damedran waited until Jehan was done talking with one of the men, who promptly rode up the trail and vanished into the woods.

The last of the sun disappeared. The warm sunset colors bleached to cold grays and blues as a wind rose, rustling through the grasses and moaning through the distant trees.

"I don't understand," Damedran said, when at last Jehan turned his way. The words seemed to wring from somewhere inside his chest. "I thought—I thought—"

"That I was a sheep," Jehan said with a quick grin.

Damedran's face burned.

Jehan raised a hand. "Don't fret. I wanted you to think that. I needed you to think that. But the time for lies and disguises is over."

Damedran's lips parted. He didn't want to say *I don't understand* again, though that was what he was thinking. It sounded, well, too sheeplike.

So what he did say was, "What disguises?"

"Zathdar the pirate being one. Besides the Fool your uncle really wanted me to be."

"Zathdar?" Damedran squeaked. He'd thought he'd had enough shocks lately. Not true, obviously. "You? But—" His mind flitted from memory to memory, then formed a question in the way that best fit his experience. "I can see how you can ride like that. Leaping horses. They do that in the west, at their academy, don't they?"

"By the time you're twelve. With your hands tied, by the time you're fifteen."

Damedran whistled soundlessly. "But they don't teach anything about the sea. I know they don't. Do they?"

"You're right," Jehan said gravely.

"Yet you have to have learned something about the sea. I mean, all the stories about Zathdar. You know ships. How did that happen?"

"Not by design. Imagine me, sent away as a small boy to Marloven Hess's military academy. Mathias thinks we need new ideas. Really, he wants to get me away from the corruption in our own academy, which, to attest to your uncle's credit, was largely gone within ten years. My father wanted me to go for different reasons. So I went west, leaving behind everyone at home who I believed were living happy lives. The letters slowed down. Then came the bad news, like my mother and father parting. My mother invited me to move to Sartor with her, but I liked my life, so I stayed."

Damedran nodded. He would have stayed too.

"Life there was good at first, but then it turned dangerous, when a good king was assassinated, and a very bad regent took his place. More news came. My father had married Princess Ananda. Not that that was bad, it just made my life seem unmoored. The old king died, and my father became king, and then the real bad news started coming."

Damedran looked subdued, but he was listening.

"The morvende have access to certain kinds of magic that delays aging for a time. I used that while I tried to reassemble the pieces of my life, but the news just got worse. Princess Atanial vanished, along with the child I never met. So I took ship for a few years to consider what to do, and ended up as a privateer on the other side of the world. When my father summoned me home, I found myself constantly surrounded by your uncle's men for my protection, but they wouldn't let me go anywhere without permission. I had Zathdar's fleet to break your uncle's increasing hold over the kingdom, since I knew I wouldn't be able to do anything as Prince Jehan."

Damedran frowned in perplexity.

Jehan wondered if he should let the boy have time to think, but it felt so good to tell the truth. "When you're away and come back, you see differences not apparent to people at home who experienced the changes more gradually. Khanerenth is full of restrictive laws. Rumors. Strife. Killings. I dedicate my life to restoring things to the way I knew Prince Math would have wanted."

Damedran flushed again. "So *I'm* the sheep. That's what you mean. But you're not saying it. I take orders and don't think. It's why Lesi Valleg hates me," he added, looking like the miserable boy he really was.

"We both had to take orders and not think. Or not appear to think." Jehan gestured, now exhilarated. Whatever happened next, he had told the truth. "The crisis came this summer when I discovered the rumors of invasion were a little too detailed to seem just rumor."

Damedran's chin jerked up. "You know about that?"

"I have suspected ever since my pirates intercepted a weapons shipment. Think, Damedran. Past the promise of glory, rank and land. That invasion would break the treaty. People on both sides of the mountains will get killed. Those plains clans of Locan Jora are not going to let their land be overrun without a vicious fight. But I don't think anyone can stand up to the king and Randart except Prince Mathias."

"*Prince Mathias?* How? I don't understand."

"I have reason to believe that Sasharia knows where her father is, and is on her way to free him. We're going as backup."

"But you let her escape! Did she tell you all that?"

Jehan smiled. "No. She's doing her valiant best to protect her father the only way she knows how. But you forget," he said gently, indicating they mount up, "who my mother is. Though I did not move to Sartor's morvende geliath with her, I never lost contact."

# Chapter Twenty-Seven

Valiant best. That's what he said, but I sure did not feel valiant. Does anyone ever feel valiant—bold—intrepid—*I am courageous, ha ha!* Well, not Yours T, anyway. I felt sulky, depressed, angry and worried by turns. Not to mention hungry and tired, for though I had earned plenty of money, and had my jewels besides, there was nowhere to spend any of it.

My trail was the straightest line to Ivory Mountain, which is not an area boasting a lot of population. I saw why when I reached the hills below the mountain: narrow trails slanting steeply upward, past waterfalls and rushing whitewater streams hidden but recognizable from their roar. Thick forest surrounded me, layers of complicated, deep green, leafy shrubs and trees. Sunlight penetrated in dapples and shafts of hazy gold. When the sunlight was strongest, sparkles of light danced on the water and gleamed in the pearl drops of moisture hanging from the edges of the leaves. When the sun vanished, I found myself abruptly closed in uniformly greenish blue shadow, guided mostly by sounds rather than by vision: unseen birds, quick thrashings of animals dashing through the underbrush, and always the trickle, drip, roar, chuckle and hiss of water. I was soon hungry, but never did I go thirsty. The water was sweet and cold, and even my mare (who did have her feedbag, and I mentally thanked Jehan several times a day for that) seemed to perk up despite my rotten mood.

So it was a long, tiring slog, though beautiful. But I was in no mood for beauty, because the density of the forest meant I would not see any enemies until they were on me. Shelter was also difficult to find. I spent a couple of miserable nights with all my clothes on and my firebird tapestry banner round me as I crouched under mossy rock outcroppings never quite large enough to be a sheltering cave.

I was on the watch for the sign my father had told me about so many years ago—three bluebells in a row, carved into stone. I'd always thought this symbol would be clear, like some kind of natural road map. As I climbed ever higher, examining every rocky scree, cliff, palisade and what have you, I began to wonder if weather and age would have defaced the carvings. That is, if they weren't overgrown by shrubs, trees or even moss.

But I kept going.

We all kept going, everyone converging on the mountain at pretty much the same time, though from different angles. Canardan's force found the tracks of the women—mistook them for warriors—and sped up their pace. Jehan knew a wood scavenger who knew where the lower cavern passages were. He and his riders made sure they left no signs behind. Randart's scouts, under threat of punishment, scarcely ate or slept until they discovered my tracks. Remember I said few live there? Randart didn't know magic, but he was far from ignorant about history. Didn't take long for him to figure that Ivory Mountain had to be my destination.

I was unaware of him on my trail until the last morning, when I woke from a miserable sleep to a misty-blue dawn so cold I could see my breath. Time to do my martial arts stretches and warm up a bit. But I forgot my morning routine when sounds echoed up the narrow valley below me.

I scrambled up, inched out onto a promontory and peered over a tumble of moss-covered stones. Down below on the trail snaked a long trail of armed men, some riding, some leading horses. They were blurred by a long grayish drift of mist, but the brown uniforms were frighteningly visible.

At their head, his dark hair and stony profile clear between dissipating wreaths of fog, was War Commander Randart.

Hunger, everything fled my mind. As Mom would say, *It's*

*Sherwood Smith*

*time to beat feet.*

&

The Duke and Duchess of Frazhan rode out with Lord and Lady Kender to meet the women.

They met on a high bridge built over a cascading fall down the side of a mountain. The road had brought them within sight of Ivory Mountain, on the other side of the river valley. It was a beautiful sight with its white crown of snow even in summer, the highest peak shrouded in cloud.

Journey's end.

Atanial straightened up as the ducal pair rode toward them. The duke and duchess were both quite old, white-haired, hard to read as aristocrats typically were. Lord Kender was a tall, lean, handsome man, but Atanial's attention was focused solely on his wife.

Lady Starveas Kender was short and round, with an intelligent dark gaze framed by wispy silver hair. Like the ducal pair, she and her husband wore Colendi-style linen over-robes, paneled up the sides, with ornamental long sleeves dagged back at an angle. Hers was pale mauve over violet; the duchess and her duke wore white over gray. Lord Kender was the most brightly dressed, his over-robe a rich green with stylized golden rye beards along the hem.

The duke's voice was thin and reedy as he introduced them all.

"Your highness," Lady Starveas said then, somehow making her bow graceful, though she sat on the back of a horse. It was clear that she intended to be the spokesperson.

Atanial copied the bow as best she could, hoping she wouldn't fall out of the saddle. Her hips twinged; the flare of a hot flash burned through her chest, tingling outward to the backs of her hands. Her face broke out with moisture. "My lady."

"We have heard word of your mission. We wish to hear the

truth from your lips."

Atanial cleared her dry throat and straightened up, resisting the impulse to wipe her sleeve over her hot face. She gave what by now had become a speech, a pattern of words she could utter without thinking, as she watched for reactions.

The four betrayed little during the speech, but at the end Lady Starveas said, "Thank you. For once rumor was not far wrong, then."

Atanial ached, itched, felt damp from the aftermath of the hot flash. She longed for a bath and for an end to this endurance test. But the cause was right. Whatever happened.

"We have been granted time to consider." Lady Starveas indicated the four of them with a graceful gesture. "For you must know that my family lands were taken by those who call themselves Locan Jorans now."

Atanial dipped her head in the half nod, half bow she'd seen the aristocrats use to one another.

The duchess pulled from her inner sleeve a golden case. She held it up.

Atanial recognized it as a communications case, which sent messages instantaneously by magic. She swallowed tightly. *Here it comes.* The only surprise was that they had made it so long without discovery.

Lady Starveas had also retrieved her own case. "We waited only to hear the words from you. We have written letters to certain friends and will send them, with your permission."

Now Atanial was surprised. She managed the half bow again, because she had no idea what to say. A trickle of sweat ran down her temple and into her ear. Ugh.

Lady Starveas smiled a little. "I cannot speak for everyone. There are some who will shut their eyes to violence in order to regain what they think was once theirs. My family..." She looked away at Ivory Mountain, crowned with snow. "We have morvende in our family. We know that land is land, it stays when we are gone. Our sense of permanence is imposed on land, it is not granted by any but other humans."

Lord Kender stirred, and the lady sent him a fast look. Atanial wondered just how much fraught emotion lay behind those subtle reactions that she could so easily have missed.

A fly buzzed by her mount's ear, causing the animal to twitch and bob. Atanial leaned forward to shoo the fly away and stroked the horse's bony neck ridge. As she did, she surreptitiously wiped the side of her face on her shoulder.

"There is the matter of holding what we'd regain by violence," Lady Starveas went on, as if Atanial had spoken.

Atanial wondered if the lady was not talking to her at all.

"Some might look forward to years of fighting. I do not. I would rather regain at least some of our holdings by negotiation. I say all this because I believe if your husband, Prince Mathias Zhavalieshin, was to return, perhaps that negotiation would occur. Many of those over in Locan Jora who sit now in our old homes and work our land were loyal to the Zhavalieshins, who once came from that area. But the king is now Canardan Merindar."

The duchess spoke for the first time. Her voice was thin and light as a bird's. "We welcome you to the castle. We extend this invitation to you all. We've been preparing."

Lady Starveas gave one of those slow, stylish nods in her direction, then turned to Atanial. It was very clear they'd planned things out. "But when you move on, we will not be going with you. Honor requires us to keep the oaths we made to Canardan, for he has not broken his oaths to us. Though, now speaking only for myself, my heart yearns for the return of Prince Math."

The duke and duchess made the low bow of accord.

Atanial lifted her voice so the women crowded behind could hear. "I thank you on behalf of everyone here. We ask no more than that."

They crossed the bridge and wound their way to the old castle whose towers were just visible beyond the lacy veil of the cascade.

# Chapter Twenty-Eight

Ivory Mountain got its name from a white stone with peculiar properties, a stone that resembled frozen ice with melted silver mixed in, or so it's been described. Those peculiar properties caused it to be nearly destroyed a few thousand years back or so. The morvende moved from the geliath (which is kind of like a cavern city a couple thousand years old), leaving it empty except for occasional retreats over the succession of centuries following.

That shows about how old the place was.

I galloped up the trail, branches whapping my face and the moisture-laden leaves dousing me with stinging-cold water. I was terrified that Randart and his gang would get me before I could find the accessway, and my fear communicated to the mare, who moved her fastest.

Up and up, the mare's head low to the trail, leaving me to watch the rocks at both sides lest I miss the triple-flower carving, which I was afraid had worn away.

I was wondering what to do if I reached the snowy mountain summit when at last my eyes were drawn to the symbol, weird as that sounds. I found out later, if you're taught the access signals, part of the magic is that image and reality will find a way to match. I mean, we're talking old, *old* magic.

In grateful relief I flung myself off the mare, who was sweating from the steady climb despite the bitter air, and fell to my knees, shaky fingers scrabbling at the smooth stone between a holly bush and a climbing of ivy that had mysteriously never grown over that portion of the stone.

I don't even know what I did, but the entire face of the rock shimmered, and there before me was a narrow fissure reaching up about nine feet, scarcely five feet wide. Dark as it was inside, I figured moss and some spiders would be preferable to a close, personal interview with Randart—backed by about a hundred buff guys wearing lots of shiny, pointy things, and probably in bad moods from missing their morning coffee.

The mare sniffed, snorted, then followed me willingly enough. Right after her tail passed the edge of the shadow cast by the sun down the rock face, the shimmer abruptly vanished, leaving us in darkness.

I stood next to the horse, who sniffed some more and turned her head, shifting her weight from hoof to hoof. Thunk, thud. I rubbed my eyes, wondering what the heck to do next.

When I opened my eyes, my vision had adjusted. A faint glow emanated from the stone in a series of purple blossoms painted impossibly long ago. The glowing signals led down a tunnel.

I stayed on foot, not sure how high the ceiling was, leading the mare by the reins. The stone floor seemed firm and not slimy. Good sign, I told myself.

We wound slightly to the left, always downhill, judging from the pressure on my toes.

Abruptly we entered a round cavern lit by a glowglobe of a kind I had never seen. Most have steady, soft light, faintly bluish, though I understand the light comes from gathered sunlight, stored by magical means. I would swear this globe was spread spectrum, for the light was soft but remarkably clear, picking out glittering bits from the rock all around, showing carvings of vines twining up overhead, and the remains of a painted sky with stars. On the soft dirt of the ground were blue flakes, showing where paint had fallen over the centuries.

Below the glowglobe's niche was a trough with running water. I could hear it rushing down from somewhere above. The horse and I were thirsty.

I cupped my hands and dipped them. The water hurt, it

was so cold, but it was clear and tasted good. The horse shouldered me aside and got a good long drink.

When we were done, I looked around. Several tunnels led off in various directions. I felt the faint ruffling of an air current from somewhere and almost instinctively turned in that direction.

Why not? Before I'd spent a couple days climbing the side of this mountain I'd thought it would be easy, like entering a big building. There's your directory, you get into the elevator, and whoosh, there's your suite. The vast size of this place was daunting. I kept trying to remember everything my father had told me when I was taught the magic, but all I could bring up was a vague sense of glowglobes, light, gleaming painted stars that looked real to my young eyes—and the spell.

So I followed the air current, which was cool and smelled fresh. I figured there had to be a hot spring somewhere down in the honeycomb of caverns, and the air was funneled upward. Anyway, I was grateful that I could see, that the tunnels were clean, no slime, no webs.

When I reached the right place, there was no warning. No trumpets, no sinister barriers or portents, no mysterious guardians. Nothing but the two of us emerging from the tunnel into a chamber with a pair of entrances opposite one another.

But I remembered it.

Here the painted ceiling was not flaking off. It glimmered pale blue in the brilliant light given off by hundreds of tiny glowglobes no bigger than a pea, the effect like the twinkling lights some people put in trees, back on Earth. The blue intensified in gradations up the dome of the ceiling, becoming a deep, cobalt glow directly overhead, the constellation depicted there glittering like a real sky.

My throat squeezed up when I recalled standing there once before, a scared little kid transfixed with wonder. I'd thought the top of the mountain had opened, leaving me staring straight up at the night sky.

But I knew it was day, and I was deep inside a mountain— and that an enemy was hard on my trail.

I had a job to do.

I dropped the reins. The mare watched me, the glowglobes pinpoints in her patient eyes. I dug through my bag and pulled out the little seashell wrapped in its homespun.

I opened the cloth and held out the shell, which began to glisten. There was enough magic—or the right magic—for the spell I'd been taught so long ago.

I stepped into the middle of the room, rubbed my damp palms down my grubby clothes, drew in a couple of *chi* breaths and began the spell.

Magic potential rushed inward through me, a feeling akin to channeling a lightning strike. I shut my eyes and concentrated on the shaping words...and finished.

Light snapped on my palms and the shell vanished.

A current of air rushed round the chamber, and the horse tossed her head and stamped as a tall man with wild gray hair appeared. His thin body was clad in a long tunic down to his knees and baggy riding trousers. He had bare feet.

My astonished eyes flicked back to his face, that hawk-nosed, kindly face I'd remembered in dreams and in waking, and then it blurred as hot tears welled up.

"Dad!"

His arms opened, and I hurled myself into them.


When Randart realized he was going to have to deal with a magic mountain, he used one of two transfer tokens the king had insisted that Zhavic make. They were instant summons, pulling either Magister Zhavic or Magister Perran willy nilly from wherever they were.

Randart had possessed these two tokens for years. He'd never thought he'd want a mage, but the time had come. The one he chose was Magister Perran, who had been guarding the old tower in case anyone tried a World Gate transfer. It was far too late for that.

Magister Perran arrived abruptly. Before he recovered from the transfer dizziness, Randart pointed at him and three of his men seized the mage, who was older, stocky and not exactly in fighting shape. They searched him thoroughly, taking away his magic case, paper, a writing chalk, several transfer tokens and the book he'd had in his hand.

In silence they handed these things to Randart, who tossed the book off the trailside cliff without a second glance and put the rest of the items in the pouch at his belt. He glared down at the mage, ignoring his faint cry of dismay. "Atanial's girl is farther up the trail here on Ivory Mountain. You will get us inside, without any trickery, or I will cut you down myself before you can gabble one of your spells." He drew his sword from the saddle sheath and kept it gripped in his hand.

Perran shook his head once, and began walking.

Randart glanced back and motioned to two of his very best trackers. They came forward and saluted. "String your bows. Be ready to shoot the girl on first sight. Do not wait for an order. Do it. The one who drops her—and anyone she's with—will get land and a title to match."

They saluted again, the fervency of their emotions expressed in the gesture. The white-lipped rage in their commander's face made it unsafe speak.

So this is how they wound their way up the mountain, Magister Perran walking, the trackers at either side, the others riding. The mage desperately looking for some way in. He had not been taught the accessway, and if you haven't been taught, it's going to be difficult to find. He knew that much, if nothing else about morvende geliaths.

As they climbed higher, woman and horse tracks fresh before them, his anxiety changed to despair and he wondered if he should jump off the mountain. One glance at Randart's angry face made it clear he was going to get no sympathy or understanding. If the tracks kept going, and all they found was a horse without a rider, Perran knew he would be murdered.

When they reached the place of the carvings, the tracks seemed to lead directly into a wall. How to get in? Magister Perran began searching for any kind of illusion, magical lock, whatever he could find.

Randart shifted impatiently, reminded yet again how much he loathed and distrusted magic and mages. The warriors watched the mage rustling desperately through the holly bushes that grew with profusion all along the cliff face. Perran's hands were soon pricked with scarlet, and his robe tangled constantly on the sharp-edged leaves. But he kept at it until Randart snapped, "Either you find a way in or die right now."

Perran turned around, flinging his bleeding hands out. "Then kill me," he cried. "Because you won't believe anything I say—"

A shimmer at the edge of everyone's vision caused Randart to start violently. The mage stumbled back. The trackers raised their crossbows.

The leaves rustled, and a small boy emerged, seemingly from the stone. He was no more than nine or ten, with brown hair and a considering hazel gaze. He wore ordinary riding clothes.

Randart stared in amazement, as a whisper hissed back down the line: this was the boy who had won at the games.

My father staggered, laughing breathlessly into my filthy hair. "Careful! I'm afraid I'm going to be a bit on the weak side until I learn to live in my body again."

I gave him a gentle squeeze then let him go, knuckling my eyes. "What? Where were you?" I looked up into his face. He had aged along with the rest of us.

He touched my cheek and gave me a crooked grin. "I had a choice. I could go right out of the world, someplace where time stops, and I would not age, nor would I know what was occurring at home. Or I could sleep in body, but in mind I could learn how to watch. I chose the latter, though my body aged, and though it took me a long time before I could master the art of wandering in the...the realm of the mind, I guess you would say."

"Then—you know Randart is after me?"

"Yes." Papa winced. "I have been watching him for several

years, now. I eventually even learned to hear his thoughts, a little. This summer, though, suddenly I could hear them all, as plain as if I were with them." He shut his eyes and cocked his head. "*Could* hear their thoughts. But those voices are fading. His is already gone. Perhaps it is because I'm back inside my own skull, so to speak. How limiting it is! Soon all I'll hear is my own yammer. I'm yammering, aren't I, Sasha?" He gave a wheezy laugh. "Never mind. I do know where we had better go, because there are two others I've been listening to, and they are also here, as it happens."

"What do you mean?"

"I think I'd better show you." Dad drew in a deep breath. "But I don't know how fast I can walk." He peered down and wiggled his toes. "Especially barefoot. When I chose to sleep, I made myself as comfortable as possible and that meant kicking off my shoes. They're back wherever Glathan hid my body while I slept." He waved a hand vaguely.

"Well, why don't you ride? I'm tired of riding. I'd as soon shake out the kinks in my muscles." I handed him the reins to the mare. "You point the way, and we're outa here."

Dad gave me a pensive smile. "This way."

Some of the men reacted with questions, but Randart raised his sword. "Are you some kind of damned mage spy? What are you doing here?"

"I was sent to this mountain this summer, to further my studies in history," the boy replied. "You saw me at your games with some friends. Just now I discovered that other humans were approaching. You can see the outer accesses from certain vantages within," he explained, pointing behind him.

"Other humans, like a tall girl who has no business being on this world at all?" Randart was angrier than ever at the unsettling situation, the sense that he was swiftly losing control. When the boy did not answer, he snapped, "Get out of my way."

For a long moment, as the boy gazed steadily up at Randart, the only sounds were the plop-plop of moisture from the trees, the snort of a horse, and in the distance, the sweet, melodic song of a lark.

The boy said, "I really think you should reconsider. Return to your royal city, as you promised. There is no cause for you to meddle here—"

A low growl of inarticulate rage began in Randart's chest and came out as a cry. He flung the sword like a spear straight at the boy.

Who sidestepped, raising an arm from which the loose sleeve fell, revealing a metal-linked wrist guard. Swifter than sight his arm whirled in a circle, deflecting the blade, which rammed into the twisted holly trunk, vibrating.

Randart gasped, "Who *are* you?"

"My name is immaterial to your purposes, but for what it is worth, it is Sven Eric."

The mage gasped, his cheeks blanching.

The boy looked his way, saying quite kindly, "Not a modern version of *that* name. I would hardly be named after a fool. It's the modern version of my Aunt Svenrael's name." He turned his attention back to Randart. "Will you return?"

The war commander, goaded by his own action as well as the result, by the implied secrecy of some name he'd never heard but which the mage obviously recognized, said distinctly, "I will not permit anyone to interfere with a lifetime of work. *Any*one. And if you do not get out of my way I will kill you or this mage or whoever is in reach, and not stop until that access lies open."

The boy stepped aside. "Then ride within."

When they passed the shimmer and their eyes had adjusted enough to reveal purplish blotches along the tunnel walls, they discovered the boy was gone.

Randart turned to the mage. "What name was he talking about?"

The mage said flatly, "Sfenaraec. The one who Norsunder was...founded on, over four thousand years ago. A name not used since."

Silence.

Randart said, "Be ready to shoot."

Dad and I and the mare walked in silence until cool air currents wafted up the tunnel, bringing the smell of running water and the low, steady rumble of a waterfall. Above the sound we heard voices.

Dad put out a hand. "The last thing I heard from Randart was his order to have us shot on sight. We cannot be seen."

I gazed at him in surprise. "Randart is already ahead of us?"

"I think he's near. There are some others as well."

We walked the last few steps and stared down at a vast lake under another domed ceiling, this one about the size of one of those super sports domes in the USA. Again, it was painted with gleaming, even glittering stars, in constellations so specific I had a feeling they were astronomically correct, and I was cast back for a moment in memory to childhood, standing on the stone edge of the lake, looking up and thinking I was outside.

Then memory was gone—thought was gone—when I recognized two of the voices.

One was my mother.

The other was Canardan.

# Chapter Twenty-Nine

Dad slid off the mare, wincing when he landed on his bare feet. For a moment he leaned against the animal's neck, his face hidden behind the wild tangles of his hair, which, uncut for at least ten years, frizzed out spectacularly, ahem, almost as wild as mine.

The eerily perfect acoustics carried the voices up to us as if they spoke from a few yards away.

Canardan exclaimed with a surprised laugh, "Is that really you, Atanial?"

Mom replied, "I could say the same to you." She wasn't laughing.

I laid my hand on my father's bony shoulder. "Come on, Dad, we gotta tell them we're here. *You're* here."

He turned his head. "I've been out of her life all these years, darling. What I owe her now is a clear choice, not an impossible one."

"What do you mean?" I asked, but my voice collided with Canardan's. "Who are these companions you've gathered about you?"

My mother stated in her Parent Night Voice—pleasant, even bright and social, but quite determined. "Canardan, we have two missions. The first, I am searching through here in case there is any chance, any possible chance, I might find my husband. Yes, you may laugh, but at least we're out of the rain. Our second mission was to confront you. Once we'd made a circuit of the kingdom gathering more women."

"Confront me?" His laughter sounded forced. "What is this? War in the bedroom? Except we are not quite there, are we?"

She said in a loud, clear voice, "The mission is to prevent you, if we can, from creating a war in spring. Everyone here has children, or nieces and nephews, or brothers and sisters, friends and lovers who enlisted in the army in order to protect Khanerenth. Abrogating the treaty with Locan Jora by invading it is not protecting the kingdom."

During the silence that followed, Dad moved slowly the last distance, with me at his side. We found ourselves on a kind of cliff, really no more than a slab of granite forming an outcropping, directly opposite the waterfall. There was a jumble of rock below it, a scree slanting down to a lower natural balcony.

Dad stood well back, in the shadow of the fissure that made our tunnel.

Canardan and his force were ranged up alongside the lake, a huge broken-walled cavern behind them with the faint glow of day stippling the rock. Apparently the lake was not part of the geliath, or at least not any more. An ancient avalanche had opened it to the outside, so people could come and go freely. During that long silence, I noticed that most of the surrounding walls had been shored up, built, torn down, temporarily housing all kinds of people, from thieves to political opponents—"people" constituting what the morvende called sunsider humans, like us. The morvende had abandoned this lake cavern way back when, leaving only that marvelous ceiling.

Mother's army appeared to be in the hundreds, far outnumbering Canardan's force. They spread all along the edge of the lake until they were quite near the waterfall, which thundered directly into the lake from a fissure high above. The women seemed to have reached the place within the last day or so, for I saw signs of a campsite, and many had wet hair, and clothing spread over flat rocks.

As Mom spoke across that leg of the lake, they gathered behind her in silence.

Canardan said, "Who is there? I cannot make out faces.

The light from this end runs reflections upward, making it difficult to see you."

Mom said, "Never mind who, if you're thinking of removing people from their places in life, for there are far more of us even than you see here. Some are on the way, others are gathering ahead, waiting for us to catch up. I can assure you, if something happens to any of us, your troubles will only begin. And that's before you start your war."

Canardan laughed again.

Then he said, "Atanial sunshine dancingstar from the far-off world, will you marry me?"

I nearly choked, but Dad did not react at all.

I whispered to him, "Speak!"

"She has to have free choice, darling. If I pop up right now, the choice is not free."

I tried not to groan as I peered down. Canardan stood among his warriors, tall, strong, with long waving hair. From the distance across the lake he looked as handsome as I remembered him—unchanged.

"Did you hear me?" he asked, his voice the warm, kingly voice I remembered from childhood, and had learned to distrust and even to hate, with all my single-minded childish passion. I'd thought Mom hated him too, but obviously I'd not perceived a lot of things. "Marry me, Atanial. Marry me and show me your right and my wrong. There's never been a queen like you, and maybe that's what the kingdom needs."

"I am already married," Mom said, her voice high and tight.

"To a ghost? If you really believe Math is alive, then set aside the marriage. You've waited longer than most would have. He'd understand, especially if it was for the good of the kingdom. Come! Come, I ask you before all these people, make peace and take your place beside me as my queen."

Mom's voice caught. "Canardan, that is probably the most generous offer I've ever heard from you. But it is impossible."

"No, it's not. That's the fun of being king. And queen. You can do things you want to do. You give the orders, make it happen!"

Mom laughed, a kind of half laugh, half sob. "If you truly want my advice, why not make me your adviser? You could do a lot better with me than with Dannath Randart, I promise you that."

"He's right," Dad whispered. "And she knows it. She'd make a wonderful queen. She might even save the kingdom. If not Canardan." He shut his mouth, frowning down in unhappy intensity.

"As adviser, you'd argue with Randart every day." Canardan laughed again. "As queen, you would give him orders, and he must obey."

"Again he's right," Dad murmured. Adding in a less neutral voice, "Until Dannath has her killed."

I fought not to yell out, *Mom, he's here!* "Dad, you have to do something."

He shook his head. "Don't you see? The important thing for all is the kingdom. Your mother would make a better queen than I would a king. The second most important thing is her happiness. He does love her in his fashion. And I abandoned her."

I kicked at the rubble in frustration, sending rocks skittering back toward the mare, who snorted and backed up a step or two, tossing her head.

Then Dad's hand gripped my shoulder, and he pointed below us. I heard vague sounds, mostly muffled by the water. Randart and his warriors had arrived through another tunnel which gave out onto the natural balcony right beneath us.

Mom's and Canardan's people were completely unaware of them. They were too close to the waterfall. Its noise covered everything but their own voices.

Most of Randart's force began making their way down to the lake, midway between Mom's group and the king's. Canardan and Mom were too intent on one another to notice.

I could only see the back of Randart's head, but even from that distance it was easy to make out how angry he was. And oh, he was angry. No, he was enraged. When I saw him bend a little to address one of the men following behind his horse, the man's reaction made it clear Randart's words were upsetting.

I couldn't hear it at the time, but he said, "Why did I not know about these women? I will flay whoever was responsible."

As always, he meant it.

He jerked up when Mom spoke. Her conviction was audible to everyone. "It will never happen. I would be your adviser gladly, but I will never be your wife."

Canardan stilled, watched by his men, the gathered women and (though he still did not know it) Randart.

Randart's eyes narrowed. Dad and I could see his profile. He raised a gloved hand, and his men stopped, everyone quiet.

Canardan's force gradually became aware of Randart's men through surreptitious nudges and head tips, but Canardan's attention was divided between Mom and memory. Atanial had spoken in exactly the same tone, the same gentleness, that Jehan's mother Feraeth had used so long ago. Though he'd ended the marriage, he'd tried to talk her into staying—they were still friends—they shared a child. But Feraeth had said, "I must go, Canardan. Your choices are no longer my choices."

Who knows. Maybe he had never really considered Mom would turn him down. Maybe he thought if he could get her to agree to one term, he could convince her on all the others. Maybe he had to seem to be the good guy, in her eyes, in the women's eyes, in his guards' eyes—in his own eyes—but he laughed again, head back, teeth flashing.

We were all watching him now, including Jehan, who had arrived from another tunnel, unseen by any of us.

Canardan threw his hands wide. "Atanial! If you will come back with me to the capital, I promise, my gift to you will be an end to any invasion—"

"You *idiot!*"

The roar of fury was almost unintelligible.

Everyone's attention snapped to Randart—who had yanked a loaded crossbow from one of his men, and fired.

Canardan jerked around, mouth open in surprise. I don't think he even saw the bolt that had been meant for his back. When he turned, it smacked straight into his chest.

Canardan's long silver-touched auburn hair flung back. One hand groped futilely at the shaft protruding from him, until he began to fall, slowly, slowly to his knees as two or three of his men who were obviously as shocked as the rest of us belatedly sprang forward to catch him.

The clang of a sword rang out, the echo ricocheting. There was a flash of white hair as Jehan leaped down from the rock fall from another of the many tunnels, unseen until now by any of us. He flung his way through the warriors ringing Randart and attacked the murderer of his father.

Randart's men had fallen back, shocked at the death of the king, but I didn't trust them. I yanked my sword from the mare's saddle sheath and vaulted down the rocky scree until I ranged up behind Jehan, whose blades whirled.

In the time I'd taken to run up, Jehan had gotten Randart off the horse, whose hooves slipped in the rubble. Randart jumped clear and the animal plunged away, ears flat, as men reached to catch the reins.

Randart backed up two steps under Jehan's furious attack, almost skidding in the rubble as he warded off blow after blow with his heavy cavalry blade. He bumped up against a flat rock and hopped up, now striking down at Jehan, who braced himself in the gravel before the rock, his cavalry sword and someone else's rapier humming.

Randart yelled over his shoulder, "Take him! Take him!"

Randart had chosen his crossbow men deliberately. They were willing to kill in cold blood. The one with the still-loaded bow yanked it up and took aim at Jehan.

"Touch him and you die," I bellowed as I dashed forward.

The man yanked the bow toward me. I snapped off a sidekick to his hand that sent the bow hurtling into the air. It smashed against the ceiling and the bolt fired—straight into the ground in front of the other riders, sending up a spurt of gravel.

Horses panicked, men in the narrow tunnel mouth fell back, some shoving, everyone yelling and slipping and sliding, as Randart glared past Jehan at me. "Kill her!" Randart yelled, with a flourish of his sword.

Most of the nearby men just pressed back, but two came at me, blades raised. I kicked up gravel at one and met the blade of the other, flinging it off. The first lunged in, but I snapped a whirling time bind with my rapier round his heavy sword, and slid the point past it straight into his shoulder. He staggered back, and as the second guy brought his blade down at me I swung inside, caught him by the wrist and used my judo to yank him off-balance. I kicked out his knee and slammed him into the first man.

Two of Jehan's men had reached me and stood over the attackers, swords upraised.

I leaped to guard Jehan's back.

Unfortunately he caught the flicker of motion at the extreme edge of his vision. He glanced back—but just as he reassured himself that it was me and not an attacker, his heel skidded.

In the second he was off-balance, Randart brought his hilt toward Jehan's head in the backswing, and brained him from behind. Jehan crashed to the ground.

Randart's men leaped forward to finish Jehan off. I whirled, sword out, to keep them back.

Randart stepped down from the rock, swinging his blade back and forth. "No, no, keep him alive. He's now the king. And he's going to take orders from me. As for *her*." Randart pointed with the sword directly at me. "Everything, *everything* is her fault. Get away," he ordered the men still ringing us, and they backed up, staring from him to me and down to Jehan. Randart bared his teeth. "This pleasure I reserve for myself."

He swung with a power stroke I could not block with a mere rapier. He had that heavy cavalry sword, and he was fighting to kill. I backed gracelessly out of the way, slipped on gritty dust just like Jehan had and dropped my rapier.

Randart laughed as he advanced.

"Your mistake," I said, though my voice quavered.

He took another swipe at me. I whirled under the blade and did a sweep kick. He was too well planted, and my feet only bounced off his heavy boots. But he looked down, and in that moment I dove to one side, rolled (Ow! Never roll on gravel!) and came up with Jehan's heavier cavalry sword that had been lying by his hand. Randart's blade flashed toward my head. The angle was too close for a power block. I dropped to one knee and flung up both hands, the tip resting on the flat of my palm, and took the blow on the flat of Jehan's heavy blade.

Shock rang through my bones, sparks flew. "You cheated," I yelled. "You rotten, cowardly slime, you hit him from behind!"

"Die." Randart brought the sword round in a deadly side-arc that whooshed within an inch of my gut. I danced back, though that put me close to the edge of the cliff.

Then something silver glittered in the air between Randart and me.

*Thunk.*

Randart lowered his sword, staring at the knife in his shoulder.

The men, who had stood frozen, some of them gazing in horror at the king across the lake, others at Randart, obviously unsure what to do, all stepped back as Damedran scrambled over the rocks.

"You broke your promise," he yelled, his voice cracking on the last word. "You *lied.*" And he began to sob, the angry, honking sobs of a teen betrayed beyond endurance.

Randart pressed his fingers over the horrible, spurting wound. "You always had...rotten aim," he snarled.

"I don't," came a voice from behind.

Randart whipped round. There was Jehan, rising to his feet, crimson blood trickling in shocking contrast down through his white hair into his face, which was as bleak as I'd ever seen it. His hand gripped my dueling rapier.

Randart shifted his blade to his left, swung at Jehan. Neatly, without fuss or flourish, Jehan blocked and, without a check, the rapier flashed straight through Randart's heart.

The warriors stirred, some starting toward me, some toward Damedran. Damedran's fellow cadets swarmed over the rocks, ranging themselves in a row, blades raised.

Everyone eyed one another, poised for action—but who was in charge? Jehan swiped blood out of his face, blinking in an effort to see.

"Hold! Everyone, hold hard! Lay down your arms," my father ordered in a voice of authority I had never heard him use.

The older army men stared, aghast, astonished. In disbelief.

"*Math?*"

That was Mom.

"Down with your weapons," Dad said, his voice strong enough to echo back from the far stone walls. "Now. There will be no retribution for those who lay down weapons. But another strike, and you are forsworn."

Clang. Clank. Zhing.

I think, looking back, many of them were relieved to get rid of the steel and the responsibility it implied. Too much had happened too fast. The pair of men holding Damedran stepped away, leaving him weeping quietly, disconsolately.

Dad picked his way down to us, his hair wild, his feet absurdly bare. But he didn't look ridiculous, he looked assured, cool, well, *kingly.*

Jehan flung down his red-smeared blade.

Dad gripped Jehan's shoulders with both hands. "You have done well, my boy," he said quietly.

Jehan squinted into his face past the blood trickling from the blow Randart had given him, and his brow smoothed. Dad was not talking about the fight with Randart at all.

I looked uncertainly from Dad to Jehan, unsure what to do now that the emergency was over.

Dad let go of Jehan and stepped to me, giving me his funny smile as he murmured for my ears alone, "He told you the truth in everything that matters."

I know it's about as trite as "true love", but I really did feel as if a weight had lifted from my heart.

Before I could cross those last few steps to Jehan, a figure hurtled between the warriors, shoving some of them aside, and then, crying as hard as she had in those early days when we first reached Earth—but this time for joy—was Mom.

She flung herself into Dad's arms, laughing, weeping, covering his face with kisses, stopping only when his arms locked around her as if they would never let her go.

# Chapter Thirty

Jehan and I had only had a single private conversation between that terrible day in Ivory Mountain and our arrival in Vadnais. And it wasn't much of one.

Immediately after Randart's death and Dad's surprise appearance, Mom got everyone organized. She asked the women to help marshal Canardan's men. By that I mean they went to the ones they knew, asking for help carrying things or help with horses or to talk—keeping them apart from Randart's men so they wouldn't get the bright idea of attacking their ex-army mates for some wholesale slaughter to relieve pent-up feelings.

Dad remained with Randart's men, forcing them to stay in military formation, that is under tight control. They were sworn to follow orders, and right now, Dad seemed to be the senior royal representative. At least no one tried to question his authority.

For the rest of that horrible day, Jehan stayed with Damedran and the cadets.

I kept out of their way as we trudged out of the cavern and began the long, dreary journey back to Vadnais. Jehan's and Damedran's faces wore twin expressions of shock; Damedran's grief was terribly close to the surface, fueled by anger and even guilt. Though he kept repeating that his uncle got what he deserved, got what he deserved. No one argued. Damedran was his own judge and jury. Finally, surrounded protectively by his cadet pack, Damedran fell into an exhausted sleep near the campfire that first night.

I eased my way through all the slumbering warriors and stable people, and sat down next to Jehan. He had been sitting alone with his back to a rock, staring into the distant fire, his hands loose on his knees.

His head turned sharply, and he looked searchingly into my face. Though we did not really know one another yet, I suspected he was bracing against an expression of triumph or some other careless dismissal of his father because he'd heard plenty from me about Canardan. And I'd never had the chance to know the king as anything but a villain.

But I'd witnessed that last exchange with my mother, during which I got a glimpse of the Canardan whom Jehan loved, the man Mom had regarded as more of a friend than as an enemy. Despite everything.

So there was no sign in me of the reactions he dreaded. All the tension went out of him, and the look he gave me, the puckered brow of grief, whacked my heart with an echo of his sorrow.

"I'm sorry," I said, and meant it. "Jehan, I'm so sorry."

His expression tightened. "If I'd been faster... I should have seen it coming—" He shook his head.

"Can I get you anything?" I knew it was woefully inadequate, but what could I do? What could I say? No action of mine would bring his father back and set everything to rights. "They seem to have gotten supper going at the other end of camp. I don't know about you, but I tend to eat least when I need it the most."

He half raised a hand in dismissal, then looked away, toward the boys, a couple of whom were also asleep, though most were awake. "I don't think I ate today. Maybe I'd better."

"Right." I got to my feet. "Let me bring it to you."

A quiet tone, practical words and sensible action eased his tension a little. He didn't want soggy sympathy, nor did he want drama. We'd just lived through plenty of that.

I went away to get in line where some of the army men and a few of the women had set up a cook tent and a kind of instant cafeteria line. I got a hunk of pan-fried cornbread, some sort of fish cooked in pressed olives and wine, sautéed carrots someone had gotten permission to pick from a local truck garden.

When I finally reached Jehan, I discovered that he'd fallen deeply and profoundly asleep, his cheek resting on the arm he'd crooked over the rock.

I set the plate nearby and returned to get some food for myself. And then I went and sat with Damedran's friends, who looked like a bunch of scared pups. Husky ones, to be sure, but pups all the same. I asked them easy questions—about homes, families, favorite activities. Things they could answer without reference to so-called Great Events.

Why do bloody events get translated into Great Events in histories? Probably because they force summary change. But here was the real effect of sudden change—the wrenches in the lives of those who would never leave behind records, the people who lived and breathed and hated and loved, feared and fought, the everyday folk whom the balladeers inevitably overlooked. They might go home and tell the story, and perhaps the sword Ban Kender gripped would be handed down to a grandson, along with the story of this day. Maybe he would even figure as a hero. Well, if he did, it wasn't like anyone would be hurt by it.

The next day Jehan rode in the wagon with his father's body. He didn't ride with me partly because he needed time alone, but also because Damedran stuck to me like glue.

From his occasional, uncharacteristically shy questions or comments, I finally realized Damedran was crushing on me, but it was a dazed crush, I think more gratitude than any real admiration for my great looks or stunning abilities. Making me into a kind of heroine probably felt better than the emotions of disgrace, defeat and attempted murder, no matter how justified everyone told him his action had been.

So passed a few days.

Before we reached Vadnais, we paused at a crossroad, and my father rode a little ways apart with Damedran and spoke to him alone. The boy separated off with a small guard leading the wagon that would be taken to his family castle, where they could have a private funeral. Dad was not having any sort of shame ceremony, too often held in the past. Those caused nothing but bad feelings.

Jehan and I traveled together after that, for the few days remaining, but he almost never spoke. From time to time he looked ahead at Dad. It was pretty plain to me he was wondering what kind of disgrace lay ahead for him, but he didn't say anything.

Mom and Dad were nearly inseparable, and from the looks of things, they didn't stop yakking except to eat when we camped. A few times they invited us to join them. Jehan refused politely; he seemed to regard himself if not as a prisoner, in isolation. So I divided my time between them, feeling like this could be over ANY time and no one would hear me complain. I mean, the bad guys were gone, where was my happy ending?

Where was Jehan's?

We *finally* reached Vadnais in a kind of procession, Dad and Mom riding at the front, me behind them, an honor guard with Jehan accompanying Canardan laid out in the wagon. Along the trip some of the women had gone home (with their men) but everyone else trailed after, including some looky-loos who'd invited themselves along now that the danger was over.

Dad had sent riders ahead. The entire city had gathered along the main street leading to the great square between the castle and the guild buildings. Whatever their private feelings, people united in throwing down white blossoms. Canardan was quite covered with a fragrant snowdrift of flowers when we reached the great square, where a quiet, orderly crowd had been waiting since morning.

There, at a gesture from Dad, Jehan stepped up. He did not give a speech. No one made a sound as he passed a torch three times over his father's still body. Magister Zhavic, with trembling hands, performed the Disappearance Spell.

Then my father lifted his voice. "I, Mathias Zhavalieshin, claim the throne of Khanerenth. My first order is to appoint Prince Jehan Merindar as continuing commander of our guard, and he is also to take command as High Admiral of the navy."

Jehan's face blanched nearly as white as his hair.

"If he accepts these tasks, I further order him to ride immediately to Castle Cheslan to lead the army back to Ellir for winter quarters. There, he will preside over a smooth change of command as he sees fit."

I was astonished, but the relief in Jehan's face made it plain to see that this was exactly the right thing to do. He bowed low to my father, setting off a group bow that rustled (with a few creaking and crackling of joints here and there) through the crowd.

After that they sent up a huge cheer.

Jehan said something to Dad. I couldn't catch the words. He turned a twisted smile to me that was so much a mix of unhappiness and desire my throat ached. Then he strode away through the crowd, his white hair floating on the cold autumn breeze, and vanished in the direction of the stable.

"I never got to talk to him," I said, hardly aware of speaking.

Mom squeezed my hand. "Let him get some space. Let people see him trusted by your father."

Space. Yes. I'd asked it of him when I left the yacht, though it had hurt me terribly. I had to give him the same chance. So I bowed my head and followed my mother toward the castle looming over us.

Mom stopped in her tracks. "Where is everyone going to stay?" She stared up at those towers with (I suddenly realized) somewhat wrinkled Zhavalieshin firebird banners hanging down.

Dad looked over at her, brows lifted mildly. "Oh. I didn't think of that."

Mom gave a short nod. "I may as well go right back up to my rooms, and you come with me, dear. In about five minutes you and I are going to be in that bath. I can think of plenty of things to do."

Though I felt closer to tears, I laughed. "Mom. There are

about thirty people earing in."

"I'd invite them to join us, but the fashion for hot tubs doesn't seem to have reached this world yet. I'll fix that." She patted my hand and turned around. "Well! Since we have quite a crowd, why don't we get those with nothing to do started on cleaning up this castle?"

She began handing out jobs. Those who didn't backpedal fast got assigned to broom and scrub squads. The surprising thing is, most of them actually went out and did the assigned jobs. A lot of them were castle servants hoping not to be fired, it turned out. Having work to do was a good thing, it helped establish a semblance or normality.

Mom then turned on me. "And you, my dear, are going to have an appointment with the royal seamstress. You have to start dressing like a princess."

"Nooo," I howled. "Not a big dress!"

"If *I* can get used to it, *you* can."


Despite her determination to polish me up before Jehan returned, when he did arrive, I wasn't in any of my new gowns. (Which I have to admit were stylish and easy to wear.) I was out in the court doing weapons practice with the guards, wearing my workout clothes, when one of Steward Eban's nieces came to fetch me. "Prince Jehan is here!" she cried, grinning with excitement.

I ran inside and straight to the side parlor that Dad and Mom had taken over as our central HQ. Dad had insisted that the servants not disturb Canardan's rooms, and Mom couldn't bear to go near them. They had agreed to let Jehan decide what to do about his father's things.

Jehan arrived just after I reached the parlor. He still wore his brown tunic uniform, now dusty from the road. He bowed to Dad and Mom, and turned to me. He no longer wore that look of pain that had so wrenched my heart on the long, awful ride. I grinned at him.

He flashed a subdued version of his old smile before

turning to Dad. "Sire, would you like my report?"

Dad waved a hand. "Sit, Jehan. I sent for something to eat and drink."

Jehan dropped down next to me. Our shoulders touched; I held out my hand. His face relaxed, and his fingers gripped mine.

"Did Orthan Randart assist you as I required?" Dad asked.

"He did." Jehan's tone was grim.

Servants came in, bringing hot food and drinks. The slanting rays of late autumn touched the table where we all kept our own stacks of to-do things, striking into gold the tea as it was poured into the fine blue porcelain cups.

Kreki Eban had gone straight from the dungeon to the steward's chambers. Mom and I had been trying to figure out how to help Kreki Eban reorganize the staff, for a lot of Canardan's servants had quit. Some had vanished when the news of Canardan's death reached the city, along with a sizable amount of silver, plate and other valuables. Chas no doubt at their head. But Kreki had unearthed a lot of the old servants, who were quite eager to have their old jobs back. Only the vacancies didn't neatly match with what people wanted to do.

When the servants were gone, Mom sighed, rubbing her temples. "Zhavic searched Randart's office down in the garrison at Math's request. He didn't find any wards or anything."

Jehan dropped his biscuit onto his plate. "I searched his office at Ellir, as you required, sire. I didn't expect to find anything like 'Future King Plans' but Orthan, who really seemed to want to cooperate, kept telling me his brother was fond of lists. Randart had had his own section of the academy archive room. We opened those chests and found the files scrupulously neat, arranged according to year, supplies, reports on personnel and exercises, for the entire army. He even noted down interrogations and the type of, um, coercion, let's call it, that was most effective for that person."

"Yuk!" Mom and I said together.

"I burned that one." Jehan grimaced. "Research I'd as soon

no one ever uses. For the rest, we had to go through it all, but in the end it was worthwhile. He kept two kinds of open lists, we finally figured out: immediate goals and long-term goals."

"Ah." Mom leaned forward and pushed the biscuit back into Jehan's free hand, for his other still held mine tightly. He obediently took a bite.

Mom smiled fondly at him. "Let me guess. Long-term goals would get shifted to immediate and when accomplished, were filed as done."

"Exactly. The outstanding ones were mostly various contingency plans, but there was one single sheet, and from the looks of it quite old, on which he'd written *hypotheticals.* All of them expressed as ideas. But if you read them mentally prefacing each with *If I were king,* they changed in meaning. It looks, from that paper and some other hints, as if he'd first considered the idea of assassinating my father within the past two or three years, if he didn't get rid of me. He was only waiting for Damedran to leave the academy and gain some sort of military triumph before acting."

"So his killing Canardan wasn't impulse so much as a long-term plan inadvertently carried out too soon," Mom said.

Jehan said, "I really believe the intention had always been there. Instinct took over."

"And he hadn't shared it with his family?"

Jehan shook his head. "Damedran made that clear enough back at Ivory Mountain. And his father was equally appalled. Almost tearfully so. I believe he was afraid he would be summarily condemned for a family conspiracy that hadn't actually existed. The invasion, yes. But Orthan and Damedran had really thought that the king would then be convinced to set me aside as heir, appoint Damedran in my place, and everyone would carry on happily ever after. Except for me," he finished wryly. "But even then, I'd no doubt run off chasing artists and bards."

"You did well." Dad rose. "No. Sit there and eat. I have to get back to the mages and see if I can get them sorted out." He winked at me, and left.

Mom leaped up, rustled over in her long blue skirts and cupped her hands round Jehan's face. She leaned down and kissed his forehead. "So glad you are back, dear boy."

She whirled around, the fresh herbal scent from her skirts wafting through the air, and she was gone.

"She seems happy," Jehan said as the door closed quietly on us.

"She's happy with Dad." I hesitated, then shook my head—which set our hands to swinging.

Jehan gave me a brief grin. "Promise me. Don't hide things. Spit 'em out. I will, too."

"Promise." I turned his hand over and rubbed my thumb over his rough, callused palm. His skin so warm. "Mom is happy when she's with Dad, but that's not nearly often enough. She was happy, oh, the first day or so here, but the talk about Norsunder and possible war worries her. A lot. She likes being social, when everyone gets along."

Jehan drank off his tea. "I sensed that, when we were here in the summer."

"Speaking of the past. I never saw your father with her, but I'm wondering if she had a kind of weird love-hate thing going with him."

"I saw them together. That's pretty much it," Jehan responded.

I nodded. "Dad won't say anything at all, but he looks worried sometimes, when he watches her, and he doesn't think anyone is looking. Not about her feelings for Canary—Canardan, sorry." I sighed. "But about these future threats, and how that relates to the queen gig."

"Gig," Jehan breathed, smiling at last. That smile, so pensive, so sweet, melted me right down to the socks I wasn't wearing.

"Jehan. Speaking of no one around. Who knows how long that will last. I have something to say."

Jehan gave my hand a brief, tentative squeeze. I got to my feet then pulled him up. We stood there in the golden shafts of sunlight, his white hair gleaming, pinpricks of light in his blue eyes.

He looked into my face and grinned. "A prepared speech, eh? If it's self-condemnation, don't do it. But if it's something you will feel the better having shed, well, let's have it."

"We call it clearing the air." I leaned up and kissed him. "And yes. I mean, I don't think I'm Princess Perfect, and I want to apologize. For not trusting you. See, I wanted to trust you, oh, way too much. So I didn't trust myself."

"Or Merindars," he murmured.

I groaned. "That sounds so awful."

"But it's true." He watched me closely. "Isn't it? Truth is, if my father were alive, where would we all be? Would he be in prison, or halfway across the kingdom drawing as many to him as possible for a civil war? I don't think he could have brought himself to give up being king. He probably expected, if your father really did turn up alive, that it would be Mathias who would conveniently go away with a cheery farewell. I am convinced it would have grieved your father to put him on trial, much less anything more drastic."

Echoing what Dad had said to Mom and me in private, two nights before: *I don't think I could have borne putting Canardan on trial, despite everything he's done. And I know what he's done, I've been inside his head a great deal this summer. Yet I also know his motives, and he was not at heart an evil man. But he was evilly educated and easily influenced to talk himself into what he wanted, and into shutting his eyes to Randart's goals.*

I said, "All true."

"So where does that leave me, I am beginning to wonder? There were some at the academy who did not like seeing me free and not in prison. Others assured me of their continued loyalty. I mislike the division between people that these attitudes imply. For surely, if there is so broad a range there at the academy, does it not hold it would be much the same across the kingdom?" He looked away, then met my eyes and said in a low voice, "In truth, I wonder if there is a place for me here at all."

*What ever happened to "happily ever after"?* I thought,

trying not to show my dismay. "Please don't decide anything without talking to Dad."

"I can't begin to decide anything." His gaze was steady. He'd tensed up again, and I could feel how important this conversation, this moment was. "Not until I know where I stand with you."

"I have been considering that. Trying to be practical. And adult. But I don't know what to think. I mean, we have an attraction thing going on that would fuel suns. We seem to know where we are with trust. What we haven't yet is a relationship."

"We have a friendship." He gave me a whimsical smile. "Or we did. Beginning on board my ship."

"Oh, we got along great when I thought you were Zathdar. Soon's I knew the truth, there was your name right there between us, like some kind of shadow. Merindar. You know, Dad asked me to do something for him. He wants me to write everything down from the beginning of the summer, when he could hear everyone's thoughts. I hadn't meant to tell you, but I think it important that I do."

"He even heard mine?" Jehan winced.

"Yes, but he hasn't told me any. That's for you to do. If you want. He not only knows what happened, but why. What people were really thinking, though he can't do it any more, and he says that what he remembers is already beginning to fade. Will you tell me your side? Maybe, I don't know, maybe I can put it all together and understand some of what happened."

"I will do that."

"Thank you. But that's for me. So what do *you* want to do?"

Jehan let go of my hands and pulled me into his arms. "I want to begin all over again, courting you," he murmured into my hair. "I want to spend the rest of my life courting you."

Whee. Even if we hadn't gotten any convenient fairy godmothers wand-waving us into happily ever after, hearing those words came pret-ty close to making up for it all. I flung my arms round his neck and this time the kiss was long, satisfying, and didn't end with sorrow, regret or distrust.

So we did it again. And, oh, a few more times.

When we did talk again, I said, "What's next?"

I meant it as a joke but Jehan let go and took a few steps away, as if proximity would restore rational thought. He looked over his shoulder. "Back to where we were. Which is deciding where my place is. Sasharia, what if the best thing for the kingdom is my leaving?"

I shrugged. "If you and I get on the same page, and I think we're going to, Mom and Dad would understand. I'm too old for them to stop me and they know it. So if you're worried about the whole princess thing, well, it was never real to me anyway. I don't hate it, but I'd rather be with you than wearing diamonds in my hair and making nice with duchesses. In short, if you've got to leave, let's pack a hammock for two."

He closed the distance again, searching my face. "You mean that?"

"Of course I do." I laughed. "Heck, when I was a girl I never wanted to be a princess even if we did come back here. Princesses were small and dainty and neat, and I was too big. What I wanted to be—" I stopped, and felt my face redden.

Jehan's eyes narrowed. "Come on. Say it."

"You're gonna laugh."

"I won't."

"You will. I know it. One snicker, and I'm outa here."

He raised his hands, smiling.

"All right. I wanted to be...a pirate!"

*How* he laughed. I whirled around to march out, he caught me, we wrestled, then fell laughing onto the couch, where I kissed away his laughter.

And when we were both breathless, he caught my hand. "I think it is time to talk to your father."

The result of which was today, New Year's Week Firstday.

This morning dawned gray with impending snow, but

despite the prospect of dreary weather, the bells of the castle, echoed by the bells of the garrison and the guildhall, all rang the rarely heard full royal wedding and coronation carillons. Bell ringers crowded into the towers, wakening the big bells and the small ones that usually hung silent. They played wonderful patterns as two carriages, drawn by pairs of white horses, rolled slowly on a circuit of the royal city.

This was New Year's Firstday, the day Mom and Dad would officially become king and queen, and Jehan and I would marry.

Mom and Dad sat in the first carriage, both dressed in the crimson and gold and silver of Zhavalieshin. Dad wore a fabulous tabard embroidered long ago with twined firebirds, hidden by Kreki Eban and triumphantly brought out last week. Mom's hair was done up elaborately with pearls and beautifully cut stones that gleamed with amber highlights.

In the back carriage, feeling very weird, I sat beside Jehan. I looked down at myself, wondering who was sitting there in the white brocade gown with the emerald green embroidery down the sleeves, round the neck and hem. Under the brocade I wore a green silk gown, which would only show when I moved. My hair had been done up by not one but two hairdressers (one joking, when she discovered the princess liked jokes, about how her arms were going to fall off, making all those little braids), each braid with a single tiny diamond fastener at the end before being looped up into a complicated coronet atop my head. Fitted against the coronet of hair, a tiara with diamonds and one single whopping emerald whose price would probably have netted me a brand new BMW, back in L.A. Nobody knew it, but I'd hauled that gem around all summer in my bag. It was left over from the bad old days.

L.A. seems unreal now, a dream—endless hot days, cars, TV and palm trees. Reality was winter slowly closing in on days of hard work, in-between all these fittings. But the good side of reality were the evenings when the four of us would gather, tired from a day of labor, talking as we ate dinner, and relearning to laugh.

Jehan told me his story privately, before he had to leave for his tour of inspection. Our going over all that old ground together—what did I think, what did he think—somehow cemented the bond that we'd always felt between us, even back on the very first day, when we'd fought side by side. We could say anything to the other, which helped us both.

He said he didn't want to hear Dad talk about Canardan's inner thoughts, at least not until some time had passed. So it wasn't until he left us to ride around the kingdom inspecting castles that Dad described Canardan's and Randart's view of events, and I wrote it all down as you've seen it here. Then it was Mom's turn. When she had finished and read over what I wrote, she hugged Dad and me, saying, "It's good to get that out of my headspace. The whole thing finally feels done. Finished business."

Jehan had not been able to decide about his father's effects. Mom helped the servants clear all Canardan's things out of his rooms, so Jehan would not have to do it. The rooms were clean and empty by the time he returned, his father's personal things put into carved chests for him to keep or sort as he wished, whenever he was ready.

Mom and Dad stayed up in Mom's rooms, and I'll get to why in a minute.

When he returned a week ago, ahead of a huge snowstorm, Jehan was able tell us how Damedran was doing. By then he'd completed his month's thorough tour with Damedran at his side, inspecting garrisons, handing out orders right and left "in the name of the king" and generally being In Charge.

Because this is what Dad wanted. Just as he'd wanted the record. Just as he wanted the wedding today—Jehan joining our family, which would add Zhavalieshin to his name—the same day as the coronation. Emphasizing how the four of us were a family.

The carriages stopped at the royal castle's grand entrance as the first flakes began to drift from the sky. We walked into the great hall, glad of our heavy clothes, our breath puffing in the cold air. All the court was gathered, the smell of beeswax candles and personal scents, most of them made of wildflowers and herbs, a kind of echo of summer.

It's strange, how sharp my memory is with some details: the pale light glowing in the long windows, a soft bluish white light now that snow was falling; tears along my mother's eyelids, and the corner of her mouth where the skin had softened over time, trembling even as she smiled; my dad's hand holding hers tightly, his thumb rubbing absently over her palm the same way I liked to rub Jehan's palm. The glow of that snowy light on the white hair of a woman with a curiously ageless face and Jehan's blue eyes, who had slipped in among the mages in their fine, light gray robes. She was Feraeth Jervaes, Jehan's mother. She stood side by side with the former Queen Ananda, who smiled fully now, for the first time in many years.

One of the clearest and most precious memories was the look in Jehan's eyes when he saw his mother, before he turned to me, smiling that smile with the deep dimple down one side.

And one of the dearest memories was the slight huskiness of emotion, the conviction in his voice as he said, "I offer you this ring, which has no beginning and no end. It is a symbol of our love..."

The funniest memory was the way I heard myself gulping for air almost every phrase as I echoed the same words and shoved the golden ring, all embroidered with intertwined leaves, onto his longest finger.

"Your prosperity is my prosperity..."

"Your hardship is my hardship..."

"...and we call upon all who are gathered here to witness the joining of this family, as long as we shall live."

And then my memory grays out, but at some point I became aware of standing at my mother's side, as Jehan stood at my father's, and how their vows to the kingdom curiously echoed the vows of marriage.

Three things my father had asked for: that I write the record, that Jehan take his name. That's two.

The third? Within the next three years, when the kingdom

has accustomed itself to all of us, my father and mother will abdicate and go to Sartor as ambassadors, Mom to stay in a court she knows she will love, Dad to study magic with the most powerful mages. He thinks that's the best way for him to prepare for the troubles ahead. He says that being king requires youth and strength. So he wants Jehan and me to take their place, and make those very same vows.

But the whole idea of me and queenship doesn't yet compute. I'm not really accustomed to the princess gig yet.

So back to memories. Like the tenderness apparent in both as Jehan and his mother met again, after years of contact only through letters. She stroked my hair, whispering how welcome I was in her life.

And the last memories are a montage of music, and dancing under the glittering lights illuminating the castle.

So I sit here now, writing it all down—

Jehan just leaned over my shoulder. "Are you not done with that thing yet?"

"I have to put in our wedding." I looked down at myself. "I have to describe me sitting in this ridiculous chair—who *is* the twit who put silk knots in the seat cushions? *What* were they *thinking*? And my first waltz in my wedding gown. Shall I put in how I tripped on my train? Then I have to get down what everyone looked like, and how your mom and mine got along like a couple of houses on fire—"

"Sasha."

"What?"

"You are not writing down everything I say. Are you?"

"Yes. So speak slower."

I can hardly write, I am laughing so hard.

"Shall. I. Describe. What. We. *Should*. Be. Doing. On. Our. Wedding. Night?"

Okay, he wins.


And here it is the next day, but as you can see, it's going to be short, for very soon all these papers will lie on the desk of

King Mathias and he can do whatever he wants with them.

Because why?

Because a little while ago, I was waking up with that happy, sleepy sense that all is right with the world. How rare, how wonderful! Outside it was cold and clear and icy, but inside warm and snug, and...

I looked over, but no husband slumbering beside me!

I sat up, peering through the open doors to the wardrobe—for I'd moved into his rooms, which were a lot less gloomy than Queen Ananda's old chambers. And what did I see? Jehan standing before the mirror, trying on the most horrible pink shirt I've ever seen—all embroidered with orange peonies.

"Jehan!" I yelped. When he turned around, I saw that he'd managed to dig up a pair of deck trousers of purple and yellow stripes. "You are not, not, *not* going out into the city in those."

"No." He strode back into the bedroom and preened, then began tying his hair up in a rose and violet bandana with green fringes. "But I am wearing it on board the *Zathdar*."

"What?"

He gave me his old, ironic grin. "Zathdar the pirate has to sail again."

"Today? Now? I thought we'd..." I waved my hand around the room. "Have some time to ourselves."

He flicked one of those magic communication boxes, which was lying on the desk. "I told you Owl rejoined my fleet. And Elva Eban's the new navigator, by the way. He just wrote. He's found Bragail of the *Skate*. Says he not only turned corsair, which doesn't surprise me. But that far too many of the very ones among Randart's old captains that I found had skipped out of Ellir are now poised in time-honored Khanerenth fashion to turn to piracy, aided by that slimy Chas, with half my father's personal treasury. It's time to do something about them, don't you think?"

"But—"

"So it'll be crowded in the captain's cabin. Won't that be cozier?" He wiggled his brows. "Get rid of those papers. You're done."

"You mean you want me to join you? In the dead of winter, chasing a slimy Randart captain and probably his entire fleet and that stinker Chas, all turned pirate?" I yelled, for he'd vanished inside the wardrobe. "What kind of a wedding trip is that?"

He reappeared. "In the dead of winter."

He tossed my winter mocs onto the bedding.

"Chasing pirates led by a slimy Randart captain."

He pitched my sturdy shirt and riding trousers into my lap.

"And desperate duels on heaving decks. For truth, justice and honor."

Next came my sword.

"Against sinister villains. Winning fabulous treasures. You know you want to," he cooed.

And I do!

# About the Author

To learn more about Sherwood Smith, please visit www.sherwoodsmith.net/. Send an email to Sherwood at Sherwood@sff.net or join her LiveJournal group to join in the fun with other readers at:

http://community.livejournal.com/athanarel/profile.

*Swashbuckling in a magic world—L.A. style!*

# Once a Princess
## © 2008 Sherwood Smith
### *Sasharia en Garde! Book 1.*

Sasha's mother, Sun, was once swept away from a Ren Faire to another world by a prince—literally—but there was no happy ending. Sun's prince disappeared, and a wicked king took the Khanerenth throne. In the years since, Sasha and Sun have been back on Earth and on the run. Mom and daughter don't quite see eye to eye on the situation—Sasha wants to stand and fight. Sun insists her prince will return for them one day; it's safer to stay hidden.

Then Sasha is tricked into crossing the portal to Khanerenth. She's more than ready to join the resistance, kick some bad-guy butt, and fix the broken kingdom. But...is the stylish pirate Zathdar the bad guy? Or artistic, dreamy Prince Jehan?

Back on Earth, Sun is furious Sasha has been kidnapped. Sun might once have been a rotten princess, but nobody messes with Mom!

*Warning: This title contains a kick-butt mother-daughter team, a wicked king, a witty pirate with an unfortunate taste for neon colors, inept resistance fighters, a dreamy prince who gallops earnestly hither and yon, and a kick-butt princess in waiting.*

*Available now in ebook and print from Samhain Publishing.*

*Enjoy the following excerpt from* Once a Princess...

Elva reappeared, braids flying, brown eyes stark in a face so pale I thought she was going to be sick.

"There you are." She clutched my shoulder. "Get out. Get out."

"What?" I looked down at my food. "What's wrong with the—"

She pulled my wrist, sending my spoon flying. "You've got to run. Now."

"Why?" I snapped, getting up to retrieve the spoon.

"Because I followed Owl. I had my suspicions." She made a terrible face. "He met up with *him* at the stable—" She waved a hand toward the far side of the brewery.

"Him? Zathdar?" I stared at the brewery, but just saw barrels of ale.

"Zathdar!" Elva repeated scornfully. "Oh, you're in for a storm, right enough, if you don't move."

Heat flooded through me, followed by the self-righteous, fire-hot anger of betrayal. And *that* was followed by the sickening, almost lip-numbing humiliation that comes of realizing one's been taken for a fool.

I grabbed my basket and followed her between the tables, the singing weavers' plaintive melody blending into the heedless roar of voices behind me.

Out in the street, glare and the rising dust of early afternoon nearly blinded us. I blinked, breathing hard as silhouettes resolved into people, horses, carts, dogs, even a family of geese squawking and flapping. Children danced in a ring to the flitting summer melody played upon a pipe. In front of the last booth before the open road, several women teased a handsome fellow in a brown tunic who seemed to be trying to buy an embroidered scarf.

All oblivious, most of them happy, and very much in the way as I scanned and scanned, resisting Elva's tugs. "This way," she urged.

I faced her earnest, anxious brown eyes and knew that Devli waited somewhere, a transfer token in hand. "Thank you for the rescue. But I think I'll take off on my own."

Her face reddened. "It's Devli. Isn't it? You don't trust him."

"I'm sorry, Elva, but I just don't trust those giving him orders," I murmured as a cart full of melons rolled toward us, shoved by a brawny fellow not watching where he was going.

She moved to one side. I ducked to the other side of it so I wouldn't have to see her reaction, and dove into a pack of sailors, several of them wearing battered floppy hats much like mine. I still felt outlined in neon, though so far the few guys in brown tunics around were not searching, merely sauntering.

*All right, Sasha, you got what you wanted. You're alone. Pick a direction.*

My pack of sailors headed toward the brewery. I stayed with them as far as the door. That sense of being watched intensified, so I slunk round the back of the Gold's stables and peered out, scanning with care.

The marketplace lay to my left, a long street of tent booths below the high palisade of sheer rock on which the garrison and academy bulked. The market street crested to the right, below the bluffs on which the academy barracks ended in the furthermost tower.

The road on the other side of the crest stretched in a lazy arc, paralleling the rocky shore against which long breakers creamed and crashed. Lines of wagons inched their way in a string that curved through mellow grassy fields to the horizon, the only tree in sight a single clump of willow growing beside a stream winding toward the shore.

No cover whatsoever, but at least that road lay outside of Ellir and its bazillion warriors.

I slipped away from my crummy hiding place and headed straight for that high point, beyond which freedom beckoned.

But right before I reached the top of the market street, not five hundred yards from the low stone wall that marked the boundary of the city, my shoulder blades itched. My danger sense had gone into the red zone, urging me to turn and fight.

I just knew I would hate what I saw. But I had to look.

Past the dancing children. Past the strolling flirts, the bargaining marketers with their baskets, past unheeding cadets and warriors obviously on leave, past the dogs and geese and sailors. I stared straight into a pair of familiar blue eyes.

Too late.

Too late, but I turned on my toes and sprinted for freedom, despite the faster footsteps behind me—much faster.

When I reached the top of the road, the footsteps had almost caught up so I plunged into a crowd of prentices in one last attempt to shake my pursuer, and risked a glance back.

The stinker was maybe ten steps away. He hadn't yelled, and though some of the people he pushed past turned to stare, and one or two began to call out in protest, stared, then quickly backed away, no one interfered.

The oblivious prentices didn't part for me. They shoved past and stampeded toward the brewery, leaving me alone to face the enemy.

The pirate caught up in an easy step, and stopped an arm's length from me.

So for a long, measureless moment we stood there facing one another at the top of Market Street, the last of the prentices flowing around us with exasperated looks and a wry comment or two that neither of us paid the least attention to.

All the things I could say chased through my mind. *You liar! Go ahead and strike me down, see if I care!* And perhaps most useless of all, *I hate you!* But I said nothing for a breathless, anguished eternity, as the market crowd walked, strolled, sauntered, pushed, shoved, talked, sang, sighed past us.

Pirate Hurricane stood there, waiting for me to speak.

And so I said, "You must really love making everyone look like a fool."

He flushed as if I'd slapped him. But then flicked his head, as if repudiating my words, and retorted, "You have no idea what you're talking about."

"Oh, so you're not a liar and a poser?"

"I never lied. I just didn't tell you everything."

"Oh." Well, that was a nasty little oopsie, but I plowed right past. "So you managed to tell one bit of truth. What did it cost you?" Take that!

"Listen. Just listen." He half raised a hand in a gesture of appeal, but when I stepped back, he dropped it to his side. His side, at which he wore a sword. And a knife through his sash. Neither of them touched, much less brandished. Nor had he whistled up his minions. There were certainly plenty of them about.

But I couldn't bear another terrible, sickening sense of betrayal, and so, without examining the motivation behind that I said, "No."

His eyelids lifted slightly, giving me half-a-heartbeat's warning. Before I could draw breath to move, or even to yell, a thick winter quilt blotted out the sun and my world was perforce confined to hot, enshrouding darkness that smelled distinctly of mold.

# GREAT
# CHEAP
# FUN

## Discover eBooks!
THE FASTEST WAY TO GET THE HOTTEST NAMES

Get your favorite authors on your favorite reader, long before they're out in print! Ebooks from Samhain go wherever you go, and work with whatever you carry—Palm, PDF, Mobi, and more.

Printed in the United States
215843BV00001B/39/P

9 781605 042961